I0635925

THE BOY ON THE TRAIN

MARTIN GOODMAN

BARB ICAN PRESS

Published by Barbican Press
London

Registered UK office: 1 Ashenden Road, London E5 0DP

www.barbicanpress.com
@barbicanpress1

A CIP catalogue for this book is available from the British Library.

Cover photograph by Jonas Jaeken courtesy of Unsplash.

ISBN: 978-1-917352-07-9
eISBN: 978-1-917352-08-6

Praise for Martin Goodman

"Goodman writes with flare and panache, and the narrative fizzes along. Goodman's novel soars."

The Times on ON BENDED KNEES

"Heralds a new dawn for British writing."

Daily Post on ON BENDED KNEES

"Beautifully structured and has a distinctive and haunting tone. Altogether a very clever and memorable piece of work."

Simon Mawer on THE CELLIST OF DACHAU

"Extraordinary ... An important, aching, artful novel."

The Toronto Star on THE CELLIST OF DACHAU

"A magical mystery tour in humility, truth, death, betrayal, forgiveness, the envelopment of nature, written as clearly and powerfully as a French Pyrenees river."

Karla Kuban on I WAS CARLOS CASTANEDA

"Such narrow, narrow confines we live in. Every so often, one of us primates escapes these dimensions, as Martin Goodman did. All we can do is rattle the bars and look after him as he runs into the hills. We wait for his letters home."

The Los Angeles Times on I WAS CARLOS CASTANEDA

"A great book about how to save the planet"

Coldplay on CLIENT EARTH

"The book is inspirational in a hardheaded, let's go to work-and-get-real-results sort of way ... There's a global vision. It's quietly amazing."

Oxford Today on CLIENT EARTH

"A treat to read – a gripping, uncanny, gothic adventure."

Clive Bloom on FOREVER KONRAD

"It combines psychology at its darkest with a genuine sense of the uncanny – a powerful and disturbing experience."

Ramsey Campbell on FOREVER KONRAD

"Goodman's attention to detail often combines with verbal felicity to memorialize even the most ordinary moments. Powerful and affecting work."

Paul Russell on LESSONS FROM CRUISING

Martin Goodman has tackled the world in a thrilling range of fiction and nonfiction. His subjects are self-experimenting scientists and spiritual masters, shamans and Nazi war criminals, eco-warriors and world-class musicians, vampires and Tibetan lamas. His books have won awards, with settings that span the globe. More and more they wave red flags about ecological crises. His recent *My Head for a Tree* tells the story of the Bishnois, a community in India who fight with their lives to protect nature. He is emeritus professor at the University of Hull, an editor for Conservation Times, and shares a life with his husband between London, Lowestoft and the South of France.

Earlier Books

With a humble nod toward Patricia Highsmith,
whose strangers met on trains to dire effect, and whose
Tom Ripley was a mid-20th century identity thief.

"Society is like a stew. If you don't stir it up every once in a while, then a layer of scum floats to the top."

Edward Abbey

Chapter 1

Tom wanted to interview online. Needless travel was killing the planet and anyway he liked to keep to his room. No, they said, the security team wouldn't allow it. Make me laugh, Tom said, you're a security company – you can make it safe. That's why we know, they said. The interview is in person or not at all.

They'd tracked him down. They'd found his identity. They knew what they were doing, Tom had to give them that. So he walked a couple of miles to the nearest station and took a train to Edinburgh.

Instead of a name, the firm had a glyph – an image of a lightning bolt – so in chatrooms the firm was called Glyph. With a thick black pen Tom had inked letters above the knuckle of each finger to read K-I-L-L C-O-A-L and in the interviews he kept the fingers splayed on the table in front of him. The two words were written the right way up for him to read them. They helped keep in mind why he was there. Throughout the interview Glyph didn't direct a single question at Tom. They just took eye measurements, gave him reflex tests, neural mapping – all that crap. They loaned him a laptop then told him the laptop was his.

From his hotel room Tom hacked into Glyph's system and found the test results. And then his counter showed a slight data charge. It took minutes to track it down and there it was: a new folder with that logo of a lightning bolt and a photo of Tom taken a minute before from his webcam. The results of his interview were posted into his machine. That was cool. Tom's gut heaved at the shock of the intrusion. He nearly vomited, but it was cool.

The train out of Edinburgh was busy. Tom chose a seat in a regular carriage. He hated the 'Quiet Coach'. People who sit there were simply waiting to be angry. One person answers their phone and everyone else is up and yelling, 'Don't you know this is a quiet coach!' Tom couldn't stand that.

Tom's window seat was on a table for four. Sit on the aisle and people knock into you. At a table there's space in front of you and you can stare out of the window. In the aisle seat a girl in a brown headscarf bent her head toward her phone and mouthed along to what she was hearing, not much more than a lip tremble. She looked safe. Tom stood near her, looking awkward. She glanced up and smiled and stepped out to let him in.

Dark glasses shielded Tom's eyes. You see lots from the window. You see reflections of people who think no one can see them. Tom didn't get out much, so it was interesting. He looked at how people moved their hands, the way they pulled at their faces, how they slicked strands of hair between their fingers.

Earbuds linked to his phone, and sometimes Tom played music and sometimes he didn't but instead listened to the talk of folk around him.

Tom stared out of the train, across scrubbed fields and through bare trees to patches of the North Sea that looked like the matte graphite of his laptop, and it was so rare to see the sea that he thought maybe he should get out more but decided not. A line of wind turbines along the horizon gave him a sudden thrill, like when sunlight breaks through cloud, though there was no sunshine out there, just a grey mass of cloud cover.

At Newcastle the train stopped and more people stuffed into the already full train. There was one seat left in the whole carriage, and it was opposite Tom. A girl stood in the gangway and stared at its reservation ticket. Then she stared at Tom. The ticket read 'Newcastle to King's Cross'. Tom knew what it said but the girl couldn't see his eyes behind his shades. He had liked being opposite an empty space.

'Excuse me,' the girl said to the old woman lodged by the aisle. The woman wore a pink padded jacket. A red velvet bow clung to her dyed blonde hair. She had tangerine glasses and mauve lipstick. You expected such a woman to be out with a carer, but she was on her own. She winced as she stood up because it hurt to go from seated to straight, but when she was upright and out in the corridor she smiled at the girl. She was glad of the company, glad to do a favour, or maybe she simply smiled whenever she could.

The girl took the seat. Tom pulled in his feet so she didn't touch him while she settled.

'You don't know what a relief this is,' she said. 'I'm exhausted. If I'd had to stand all the way to London, I'd have cried.'

She was talking to him. Tom didn't respond, but it made no difference.

'Sorry to stare,' she said. 'It's just you're the image of my little brother. You're older than he was – well, I guess you are – but you're so alike. He was a geek. A geek angel. He had a mass of black curls, like you. And a face like a ghost's. It's weird. Where are you from? What's your name? Your last name, I mean. I wonder if we're related, like cousins or something.'

Tom thought about telling her: Snelling. Daventry. No more than that. To see what she'd do with it.

'Arkwright,' he said. It wasn't the new identity he'd been working on. It was a made-up name that popped into his head. 'Potters Bar.'

'Oh.' Her mouth formed a perfect circle then closed itself. Her face was an oval. Her hair was short and some kind of blonde but darkened by wax with no misplaced strands. Her eyes were light blue with points of dark grey as their pupils. Her eyelashes were so pale it was hard to be sure they were there. A silver butterfly was pinned against each earlobe. Those were more details than Tom cared to take in, yet he found himself looking for more.

'Arkwrights of Potters Bar? No connection there, then. We're Snellings.'

His name in her voice hit Tom. It was like the breath had been pushed inward from his chest.

4

'I'll change my name someday. When I get around to it, not when I marry – I want to be a single mum through a nameless sperm donor after some drunken fuck – but a deed-poll thing. I've never liked Snelling. Smelly Snelly, all that stupid school insult stuff – I'd never wish that on my kids. Do you know what was worse? My first name's Melanie, Mel, so kids at school called me Smelly Melly Snelly. Max was the last of the Snellings, I reckon. It's weird. You do look just like him.'

'He's dead.' Tom meant it to be a question, but it came out wrong. He wasn't good at chatting.

'Too weird.' Mel stared at him hard. 'You've got the same voice. He wore black too, black T-shirts. You probably smell the same as he did. I bet you like the same music, hate all sports, are allergic to cats, get a rash in the sun. Go on, tell me, what's your favourite food? No, wait a minute.'

Mel reached into her bag, simple denim, and pulled out a miniature notebook. Its glossy cover showed a white mess of a chick with splayed yellow feet and a gaping beak. Not a pretty cover. Tom guessed the chick was an eagle. With a plain wooden pencil Mel jotted something down on the pad. She tore out the page, folded it in half, then set it down on the table with her hand flat on top of it.

'Now tell me.'

Dill pickle. That was Tom's favourite food. He was set to lie and tell her corned beef though he'd sooner starve than eat that, but his mouth went ahead and did the talking.

'Dill pickle,' he said.

Her face had the wash of a light tan and there was pink in her cheeks, but that all blanched away. Mel went as pale as he was.

She pulled her hand back.

'Turn it,' she said. 'Go on. Turn it. Read what's written.'

He was about to. Tom reached his hand forward. Another hand appeared. It slammed down on the table, provoking a draught that lifted the paper and sent it to the edge of the table and off on the drop to the floor.

The hand arched up and the fingers pushed forward a train ticket.

'Carriage C, 34, facing. I believe you're in my seat, miss, if you don't mind.'

The intruder left his hand on the table so people could study it: the manicured fingernails, the whorls of blond hair on the knuckles, the platinum band on the wedding finger, the starched white cuff and the monogrammed S.M. on the cufflink. His watch was a Patek Philippe with a gold strap. Once everyone had had time to notice, he lifted his hand away.

'Sorry and all, but I've got work to do and I can't do it standing up. You should have made a reservation.'

'You're too late,' Mel said. 'If you don't take your seat straightaway, it's forfeit. That's the rule.'

'You're kidding me. I was in first class. I always travel first class. My PA screwed up. She's stuck me in with you lot. Now first is sold out. The ticket collector sent me back here. Back through five crammed and stinking carriages. You want me to go and get her to throw you out? That's what you want me to do?'

Mel pulled a phone out of her bag, and angled it for a moment so Tom could read *Librem 5* on its back. He'd read about Purism phones but never seen one before. It flashed Tom two signals: it was expensive, and Mel cared about security more than anything else she might get from a phone. She clipped an earpiece over each ear, tuned into a stereo world, and looked out of the window. She winked into her reflection. For the boy opposite. She knew he watched out for reflections.

'I don't believe this.' The man held up his hands and looked around, like this was a reality show and he had to win the audience to his side. He aped his disbelief so everyone could look at him.

Mel was quick. She kept looking into the window but her left hand shot out. Only Tom watched the ticket. It lay on the table where the man had slammed it down and then it was gone.

'The ticket,' he said. Did he do that when he was on his own, mouth his thoughts into the air? 'Where's my ticket?'

He reached across the table and tapped the girl on the shoulder. Her body convulsed. It was great how she could do that, like she was little Ms Innocent and this hand from nowhere had just groped her.

'You get your hands off me!' Mel yelled.

The guy snatched back his hand. He knew the danger; press up against a woman in a crowded lift and she alleges assault, so no hands.

'You stole my ticket, you bitch,' he said instead, and turned for help. 'You saw it,' he said to the doll woman in the red bow.

The old woman cringed, looked up at him, twisted her lips into a thin smile, like that would keep him away. He leant in close, the way an oculist would, maybe.

'Fuck me,' he said. 'There's fuck all there.'

He wheeled around. 'You,' he said to the girl next to Tom. 'You saw her.'

She was quiet, this girl on Tom's right, earphones tucked in beneath her headscarf and volume so low Tom could hear nothing. It was the Koran maybe, soft murmurings of the Prophet's words to keep her on track in this alien world. She looked down at the edge of the table, as she had been doing all trip.

'What is this, the see-all-say-nothing table? You, kid in the corner, the kid in shades, you missed nothing. Your type never do. Are you man enough to say it out loud? Tell her. Tell her to give me back my ticket.'

'Has it got your name on it?' Tom asked.

'What the fuck sort of question's that?'

'You say "my ticket" like you've got proof. This lady got here first. She sat down. I presume she's got a ticket. If so, it'll be her ticket. Unless it's got your name on it.'

'You sick punk.' The man took out his phone and started scrolling through his messages.

'That's mine.' Tom pointed. 'That Apple phone. It's mine.'

The man stared.

'The watch on your wrist. That's mine too.'

'You mental? They let you out on your own?'

'I'm playing your game. You see something and claim that it's yours. That watch. That phone. They're mine. Give them back.'

The man pressed speed dial and faced away. It spoke through Bluetooth straight to his ear. He punched in numbers till he got a live voice.

'Pam? Where's Pam? Sick again? Her kid's sick. How many days is that? That kid's so sick I'm shocked it's alive. Well, Pam's screwed up big-time. Who is this? What do you mean, who am I? Steve McInnes, that's who I am. Well, Sheila Fogarty, whoever the fuck you are, Pam's left me in a crisis and it's your job to fix it.'

Tom took out a pen, scribbled his email on the back of the ticket and stared at the girl. She was catching things in loose reflections in the glass, gave a wilful who-gives-a-fuck? look out of the window, but turned when Tom didn't look away. A quick glance at this Steve McInnes first.

Steve was still at it. 'I'm on a train, Newcastle to London. First class is full. Pam Well-it's-not-my-fault-my-kid's-sick figured what the fuck, let's stick Steve in cattle class. We'll sort out her priorities later.'

The shift of Tom's eyes, the flick of his fingers, Mel got it. She turned back to the window but her hand reached down and under the table. Tom and Mel touched fingers. Swapped tickets.

Steve was on a phone jag. Couldn't stop. Talked so the whole carriage got to tune in. 'Your priority, Ms Sheila Fogarty, is to root through files and get some confirmation of my seat booking into my inbox right now. You're a fill-in at Hardbridge. You want a real job. Pam's is a real job. It pays well. It's just become vacant.

See if you're up to it.'

He tapped an end to the conversation.

'Hey, you, Ticket-inspector woman.' A uniform was working through the crowded vestibule. Steve shouted at it. 'We've got an incident here.'

The inspector entered their carriage. Black hair tied back with strands loose, black-rimmed glasses, she looked up and the effort of smiling dropped from her face.

'All tickets, please,' she called, and kept to procedure, refusing to be hurried.

The woman with the red bow and mauve lips heard the inspector's call and got flustered. Her hands clawed through the insides of her bag and a packet of throat sweets and empty wrappers and crumpled tissues with lipstick stains and a chapstick and receipts and store cards and her ticket and a travelcard hit the table. The receipt for her train journey looked like a ticket. She picked it up and smiled.

'That's your receipt,' Tom explained to her. 'You need the other bit. And this.'

Tom picked out her Senior Railcard. In the picture she had the same red bow on her head. And he dropped the ticket in his hand on to her pile of stuff. He took hers away. The switch was easy.

'Here you go.' Tom picked out the ticket he had just dropped. The old woman took it and smiled at him.

The guard reached their table and squeezed out a smile of her own. *The guy in the aisle's a jackass*, it said, and *this was the kind of kid who helped old ladies*. She had noticed and she was onside. She scribbled a cross on the woman's card and the woman held it a while, blinking, then slipped it back into her bag, along with the rest of her crap.

'She's the one to check.' Steve McInnes stabbed a finger toward the girl. 'She's in my seat.'

'That's your incident?' the inspector asked, as if she found this man pitiful. 'Someone's in your seat?'

'It's my seat.'

It came out like a toddler's whine. The guard gave Steve the silent look then held out her hand. 'Show me your ticket, please.'

'I've not got it. She's got it. She stole it. That's the incident. She stole my ticket. I'm reporting a theft.'

'You've not got a ticket?'

'No, I have not got a ticket.' Steve articulated each word, as if the guard were a dodgy voice-recognition program. He leant forward, his hands stretched behind him, and gusted the words in her face. 'That bitch has got my ticket.'

'We don't tolerate abusive language on the train.'

'I am being nice,' Steve said, and straightened up. 'This is me being nice. Why not stop being some high fucking moral guardian and do what I'm sure you're very good at. Be an inspector. Inspect that girl's ticket.'

Mel held it out. 'Here you are,' she said to the ticket inspector. She pinched her shoulders tight so she looked cornered, vulnerable.

The guard was in two minds. Enjoy the face-off with the guy or check the tickets.

The girl in the headscarf held hers ready. Tom did the same. They were cooperating. It became the way to go.

The guard took Mel's ticket first. Checked it, scribbled her little cross on it.

'What the fuck are you doing?' As the guard was handing it back to Mel the man reached out and snatched it. 'This is mine. She stole it. You can't deface it and give it back to her. It's evidence.'

'Sir.' The guard was turning icy. 'You have no ticket. You're causing a disturbance. I'm going to have to ask you to calm down.'

Steve's phone buzzed in his hand. He pressed buttons and barked a laugh. 'Look!' he shouted, and showed her his screen.

'This is a receipt,' she said. 'Where's the ticket?'

'Here's the fucking ticket.' Steve waved it in her face. 'And here's the receipt that matches it. Can she give you that? Has she got a receipt? Ask her. Go on, ask her.'

The guard held out her hand and waited. Steve passed back the ticket. She studied it.

'This isn't your ticket,' the guard said. 'The numbers don't match.'

Steve went still. Checked his phone. The guard showed him the ticket.

'They're both in on it.' Steve pointed his phone at Tom like a ray gun. 'She stole mine and then they swapped. He's got my ticket.'

'You have no ticket because everyone's stolen it,' the guard concluded.

Tom slid his ticket across the table. He used his right hand, the word COAL still written across its fingers. It was upside down to Steve but even so he seemed to quicken at the sight of it.

The guard inspected the ticket. 'You're in the wrong seat.'

'I told you!' Steve said.

'That lady was settled in when I got here,' Tom explained. 'I didn't want to disturb her.'

'And he was in my seat,' Mel joined in. 'This was empty so I sat here.'

The guard inspected the ticket of the girl in the headscarf. It checked out.

'Sir,' she said to Steve. 'Everyone here has a ticket except you.'

'I've shown you the evidence. Here.' Steve shook the phone in her face.

'A receipt is not a ticket.'

'She's got it.' Steve nodded at the old woman, who looked up at him and tried a smile but her upper lip was trembling. 'You just scrawled on her ticket. You didn't check, did you? You didn't check for the seat number.'

The old woman was holding her bag on her lap. Steve grabbed it, slammed it on the table, opened it and started to rootle inside.

'Stop that right now!' The guard held her phone in front of his face. 'Behave or I'm calling the police. They'll board at the next station and remove you from the train.'

'Here it is.' Steve pulled the ticket out of the bag.

'Put that back' – the guard still brandished her phone – 'or assault and robbery will be added to my report.'

Steve thought, dropped the ticket, clipped the bag shut and stuck it back on the old woman's table.

'Better.' The guard held her phone a while till she spotted him relax, checked its screen. 'That'll be £112.'

'But I've got a ticket.'

'You have no ticket.'

'There are no seats.'

'We can't allocate seats after the train's departure. Are you going to pay or am I going to make my phone call?'

Steve hesitated. It wasn't the money, it was the principle. But what the fuck. He pulled his wallet out of his jacket pocket and took out a card.

'We don't accept American Express. Cash, Visa or Master-card only.'

Steve's wallet was thin. Who used cash? He handed over his Visa.

It was time for Tom to go. First he managed to reach down to the floor and pick up the scrap of paper Mel had written on. Then he stood and took his bag off the rack. The girl in the headscarf moved into the aisle to let him pass.

'Have my seat,' Tom told Steve. 'I'm off next stop.'

He wasn't. He just didn't want to be stuck in his seat while Steve wandered out of range to find somewhere to sit.

Steve glared at him.

'I suggest you take up the young man's offer,' the guard told him. 'I don't want any more trouble from you.'

Steve made a drama of it. His body, his hip and his thigh pressed into Tom's and pushed him against the Muslim girl, then his elbow jabbed Tom in the chest as he moved past. Tom gasped. People looked. Tom wiped the pain from his face and stepped away.

Steve's arm and hip and thigh, the heat of it, the hardness of the bone and the slight yielding of the man's firm flesh as it pressed against Tom, stayed etched in his body. Like it left a dent. Tom would lie awake at night and trace the lines of Steve's body's contact with his own.

Shifting a bag, Tom made a space for himself on the floor of the vestibule.

An email came in.

'You've left me sitting opposite a jerk,' it read. 'Still, thanks.'

He checked the email address: xgvsu@tvskvjty.net

She was not giving much away. Tom had an email address and the name Melanie Snelling, which he was keen to know more about because he was sure she had made it up. He looked at the scrap of paper with the words DILL PICKLE in small block capitals. He had known that's what it would say but still it gave him a jolt to see it. This was his sample of Mel's handwriting. That was all Tom had.

Still, it was a start.

Tom's phone was not as easy as his laptop to work from but it knew what it could do. Steve's phone was putting out its own signal. Tom sidestepped the train's Wi-Fi and locked in.

For now, Tom didn't bother with taking control. He made

do with a shared view of Steve's screen. As Steve scrolled through his emails and flashed back responses, Tom simply read what came up. He was in learning mode. And he learnt that Steve was a commodities broker. And that the main commodity he traded was coal.

Tom was seventeen and lived in a bedsit and he was vote-less and a loner and because of its addiction to fossil fuels the world would be fucked one way or another before he was thirty and what could he do about it? That was the question and the answer was like tipping over into a chasm. There was no answer. But now he had been to Edinburgh and been recruited and that gave him some ideas. And it turned out that the arrogant shit who had just made it so that Tom was sitting on the floor of a train grew rich from selling coal.

Steve McInnes thought he could screw the planet and throw his shit at a girl and knock into Tom so hard it still hurt and get away with it all.

Well think again, Steve.

Chapter 2

Tom wasn't big on human contact because human contact was all one way. People notice you, and they find a way to hurt you.

It never paid to be noticed. That made the train trip stand out. It gave Tom two significant adult encounters to dwell on.

Tom could still recall the press of Steve McInnes's body against his own. He checked for bruises and could sense them there, a light grey stain beneath his skin.

With the girl called Mel the fast flash of conversation is what stood out, the way she played him, and knew secrets of his life. Had she hacked him? He guessed so. That's how you come to know secrets of people.

Was she hacking him still?

Tom kind of hoped so. The thought that she might be watching him gave an extra spin to his attacks on Steve McInnes the coal trader. Turned them into a performance.

✎

This is what Tom saw when he looked out through the lens of Steve's webcam into scenes around Steve's home:

A Shih Tzu called Millie, a little scruff of a thing. Steve took her onto his lap and scratched her scalp while he scrolled the screen and the dog closed her eyes in bliss.

Woman's voice off camera: Look how she loves that. The birthday girl gets all the treats.

Steve: You jealous?

Off camera: Millie's forty-nine in doggy years. Let her soak up whatever you can give her.

Tom worked it out. The dog was seven. Tom had seen the couple's two kids run past in the background. The oldest, Amy, looked about five. The boy was Colin and was around three. So, first Steve and his wife got broody and made do with a puppy, the way couples do, and after that practice run they had their girl and then their boy. Now all they needed was a nanny to make their family complete. So they got one.

The access codes for Steve's phone and laptop were both the same and the kind you crack with first guesses, but now Tom stayed tuned for personal information that only Steve would know. He needed intimate touches to form credible passwords for new accounts in Steve's name.

Drip by drip, Steve supplied those needs. He had a pet name for the dog. He lifted her up so her back legs dangled and murmured the name into her ear. Soft, but not so soft a regular microphone couldn't pick it up. Millikins. Steve in his new online persona was the sentimental sort, Tom decided, who would take a pet name, turn letters to numbers, and be smug about having a coded password he could remember. One like M1ll1k1n5.

His wife's name was Karen. Steve's secret name for her was Hots. Not much to work on there. h0T5. Steve was the type who would add his wife's pet name to her date of birth, Tom thought, and think himself smart because he had made up a unique yet memorable password. Tom would find Karen's date of birth through the regular channels. He would do the same with the kids'.

Through the lens of Steve's webcam Tom inspected what he could see of the room. This was a home office that doubled as a guest bedroom. A signed Miró print of red-and-blue squares in an overlarge silver frame hung over the bed. Below it, a visual joke to reflect the picture, square red-and-blue cushions were stacked against the headboard. So far as Tom could tell from overhearing quick asides, the couple's marriage was hanging together OK on the sex front. Steve didn't sleep in this room, nor did Karen, but Steve kept odd hours so he made use of the guest room's en suite bathroom when he was up and about in the night.

The screensaver on Steve's laptop was a photo from a couple of years ago. Two little kids, one taller than the other, stood bare-bottom naked and stared out at a broad and calm sea. A small dog sat beside them and Tom recognized it as Millie. It was funny, the way people gave the game away with their choice of screensaver. The pictures showed what they loved. Sometimes that gave Tom all the clues he needed. This was the case with Steve. Tom's instinct to mix the names and birthdates of Steve's kids and dog was spot on. That's what Steve had in fact done to make four of his own passwords.

Tom had no time to think of that now, though.

Noises off camera: The whirr of the extractor fan. The water rush of the shower. The jerk back to silence.

The shower had stopped. Tom didn't want to give Steve time to dry. He needed him wet. He worked the keyboard. The screensaver of kids, dog and sea disappeared and a car advert popped up in its place. It was for a Jaguar F-type convertible.

On the screen of Steve's laptop the volume control slid to max. The cursor zoomed in on the full-screen button and the image of the red sports car in heather-decked Scottish mountains snapped tall and wide. The cursor clicked PLAY.

Sitting in his room in Daventry, Tom switched the view on his screen to a live relay from Steve's webcam. The electro-beat soundtrack of the Jaguar ad pulsed through his headphones. The ad would last seventy seconds.

Sixty-six seconds left. Where was Steve?

Tom planned for Steve to show up naked and wet, not with some towel wrapped round his waist. That would be no use at all.

Come on, Steve. Sixty-three seconds. Where was he?

Sixty-two. There!

A blur of flesh on the right of the screen, some limb – an arm – and then Steve stepped into view. His blond mop of hair was tousled. The vain prick had been drying it even while the advert blared music that would wake the wife and kids. He did carry a towel, a white, thick one, but it draped from his hand and hid nothing. Steve's dick was not erect, as Tom had hoped, it was hanging, but it was engorged. That would do. Steve had just had a wank in the shower.

Steve stepped closer and looked. 'What the fuck!'

Tom heard him and his mind raced ahead. He could edit the speech. A slight tweak and Steve would be seen to mouth, 'Want to fuck?'

Steve leaned in close, reached forward, then took back his hand to dry it. He didn't want to drip water on the keyboard. *Don't just take the bend*, the voiceover on the ad said, *Own the bend.* Smoothly, the Jag swerved on the mountain road. Its engine roared. Steve watched it. He liked it. As the red Jag hugged a curve in the road Steve smiled.

Was it a come-on smile? It could be, Tom thought. It was a matter of context, of interpretation. He would make use of it.

The ad pulled back to a wide shot with the F-Type a red speck among Scottish peaks. Steve jabbed at the keyboard to close the ad. He didn't bother to shut down the camera. Of course he didn't. The ignorant fuck didn't even know it was active. It kept filming as Steve trod back to the bathroom.

Tom scrutinized Steve's body. The man had good musculature across his shoulders. And a trim arse. The tan line around his waist told a story of slender Speedos worn in the sun. No doubt Steve had topped the tan up at half-term, taking his wife and kids to some sunny foreign beach. Enjoy that tan while you've got it, Tom thought. It's set to fade.

You do one thing and think about another. Just because the soundtrack of Steve's life looped through Tom's Bluetooth all day, it didn't mean Tom was listening. Nodes of Tom's brain were scanning, that's all. Words weren't Tom's target. Steve wasn't an interesting man, he didn't say interesting things. What sparked Tom's brain was *how* Steve spoke. There would be some inflection, a little gust of heat behind his voice, and that was when Tom tuned in.

When did life get personal for Steve? That's what Tom wanted to know. When Tom was awake, and he was awake a lot, the soundscape of Steve's life was looped to his ear. The only trouble was …

Steve (talking to Karen, some everyday guff about childcare, but then the sudden flare of anger in his voice and Tom blinked away from his task and listened): This phone's shit. It's lost half its charge already.

Tom stripped apps from the phone and bedded down others but still the constant run of the microphone drained the battery. The thing about secrets is you don't know when you'll hear them. Tom was loath to turn the mic off and stop listening.

He worked his way around it. When Steve was at his workstation, Tom took his live feed from that and muted the mic in Steve's phone.

Steve's home was wired for voice command, so Tom could follow him round that way if he had to.

Tom popped in and out of Steve's phone on a needs-must basis, and made do.

Tom was learning more about the nanny. She was Hungarian. They called her Hanga. Both Steve and Karen, when they talked to her, used a slight up-inflection at the end of each sentence, like they needed to stay on her good side. She was in her early twenties. Tom glimpsed her once. She was a thick-set young woman with round glasses, a round face, even a round hairstyle. Sallow skin and dark hair. Her voice was husky, almost sultry, like she was putting on the accent for effect.

Steve to Karen: Can't you get her to wear deodorant?

Karen to Steve: She does. A special brand. No aluminium. Says she's too sensitive for anything stronger.

Steve to Karen: What about my nose? That's sensitive. [Pause] Can't you get her to shave?

Tom had thought to make use of the nanny, but when he heard Steve's take on her he saw it was a stretch.

Unless the young woman's stink, the body hair, was what Steve was into. Tom could plant evidence that Steve stalked her. That he got high on nannycam. Hanga takes her phone to sit down for a crap and Steve turns on its camera, downloads the footage, and keeps it on loop play on his laptop.

Blood pulsed in Tom's dick.

Whoa. Where are you going with this? he asked himself. Keep it simple.

He played back his thoughts. Was he getting off on thoughts of Hanga taking a crap? No way. That wasn't him. He was acting like he was Steve and getting off on some sick fantasy he had made up to stream in Steve's head. Get too close to Steve's mind and that's what happened. You got infected. Time to take a break.

Tom placed his phone beside his headset and shut his computer down. He got up from his desk. Tom knew what he had to do.

Chapter 3

Tom had quit school when he legally could, and it hadn't been that long ago. During his so-called schooldays he didn't show up much. One day when he did, his class was already on a bus. Tom got on without thinking and before he could panic and get off again he spotted a toilet. He didn't need it but he needed one to be there. He went inside to check it out. It was narrow and the lock was a thin metal tab you flicked over and into place, but it worked. If Tom got a seat right next to it he should be OK. He was about to get out when the bus started to move, so he figured he would sit down on the toilet seat. That would be best.

In time the bus stopped turning corners and wheeling round roundabouts and settled onto the straight of a motorway. Tom figured it was time to come out. He hadn't paid for the outing and he had no signed letter from his parents but he stepped from the toilet and found a seat near a window, and that's how Tom came to go on a geography field trip. It was the most memorable day of his life.

You don't need many days like that. You need one, and you can replay it in your head.

For Tom, that day out put stuff in his head he didn't know he needed and taught him what he didn't know he didn't know. He didn't know, not in a gut sense, that he lived on an island and that that was what kept his head so tight. His hometown was in the Midlands and his home was on a narrow street packed with small, dark houses. On his way off the bus a teacher looked shocked to see him but gave him a geology questionnaire to fill in and pointed him across the car park and down to the sea. They were here to do a recce of Lulworth Cove.

Fuck that. Tom checked out the public toilets so he knew they were there, and he found you needed coins to get in. He walked around looking at the ground till he found some. In case the need struck.

The other kids had gone. Tom looked over to where people funnelled into a crowd and headed for cover. In the opposite direction a path led up a hill through scrubby grass and Tom took that. He had to lean his body into the wind it was so fierce, and head up and up. Angle his head and he saw the steep path, but angle it more and he saw the first crest of his first big hill and above that were thick, banked clouds of sky. Tom kept going till the path grew flat and he could stand still and look out.

Down below was Durdle Door. Tom learned the name later. Waves had knocked a limestone cliff into an arch that edged one side of a cove. Tom looked out over the whites of waves and the rippled dark of sea to a sharp horizon. Grey sea met grey sky like a study of darkness, but that was OK. Tom didn't need blue. He needed expanse.

He filled his head with all that space and locked it in. He shut his eyes and took in the roar of wind and sea and felt the blast of cold on the skin of his face. He looked out again, from left to right and right to left, and then stared ahead. Tom stood on a hill and stared out over Planet Earth and let it fill him so he would never be small again.

Back on the bus, while they were still in the run of narrow Dorset lanes, Tom threw up. Happily he was sitting in the toilet at the time. The trip was worth it though because its memories clung. On that day away from school Tom learned that a patch of sky can be an antidote for what life does to you.

Tom's maths teacher told the class he had just invested in Bitcoin, only he called it Britcoin, like it was some British currency complete with a virtual queen's head. He had spent thousands, the schmuck said, like he was proud.

Tom had bought his own stock of Bitcoin for near nothing and investigated and decided it was time to get out. Most Bitcoin got mined in China, burned up vast energy powered by coal, and in effect was killing the planet. Tom sold up. He was sixteen. He used the money to leave school and set himself up in a flat of his own.

You had to be eighteen to sign a rental agreement. Tom used his dad's name and bank statements and stuff for proof of ID. He paid a year's rental in cash.

Go down the stairs from his house then left and across the street and through an alley cut between the row of cramped houses, it smelt of piss but it wasn't far, and Tom could hold his breath and he was out the other end and over the road to where there was only park. It was proper park too, with railings and a gate. Inside was grass and trees, no flowers. Tom didn't like flowers, they were vulgar, though he did once buy a tub of lavender from outside a shop and planted that in a triangle of the park's dirt. He thought it would attract bees, and it would be cool to hear bees.

Someone ripped out the plant. Some grass and trees was what there was.

It was a shitty park, truth to tell, pocked with burnt holes from barbecues and slimed with dog turds. Tom minded his feet as he walked across the grass to the far edge where wooden fences rimmed with barbed wire screened the houses beyond. This side of the fence, grass was left to grow tall as a concession to wildlife. Cats prowled inside it. Strips of fence had fallen away and Tom looked through to the tangles of brambles on the other side. Nobody went in for gardening in this part of town.

A dusty green shrub poked branches and sparse leaves above the fence. Tom heard the chatter of birdsong. Up came a house sparrow. It was April. They were nesting. Another bird joined it till there were five, chirping and singing. They hopped down and out of sight but kept singing, and Tom laughed, a soft gust of laugh that was relief, really. That's all it was.

Hear a bird and it quietens you and you know you've got something to fight for.

Away in London, Just Stop Oil was doing its thing. Protesters were marching and parking their bodies in the street to block bridges and roads and disrupt the flow of work in the capital. Stop climate change and stop it now, that's what they were about. Part of Tom roared them on and ached to join them, but that was the ache of Tom's life, this want to be able to join in. He could keep it in the background.

Tom watched film of the protesters. They were mostly white and older than him. For them, this was novelty rather than everyday stuff, going against the police. Mass unrest led to mass arrest. The protesters were gifting themselves to the state. The police took your prints, added you to their database, gave you a fine and a criminal record.

Tom was shy of databases. His type of activist stayed under the wire. You don't see them coming and you don't see them go. It's a lonely life, but you get to live it.

On his walk back across the scuffed grass Tom's mind never stopped, and it recalled a scrap of film he once found on YouTube. It showed rich prats on a yacht out at sea. They held long rods and pierced sprats onto hooks to act as bait. From the back of the yacht they cast high, the little fish catching silver on their scales. Seagulls swooped from the sky and snatched at the bait. Fishhooks clawed at the insides of the birds' stomachs and the young men reeled the gulls in. That's what they were doing, fishing for seagulls. For them it was fun. The seagulls flapped and the line stayed taut and the birds were pulled toward the boat. The men laughed, big, open-mouthed, perfect-teeth bellows of laughter. Haw haw haw!

Tom shuddered. This was a bad image to have in his head. He had to rush back home before he threw up.

He raced with tiny steps in case long ones loosened his bowels. He was scared he might crap his pants. You see into the world, see how mean it is, and your guts can void themselves. It can happen.

Chapter 4

At school, Tom's French teacher had graded him E for Effort. Tom made up a matching alphabet of grades in his head, starting with A for Arselicker. 'If only you'd try, Tom,' the teacher had said. He liked her for that, for talking to him in a soft voice and for using his name.

She was right, it turned out. Tom wasn't thick at languages. He simply had to put in the effort. It took five hundred hours of study to become fluent. Tom left school, set himself up in his own place and programmed in two hours of language learning a day. First up was Spanish.

And, for Spanish, Tom began with sounds. That was stage one for babies when they were picking up language and it worked well for them. Tom listened to Spaniards giving voice to vowels then copied and recorded and played back and listened and tried again. It taught Tom something about himself: that the slither of tongue he had in his mouth behaved in an English way. To make his vowels sound Spanish he had to make his mouth more open and shift his tongue lower and further back. He had to stop curling his lips in order to keep the vowels short. Tom soon moved on to words and meaning, but he kept this lesson in mind: that little things like the habits of his tongue could betray him and keep him stuck as Tom.

Tom monologued in Spanish. For listening skills, he sought company. In Argentina, Mexico, Chile, Venezuela, Panama, Bolivia and Spain, Tom sat in on Skype and Zoom and Googlechat and Teams conference calls, and it was as if these computers in other people's offices came with Tom's ears attached. Tom became particularly fond of sitting in on conference calls between engineers. They didn't speak tourist Spanish, and the Spanish itself changed between countries, but in a couple of months he began to understand.

Once he had found his way through all their technical terms and acronyms, he took on board their skillset. How does an oil refinery work? What are the weak points of an electrical grid? How much notice does a coal-fired power plant need to fire up? Some of the answers were plant specific, and he needed them all. He found them.

With Spanish in the bag, Tom shifted to Arabic. The prompt was a sign on the local mosque he passed on a back route that kept him away from most traffic and diesel fumes. Its calligraphy was in a font that used the effects of a broad-nibbed pen. It would be fun to make use of a font like that.

To begin, Tom had to read from right to left and convert the pen strokes of the Arabic script into sounds. It meant utilizing his tongue in a fresh way, like it was a whole new creature exploring his mouth. He had to discover and put to work the muscles in his throat. Open sounds resonated in his skull, a hum scored a line inside his forehead, and clicks uncovered sinews in his mouth. Tom's tongue and lips spun effects from each other, spitting air into meaning. Language was a physical work-out.

Not that he got to converse in Arabic. Tom sat in on the meetings of Saudi Aramco's oil engineers as an unnoticed observer.

July and any grass in the park had turned brown. Back from a walk and in his room, Tom sat on his chair. It was a beech-and-elm Windsor chair made hundreds of years ago – that's what Tom liked to think – by a carpenter on a lathe in Chilterns woodland. Tom bought it in an online auction for next to nothing because few others give a fuck for traditional crafts.

His desk was a scrubbed oak table stained with the rings of other people's plates. His bed was a thin mattress on the stripped pine boards of the floor. Books formed one neat stack beside it. These were Tom's classics. He did his research in the town library but didn't borrow their books because that would give them a record of his reading habits. He waited to see what titles turned up on the shelves of the town's charity stores. Most books there were crap, but he found *The Book Thief*, *Life 3.0*, *Dune*, *The Perks of Being a Wallflower*, *Why I No Longer Talk to White People about Race*, *The Talented Mr Ripley*, *Sapiens*, *Disnaeland* and *Burn Out*.

Tom read for two hours a day, in half-hour bursts. It was more for discipline than for fun. Tom's eyes strobed the print on paper while his head was still processing what he had captured onscreen, but after a few minutes he relaxed and was present in the paper book.

Otherwise, the room held a rail and a shelf that were home to his clothes. And there was his computer.

Currently, he had the view from Steve's webcam at work.

Steve was not at his desk. When he went on a proper break such as lunch, Steve followed company rules and logged out. When he just popped away for a moment he didn't bother. Tom checked. Yes, Steve was still logged on. That meant he was grabbing a coffee, having a slash, whatever.

Normally such moments were when Tom got to work. If Tom did his stuff while Steve was logged on, Steve was responsible for it. Records would prove that. Served him right.

Now, though, Tom didn't know when Steve had left so he didn't know when he would be back. He could try and track Steve through his phone, but relax, Tom, he told himself. His heart was racing.

It was oddly calming, to stare out at the office when Steve's head was not in the way. Tom saw the backs of rich young men who sat in plywood cubicles in front of make-do Dell computers. He looked out at the centre of this still hive of activity and his heart slowed to its regular, fast beat.

✎

It was a surprise to Tom that he now had a job of his own. His job was odd, of course. The company that recruited him had no name or existence in Companies House, just that glyph and a workplace that was virtual. Instead of paying him a monthly salary they took over Tom's finances. Money went out of his account and it came in. His bills got paid. 'We think you're one of us,' Glyph told him on his interview day. 'We see the world in the same way.' Nobody told him what to do.

Sometimes, at the start, Tom would be staring into Brazilian timber interests, Canadian bauxite, Nigerian oil, and the screen went blank. Not there, that meant, not where you're looking, look somewhere else. The screen would come back with the staff directory of a coal-mining company or coal-fired power plant.

Always coal.

Tom knew his stuff: coal chucks out way more CO_2 than all other fossil fuels and belches arsenic and mercury into the mix; kill coal or kill the planet, that was the choice, but shoot for oil and gas at the same time, that was his take, and while you're at it kill meat; the whole planet was at last gasp.

You're on our coal team was all Glyph said. So Tom picked a name from the staff lists and set to work.

Tom's aim was to turn employees of these coal companies into sleepers. Think of it as parasitizing. You start with locating their password and soon you're cruising their online domain. They're your avatar. You don't control them, but you could. They do what they do by your grace. At any point, you can activate them.

Tom ventured out from coal mines and into utilities and targeted those who commanded the transmission of energy from coal-fired power plants. Once he had these people in his power, it hurt Tom to know that a coal-fired power station was working because he allowed it to; that a night-time switch from renewable to coal-fired energy was happening on his watch. Banks funded the building of coal-fired plants, which was like funding the gas crematoria in Auschwitz. Tom needed to get at the bank staff and shut the funding down. Every day of inaction deepened the climate crisis. Tom was desperate to act now.

Wait, Glyph said. *Create more sleepers. We'll activate them all at once. Collapse the whole system.*

Tom didn't think there was time to wait.

And so, with Steve, he didn't.

Steve's specialty was coal, which would be a stranded asset before Steve turned fifty, yet that prick was out there selling coal futures.

Tracking Steve started as a hobby, but when it leached into Tom's work time his screen never went blank. Somehow, likely because of the coal link, Glyph approved of what Tom was doing. Or didn't disapprove.

What was different was this: Tom would not stop at the normal point, with Steve under his control, and hand him over to Glyph. He had rubbed up against Steve on the train. Steve was a loud-mouthed, arrogant prick, who stood for everything in life that Tom detested. A world wiped clean of any trace of Steve would be a much better place.

Tom spotted Steve's message to his new PA. Steve needed a flight. She alerted the company's designated travel agency. They went ahead and booked Steve the tickets he needed. It was a package: a business-class flight to Hanoi on Vietnam Airlines and a luxury car to take Steve from the airport to an executive suite at the Golden Dawn.

Tom had taken that one train trip with Steve. He knew how Steve went ape when he didn't get his first-class travel. Tom headed for the Vietnam Airlines website. With Steve's booking reference details duly entered, he clicked Manage Flight. Click click click, and Steve had a new seat. Economy, near the toilet, one seat back from the front so no extra legroom, right behind the babies that wail in their cribs. The same for the return flight. Next Tom would go to Golden Dawn and cancel the pick-up car.

First, though, he paused.

Why would Steve head to Vietnam?

It took a second to guess. Look inside Steve's head and you found a lump of coal. Tom scouted around for facts. Vietnam was set to hit two exajoules of coal consumption. That was ten times worse than the UK. And growing. As the West cut use of coal, the market for the stuff moved to Asia. It looked like Vietnam might double its coal imports for the year. Coal-fired power plants were being built. More were planned. Steve was the coal broker flying to Hanoi to get his cut out of choking the planet to death.

Tom stayed on the Vietnam Airlines site and started to cancel Steve's booking. It was best if the man didn't fly at all.

Then Tom thought again.

Keep Steve smug, that's what you need to do, so he doesn't see it coming.

Tom aborted a change he had made. Keep outbound Steve in business class and let him take its luxury for granted. Give him that to look back on from his cell.

And switch him to coach for the return flight.

Chapter 5

When Tom went online and played with the seats on Steve's flight he did so as Steve. He was now the world expert in doing things as Steve. For other stuff, he reached out. Since Vietnam had wedded its future to coal, others on Glyph's 'coal team' must surely have the skills he needed.

They did. All three of them were based in the UK but one kept a keen focus on Vietnam, while two more worked a young Australian coal exec who included Vietnam in his frequent visits to Asia. He was Trip Bailey. Because Trip mustn't guess he had lost control of his life, Glyph mostly just watched him. But this was urgent. Knowing what made Trip lower his guard, they concocted a plan.

On his home territory, around Sydney and Canberra, Trip's Grindr profile hooked him up with young Asian men. For his upcoming trip to Hanoi, Glyph's team switched his hotel booking from the Grand Vista to the Golden Dawn. On his arrival they monitored his phone, and heard him making sweet with a waiter called Kim who was in charge of the breakfast bar.

Game on. Kim was now their target.

Tom didn't hold out much hope. Steve was already on his way, getting ready to tuck himself into his luxury sleeping pod on the London to Hanoi flight, and they still didn't have the passwords they needed to access the hotel's systems. Trust us, the two who ran Trip as their sleeper said. We know Trip. He fishes local when overseas and won't sleep alone. Kim will come good.

And he did. It worked just like they said. Drink and food were brought to Trip's room, and shortly after that came a knock at the door. Kim entered. There was the usual small talk, the promises made. Then came the grunts and calls of sex on the audio stream and not long after that the snores. It's always Trip's snores, the Glyph duo who tracked him said and they laughed. Just wait. Trip's sound asleep. Kim's young. He's awake. Trip's Dell XPS 17 is sitting on the desk by the window. What else has a young man got to do?

Trip hadn't closed the screen. He seldom did. It was a business laptop, needed his long password to wake it up from standby, so the team typed it in. The laptop's light worked like a beacon and drew Kim across the room. Click click click, he was at the keyboard. The only screen that came up was the Golden Dawn's home page. Kim typed in his username, clicked on the box beneath it and typed in his password.

And in doing so, he handed the Glyph team access to the hotel account.

Thank you Kim.

By the time Steve's plane landed the team was far enough

inside the system to recall his pick-up car and buy themselves an extra hour.

It was just enough. As Steve was being driven by a taxi across the Nhat Tan bridge and into the city centre, the team unlocked the Golden Dawn Hanoi's security systems. They settled Tom on the inside. He was able to pick his view from among the Golden Dawn's network of security cameras.

Tom chose a camera which was high in a corner of the Golden Dawn's lobby from where he could look down. Up here he felt like a spider. Or a whole host of spiders, because he could move between cameras and enjoy angled shots down into all the public corners of the hotel.

Tom hated the empty marble gloss of the lobby, but it didn't matter. Hate was simply a quality that made Tom human. The spider in him had built its web and Steve was coming. It was a meticulous web, built from keystroke after keystroke. Steve wouldn't escape. Tom would wrap him strand by strand.

Here he came.

That thatch of Steve's blond hair gave Tom the signal, and his heart jumped. The plate-glass doors slid open and he strode on through, bold, like he knew where he was heading.

This was Tom's first view of how Steve walked across an open space. The man moved like a big chimp, down from the trees and out in the clearing, looking for something to piss on to make the place his own.

He spotted the reception desk and veered left. A little Asian woman dressed in black was in his way. She had stopped a few feet short to pull her documents out of her handbag and now had them in her hand. Her pause gave Steve his chance. He nipped ahead of her, stood at the counter and took his time, pulled his own documents out of the calf-leather Coach briefcase hooked over his shoulder.

Tom gave it some thought. If Steve had stopped, smiled at the woman, let her go ahead, would Tom have let him off?

It was an idle thought. The Steve who did that would not be Steve.

Steve was Steve. He had it coming.

Back in London, Karen was asleep. Tom was in Daventry and needed sleep too. His head kept nodding forward and jolting him awake. Out in the Hanoi hotel lobby Steve slipped his documents back in his briefcase, took his key card in its little folder, and when he turned to head for the lift Tom could see his look-at-me grin. The big, sick dolt was pleased with himself. Tom took all this in and felt bile rise and burn his throat. He was enraged.

Step back, Tom, he told himself. Remember, you don't do rage. Get some sleep.

Tom had his own shower room with a toilet and sink. The light switch turned on a fan; he hated its noise and didn't want to see himself in the mirror. He left the room dark. He guided the eucalyptus toothpaste onto his brush with a finger, cleaned his teeth, rinsed and spat and rinsed and spat. That would do for tonight. He kept on his black T-shirt but took off his other clothes and folded them onto his shelf. Just one more look at the screen before bed.

Steve was now in his room and had sent Karen a photo of the view from his window. His room was up at the top of the hotel's tower and looked out across a lake. The picture captured the early dawn light. Above the buildings on the far shore, a brown smudge of pollution rose into a washed-white sky.

Now Steve had another shot ready to send. It was from the bathroom and showed a hi-tech toilet, green lights on its side unit set to glow. It was one of those toilets that jetted water to clean shit from the crack in your arse and warm air to blow you dry. Steve typed a schoolboy quip about his squeaky-clean bum and the rest of the message for Karen to wake up to, stuff about a long flight but he got some sleep and was there safe and set to work. Stuff about him.

He did it on his phone so the top of the message scrolled out of sight. While Steve was writing at the bottom of his message, Tom added to the top: 'A toilet to blowdry your cunt and me here to make your cunt wet and you there fucking shame what's a man to do?'

Tom typed quickly and didn't bother with punctuation. They'd take away Karen's computer too, they'd check her emails, it'd give them a pattern of behaviour.

Tom finished his edit just in time as Steve stuck kisses on the end of the message and clicked send.

That was enough work for one night. Tom set his computer to sleep mode and went to his mattress, where he lay flat on his back and shut his eyes.

Chapter 6

Tom's studio flat had a front and back window. The front one was boarded up. Twice in one day a van had parked outside and left its engine running. First Tom heard the noise, that echoey rattle that diesel grinds out, he smelt the pollution, and soon he felt the diesel particulates scouring his throat. They were on their way to burn his lungs and screw with his brain. It was intolerable.

Tom waited till the second van had gone and went out and bought a sheet of plywood and a roll of flue-sealing tape. He fixed the plywood across the window frame. In a charity store he found a poster of a Swiss mountain. It included snow and a bright blue sky so it could pass for all seasons. Tom taped it up to cover the plywood and it became his view.

From the back, enough light still filtered into his room to tell Tom the time of day without the need of a clock. It was 11.20. He got up from his mattress and checked the computer screen. 11.23 a.m. – 6.23 p.m. in Hanoi. Where was Steve?

The panels from the Golden Dawn's security feed were live on Tom's screen. He checked the corridor outside Steve's room.

Empty, as expected. The camera on the same floor showed Tom the entrance to the Club Lounge, where a young Vietnamese woman in a cotton dress the colour of pistachio ice-cream was standing with a smile.

And there, yes, that's Steve. The camera was poorly angled but Steve was leaning forward in conversation. Steve was wearing his smile and brought a glass to his mouth to drink some white wine. There were three others at his table, Koreans in grey work tunics. Steve had made himself new friends.

Good luck to him.

Steve was otherwise engaged, that was all Tom needed to know, and he didn't have his laptop with him. Steve's drinks should lead to dinner. That would keep him busy.

Tom needed an hour of unfettered access to Steve's email account, maybe less.

Steve's calendar showed that his morning had been pocketed with meetings in the hotel's business centre. Steve was selling coal into Vietnam but also to South Koreans, whose principal focus was cement. Cement, of course, was made in kilns fired by coal. It took two hundred and twenty kilograms of coal to make a tonne of cement. Steve was buzzing with the possibilities.

In the afternoon, Steve had joined the Koreans on a road trip. Images from the outing filled seven rows of Steve's Google Photos gallery. In one picture Steve stood at the centre of a line of Korean men, his shoulders level with the tops of their heads, his grinning face like a moon in their sky. The backdrop was a mountain range with God-size bites chewed out of it. For a twenty per cent annual rise in cement production, you need a lot of limestone. You have to quarry out a mountain or two.

The dark blue suits of the Koreans bore the dust they had gathered as they trooped around on a cement plant inspection. In the last photo of the sequence a Vietnamese man with black glasses and a peaked hat was pushing the palm of his hand flat against the air and seemed to be snarling a command. You could see his teeth. 'No take picture here,' Tom guessed.

Then it was all off on the company jolly, lines of men in flat-bottomed boats behind oarsmen who shaded themselves with old umbrellas and worked the oars with bare feet. The karst landscape bulked its rocks into dark and rounded hillocks which turned the men in the boats beneath them into figurines. Well done for the photos, Steve, Tom thought. It's good to capture the jungle beauty of your last happy day on Earth.

One image was simply a study of nature, a tree dropping green tendrils to meet their reflection in a smooth spot in the water. Steve had a good eye.

Tom sent the image to Karen. No message. A gesture, something beautiful to look at. She'd be glad of that.

That was the break away from sordidness Tom needed.

He dived deep again and entered a website he had scoped from a distance. Rooms were lit by candles in dirty glass jars so the figures on the bed were shapes, the curves of limbs, the occasional glint of light in dark eyes.

Tom was acting as Steve so he had Steve drop a pre-paid digital token, but hated Steve for what he had Steve do. Pay for stuff like this and it's your fault, you're making it happen. So Tom had a plan to mitigate the bad that Steve was doing. It was a wild plan, as unlikely as setting up Kim to deliver the hotel passwords they needed, but hey, that had worked.

Steve's digital token triggered a light that flung a beam that pinned a shadow of a girl to the bare wall behind her. She was clothed; there was that. A scrap of a red top hugged tight to her chest, and matching mini pants topped legs like a chicken's.

She blinked. Her face froze. A man shouted. The girl's face winced into a smile.

Tom's spine ran cold. His mouth hung open and his face froze a while. It was like he was the girl, so locked in fear he was unable to move. He knew what it was like, he had been in situations like that, but he wasn't there now. He clicked back into action. He couldn't find the girl's location, the police couldn't, nobody could, it was buried inside a whole chain of VPNs, but the site offered home delivery.

Tom dropped another token in Steve's name and added the address of Steve's hotel and his room number. He picked a time from a drop-down menu and booked a girl for early the following morning.

If Steve had any vestige of decency he'd refuse delivery. And if Steve simply acted as Steve, he'd make a scene. Start badmouthing hotel security. Set them on red alert. That's not what's meant to happen when you have young girls shipped to your room. These things are meant to stay in the dark, not be brought out into the glare of security guards and CCTV cameras.

For a back-up, Tom booked a second girl to come an hour later.

Tom signed off and took a shower. He towelled himself dry, stood there a minute and felt the air move against his skin, then got into the shower again. He turned up the heat and felt his scalp turn red.

Girl one.

Tom got there early, staring through the lobby camera, but the girl might be early too.

How far would she get? The girl was streetwise. Tom had guessed that much from the tilt of her head and the jut of her chin as she stared into the camera when 'Steve' had booked her. Or, at least, she wasn't drugged out of her wits. But it took more than attitude to get you up to the executive suites. The hotel staff were streetwise too. They knew what to look for, and this girl was barely into her teens. Would she know not to pause, to look like she belonged, to march across the marble floor and straight to the lift without catching anyone's eye?

Tom doubted it.

Idly, Tom checked on Steve's phone. While Steve slept, Tom had gone into it and turned off the alarm. Tom figured it would be better to have the knock on the door, or perhaps the call from reception, wake Steve slug-headed to face the day while still shredding his latest dream.

But the phone wasn't powered down. It was still on charge, but activated. Steve was awake. Was he still in his room? Tom checked Steve's iPhone's screen. A live playlist. Steve had synched the music to his Apple Watch.

Tom switched to listen in to it. An electronic beat through his headphones blasted his head apart. Tom had turned the volume full tilt to catch the regular sound of Steve's sleeping breaths in the night and hadn't turned it back down.

His fingers slashed at the keyboard to drum in silence. He took off the headphones and shook his head side to side. Onscreen, Tom pulled up Steve's playlist. Steve was into the band Tough Love and was blasting their song 'So Freakin' Tight'. It was one of his favourite running tracks.

So where was he?

Tom's fingers flashed in more code to track the phone's GPS signal. A blue arrow popped up and obscured the name of Hanoi on a map of the world.

Tom pulled in close, closer.

There it was: the Golden Dawn Hotel.

Closer still.

The hotel overlooked a lake. Turn left, hug the lakeside, and you reached a bridge. Across the bridge was an island. There was the blue arrow, on the far edge of the island.

It was moving. Moving fast. Tom understood. Steve was out on his morning run. Tom watched the blue arrow complete its circuit back to the bridge then skip it on by. Steve wasn't done yet. He was up for another circuit.

Fuck Steve. He had an appointment back at the hotel. Didn't he care?

Tom switched back to the view of the hotel lobby. No young girl skulked at its edges yet. No bold thing was doing her strut to the bank of lifts. No concierges lined up to block her way. Was she late?

Tom checked his computer's clock, which he had adjusted to Vietnam time so as to make no slips. She was already late by a minute. Was she coming? What did time and appointments mean to a young girl who had been worked through the night?

Tom had stopped breathing. He noticed this, the breath caught like a pain above his heart, the heart beating like he could hear it, like it was trapped. What was it? Anxiety? Adrenalin?

It didn't matter.

First, close your eyes. Breathe in. A gasp. Breathe out. There you go. Breathe in again. Hold it. Let it go.

Tom brought his hands back from the keyboard and settled them in his lap. He felt the tension in his fingers and flexed and relaxed them to let that tightness go. Keep breathing, in and out. Better.

Sometimes, you look into your screen and out through some distant lens and you forget you're not there, that nobody can see you. That's all it was, Tom told himself. From his global distance he had set things in Hanoi in play. The show he had set up didn't need him to spectate.

Tom managed a couple more minutes, his eyes clamped shut until the eyelids relaxed, and then he opened them.

First he checked the GPS signal again. The blue arrow located Steve on his approach to the hotel, running at moderate speed. Tom flicked back to his view of the lobby.

Was that her?

He cut to a camera fixed to the wall behind the reception desk. A girl had wandered in and turned right, toward the restaurant. She must have looked for Steve in there. No luck. The breakfast team had turned her round and sent her to report in at reception.

Tom didn't know what he had imagined but he must have imagined something, a tarty skirt like a tight band above her thighs maybe, or a gym slip to bring out the schoolgirl, but whoever ran this girl knew their market. A linen skirt stopped at her knees and a collarless jacket hung over a simple white blouse. Her bare ankles showed above black leather shoes.

The shoes were the flaw, at least a size too big. She had to shuffle, geisha like, to keep them on her feet as she crossed the marble floor. The girl looked like a child dressed up as an adult.

Which is what she was.

Maybe that was deliberate. Maybe that's what her customers wanted delivered to their bedrooms. But first she had to make it past the desk.

The girl came close. All Tom could see was her head above the counter. Her hair was cut to a thick black fringe and dropped to ragged wisps by the sides of her face. The on-monitor image wasn't clear enough to see, but from close Tom expected he would note dabs of glue holding the girl's eyelashes in place. They were too long for real, like a baby doll's. The eyes were rimed with mascara, and her face was masked with foundation. It turned her skin a pale matte.

She looked up at the receptionist and stated what she wanted. The receptionist paused then reached for the phone.

Tom could have routed himself through the Golden Dawn Hotel switchboard so as to make and answer calls from Steve's bedside phone – that must be possible to do – but it was too late to think of that now. One for the future.

While the receptionist let the phone ring out in Steve's empty room, Tom thought the possibilities through. He had enough recordings of Steve to utilize Steve's voice; an algorithm would allow for a credible flow of conversation. Tom noticed the lift of the receptionist's head and looked at the screen to see what had caught her attention.

Here he was.

That blond hair had darkened with sweat and stuck to his scalp, the fringe clasped inside a pale-blue headband branded Prada. For his morning jog Steve had trimmed himself out like a fashion video crew was in tow.

Could that be right? Did Prada do headbands? Or did Steve think he could get away with rip-offs in Hanoi? Judging by the way his head did miniature shakes from side to side, a matching sky-blue wireless headset was still spitting music into his ears. The Apple Watch was on his left wrist, face down, but Tom knew the make. Tom had been there online when Steve ordered it: Series 4, the stainless-steel one with the silver Milanese band.

The prick wore thin reflector goggles that shone dark blue. His white sleeveless top arched low to show his nipples and the fuzz of chest hair matted to his skin. His meagre shorts, an electric blue, barely pouched his balls. Sport socks showed above his trainers which were simple, Steve's five-hundred-quid runabouts, Adidas Futurecraft 4D in Onix Aero Green.

Tom knew all that crap about the brand because, like with the watch, he had been there when Steve ordered them online. Tom hadn't been tracking Steve all that long, but every day Steve dragged him through some high-end emporium, like an addict needing a fix of the brand of the hour.

Steve jogged on the spot and pushed his goggles up on his head.

Even from his global distance Tom could smell Steve's animal sweat. In this Vietnamese setting of modest sizes the guy was a tall, blond, broad-shouldered freak. Steve stood out, but lots of people stood out. The hotel sucked in foreigners. The staff couldn't know everyone by name, yet all the little girl had given them was Steve's name.

Tom saw the receptionist nod at the man on the small front desk, who tripped away from his console and sidetracked Steve. That meant they did know him by sight and by name. Were the staff that good with everybody?

Steve pushed down his headset to collar his neck and let the man lead him to the main desk. Where the girl was waiting.

Tom didn't have an audio feed, but it was clear what was being said. The girl looked up at Steve. Her lips fluttered away in a constant jabber. Steve worked to ignore her and focus on the receptionist. Tom could lip-read 'No' and 'No way' as Steve shook his head.

The girl moved closer, the fingers of her tiny hands stroking Steve's right arm. The words on her mouth looked like English: 'You pay me you pay me.'

Steve backed away, two steps, but it brought more of the girl into Tom's view as she followed. She kept looking up at Steve's face, imploring him, while her left hand dipped into the pocket of his skimpy shorts.

He slapped her hand away.

No money there, that was clear.

Tom spotted two concierges closing in across the lobby. The girl didn't have long now. Her fingers stroked back through the hairs on Steve's arm. Her mouth made bigger word shapes; she had increased the volume, but she didn't frown. She was a little girl pleading, not threatening.

With one swift sweep the girl slipped the Apple Watch from Steve's wrist. She raised herself onto her toes and snatched the headset from around Steve's neck. Then she was off.

The move was so quick Tom had to replay it in his head to make sense of it even as he watched the girl scamper across the lobby. Steve stood rooted a moment. He lifted his right arm and gaped at his wrist, bare of his watch. He reached his left hand up to his neck and felt for the headset but stroked collar bone. The headset, too, was gone.

The girl kicked off her oversized leather shoes. Who cared? They were cheap. She had her prizes. She wouldn't be slapped about for not doing her job. She ran barefoot.

Steve started to run, but it was as if it were in split screen, the Englishman lumbering in slow motion while the Viet girl pelted like a rabbit.

The Golden Dawn wasn't a place where children ran free. The hotel didn't have the protocol to prevent such grab and runs. The girl scarpered and nobody moved. She was out and away, gone down the ramp and into the street.

Steve gesticulated and shouted orders at any man he could see. Go catch that girl. It was like shouting go catch a cold. Steve came back to the reception, still shouting. He slapped his right hand, empty of his watch, flat on to the counter three times to beat home his point. He had been robbed and the hotel was liable.

That was Tom's best guess at Steve's complaint. Steve wasn't a man for self-reflection. The world went Steve's way, and that was fine by Steve. If it didn't, it was your fault.

Keep it up, Steve, Tom thought. Behave like a jerk. You're being recorded. The hotel will share the footage of this incident with the police. The police will then share every second of it with Interpol, should they ask.

And they will ask, Steve.

Believe me, they'll ask.

Chapter 7

Here was girl number two, right on cue.

This one played it right. She breezed in through the lobby doors and didn't hesitate. She caught nobody's eye but walked directly to the lifts. Her jeans were skinnies, and she had beige thong sandals on her child-sized feet, and a satin top of olive green with a neck that plunged between where breasts might grow someday. Her hair reached past her shoulders and was brushed back behind her ears. She could pass for a teenager. The lift doors closed on her.

Tom had no access to the upper-level cameras that watched the lifts, they were in a blind spot. He switched to the view of the topmost corridor. Steve had just walked along it, off to catch breakfast in the Premium Lounge, and now the corridor was empty.

Here was the girl. Again, she showed no hesitation. She walked along the corridor and counted down the numbers on the doors to her left.

When she reached Steve's door the girl did not pause at all. She might have brushed her hand through her hair, sucked in her cheeks, shrugged her shoulders, but she was brisk, out on a business call. The door had a bell, and she rang it. No one answered. The girl bunched her right hand into a fist and rapped on the door. Still Steve didn't answer.

Tom glanced across at the monitor that showed Steve at breakfast. He was sitting at a table with a bunch of Korean delegates who were more casually dressed for the day in grey cotton uniforms. Steve's sleeves were rolled up so his Patek Philippe flashed its gold. Somebody should tell Steve: only teachers and men over fifty wore a wristwatch. Steve was an embarrassment.

The girl walked back down the corridor. She bypassed the lift and kept going straight. She must have worked this executive layer of the hotel before. She knew about the Premium Lounge.

From a camera fixed to a ceiling behind the lounge's morning hostess, Tom watched the girl approach. She turned on a smile that looked convincing, and spoke words that Tom presumed were in Vietnamese but included what looked like the shape of Steve's name. This was a young girl. She didn't look like a threat. The hostess nodded and allowed her to pass.

It wouldn't take much for Steve to avert the danger posed by the girl. He could take her to the buffet, give her a plate, ask her to fill it, have a discreet word with the hostess, say something was clearly going wrong with hotel security, that he kept receiving these unsolicited visits from young girls. If she caused a scene, he could fetch cash from his bedroom and pay her to go away, but keep her away from the Koreans, please. He had business to transact.

Tom thought through this whole strategy while the girl walked the few feet to Steve's table. It would have worked.

Steve wasn't as sharp as Tom, though.

The group of grey-clad Korean men plus Steve were situated by the window, a lakeside view across all of Hanoi beyond them, but the girl wasn't interested in panoramas. She checked a picture on her phone and looked up at Steve to make sure, decided she was sure, and stood close to Steve as she spoke at him.

She reached out first and touched him, her fingers making contact with the skin of his arm and stroking. She smiled. Steve had booked her, he wanted sex, here she was at the time he had requested, he must be pleased to see her. The girl didn't know Steve's recent history. She didn't know that the last young girl to stroke Steve's arm had run off with his headphones and Apple Watch.

Steve jerked his hand away as if the girl had committed sexual assault. He turned to face her. Tom was watching from behind Steve's head and didn't know how he was playing it, but it looked like the girl had decided things were not going the way she expected and changed tack.

Tom couldn't make out the words on her mouth, but she was trying to make Steve admit to something because Steve started shaking his head. This wasn't him, he wasn't Steve, he hadn't booked her, he didn't want sex. Whatever it was the girl was asking of him, Steve's head kept denying it.

The girl got louder, or at least her mouth moved faster, and Steve got up and tried to walk past her. He was going for help. The girl reached out and took hold of Steve's arm to stop him.

Steve had already lost one watch that morning. That had been an Apple, which was bad enough, but he sure as shit wasn't going to lose his Patek Philippe. He pulled his left hand away, holding his wrist high in the air, and used his right hand to push her clear. She stumbled against the table. Two of the Koreans got up from their seats and shoved back their chairs with their legs, startled, but another, a young man, chose to be gallant. His face showed concern and he said something kind to the girl.

Here, she said to him. Without an audio feed, Tom had to interpret, but the meaning was clear enough. The girl reached out her phone so the young Korean could see it, pointed at it and then at Steve. She spoke and nodded her head and pointed again. This man in the picture, she was asking, it was Steve, wasn't it, it was this blond foreigner at their table?

The young Korean's face turned blank when he looked at the picture. He looked from it to Steve then back at the girl and nodded. She waved with her hand: go on, show them, let them see the phone.

The phone travelled around the table, between the Korean men's hands. They all looked solemn and gave slight nods of their heads.

Steve was out of the camera's range. He had gone for help. He returned with the hostess. Show her, the girl said, or that's what Tom read from her lips and gestures, and that's what happened. The phone was passed along the row of Korean hands to the hostess. She took it and her eyes widened when faced with the picture and blinked at Steve.

Now it was Steve's turn. He took the phone and stared at it. And stared. Tom could see Steve's face now. He could read his lips. Steve's mouth made big shapes, like he was shouting, 'Where did you get this?'

Tom didn't need the girl's explanation. Not that he could see the picture, but he had only had Steve send out the one. The one he had taken when Steve was watching the ad for the Jaguar F-Type. You sent it to her yourself, Steve, Tom could have said. It's your favourite selfie, you fresh from the shower, your blond hair dark and plastered to your scalp, your towel in your hand and hiding nothing, your sizeable dick still engorged from its wank. You're proud of this picture, Steve. You've pinned it to message boards. It's an attachment to a score or more of your emails. There's no point denying it now.

Two of the hotel security staff, both men, entered the picture. Perfect. This was set to work. They kept a distance while a man with a trim haircut and light grey suit, a representative of management, came to the table and started talking to Steve. The hostess passed the girl's phone to him. The screen had gone blank. The hostess handed it to the girl, who pressed a finger against the phone's sensor and nodded when the image of Steve reappeared and handed it to the manager for him to look at.

This was all too much for Steve. He started to argue, but you can only get away with so much without losing Premium Lounge rights. The manager stood firm, his left hand held out to indicate Steve's way to a private one-on-one meeting out of view and out of earshot, but the girl wasn't much for a one-on-one and the manager now had her phone and pulled it out of reach when she grabbed for it, and the two security men closed in so she followed the men from the room.

They'd ask for her identity card. Would she have one yet? The Vietnamese government gave them out when citizens were fourteen. If she had one, the security men could collect her data. If she didn't, it meant she was thirteen or younger. Either way, the hotel had to stop and think. Surely they did. This girl didn't run solo. Some operation was running her, sending underage girls to clients in the hotel's rooms. That didn't suit the hotel brand. They'd call the police. The police would question the girl. They'd locate the gang that ran her. Raid the place. Rescue every girl.

It could happen.

Tom had done what he could. It was out of his hands.

What was certain, was the hotel would now be utterly sick of Steve.

Steve would be sick, too, of course, but Tom had done him a good turn. Hell could have broken loose without warning when Steve was back in the bosom of his family. Instead, Tom had delivered this twenty-four-hour notice of doom. Two girls had turned up with Steve's name and room number. They claimed he had booked them. Steve believed that he hadn't. The second girl showed up with that picture of Steve in her phone.

How did it get there? And who had snapped Steve, naked and smiling and wet?

Steve's brain was now fuelled with questions to resolve.

Tom retreated to the confines of Steve's laptop and waited. It took Steve forty minutes to talk himself clear and retreat to his room. Tom wasn't watching. He had even disconnected the webcam so he couldn't be tempted.

Tom knew Steve was back, though, because he did what Tom expected him to do. Steve brought up his settings and changed his password. He did the same to his email accounts, both his work one and his private Gmail account. As though there was such a thing as a private Gmail account.

A text arrived on Steve's phone with a code to authenticate the change to the Gmail password.

Tom had sent it.

Steve typed the code into his screen.

Tom laughed and laughed and laughed.

Chapter 8

At thirty-six thousand feet, half the globe away, Steve was scrunched up in his economy seat, journeying back from Hanoi. He had taken one of Karen's Valiums, which combined well with the airline's champagne. The effect wasn't sleep, but it was groggy enough to pass.

Meanwhile it was an early start of day at the Hardbridge offices in London. Steve's desk was vacant, which opened a clear view for Tom.

Tom had come to know the human traffic that passed behind Steve's back. Since Steve had left for his short trip to Hanoi, there was a new guy seated in the carrel across the way. Ginger hair was shaved into the nape of his neck and wire spectacle arms hooked behind the button ears under his headset. His head made tiny shifts from side to side, as if he was tracking numerals on screen. He could be seventeen – he looked that eager – but Tom guessed more like twenty-two. He had snuck into the profession with a few years to go before he was replaced by AI.

Robotic control would be an advance, was Tom's view. Tom was amused but more often offended by the layers of human incapacity he found on trading floors. To him, this chase of stocks and funds was nothing better than a high-stakes video game. Men and a scattering of women skimmed waves of data while algorithms did the actual work.

Tom had been tempted to intervene. With a few strokes he could have boosted Steve's hit rate or squandered multi-millions. It was just a temptation, though. Tom practised to kill off such urges when they arose. They led you astray. They made you forget to want what you really want.

Get what you really want first and then see.

When Steve chatted with experts, Tom had listened in. After these chats Steve would pull up spreadsheets for a bout of what he called analysis, but Steve knew squat. His decisions were punts. Commodities were about supply and demand, but supply was always limited so all it came down to was profit now or profit later. Now was better but later wasn't so bad, and a bonus would come at end of year whatever Steve did.

At Steve's home Tom had listened in as Steve and Karen worked out, for fun, how they would spend that year's bonus. They had their eyes on a cottage in Southwold. It wasn't on the market yet, but friends of a friend owned it and were thinking of letting it go. It wouldn't matter what Steve and Karen paid for it because the town was like Notting Hill-on-Sea and prices shot up so fast they'd clear a profit in a year. Karen's semi-best friend had a place across the river in Walberswick, and it was good for the kids to have a break from London and its pollution and get some salted air into their lungs.

It took a while for Tom to come to know Hardbridge's in-house IT team, because they kept close to themselves and had little to do with the brokers. They played their own speed game: algorithms for the trading floor flourished on speed and whoever squeezed an extra millisecond faster in response time got the team's entire doughnut fund for that week.

Hardbridge outsourced its cybersecurity to 4tknox who Tom found laughable. 4tnkox bought in almost all its software. The Comms girl who put together Hardbridge's weekly staff newsletter put that week's stats for cyberattacks inside two rosettes, one red and one blue. The red showed the number of attacks. The blue showed the number of attacks prevented. Both figures were high and both were the same. Attacks were a source of pride.

Tom knew hackers that played along and gave those special-ists the attacks they needed. These hackers worked in bands. Their game was the equivalent of setting the sky ablaze with fireballs while tunnelling beneath the walls. Most would be caught but that didn't matter so long as one or two got through.

In the weeks Tom was watching, one attack did sneak through Hardbridge's firewalls and connect. Tom was the first to notice and he shut down Steve's account till 4tknox got the problem fixed. You protect what you own. By now, Tom owned Steve.

Steve had full security clearance. Tom had simply studied his moves at first, and he became Steve, and now as Steve he had gone quietly rogue.

The computer was a made-to-measure Dell. Steve's work-station was a cubicle separated from the next by a sheet of brown MDF. Pipework was exposed in the ceiling and strip lighting hung low on chains. To Tom the trading floor was a mix of downmarket and brash and he would be glad to see the back of it.

The set-up was easy enough, just a cut and paste of the long URL and the answers he'd had Steve give to three questions. Favourite TV show: *Blue Peter*. Favourite Film: *Back to the Future*. Favourite food: Banana sandwich.

The answers made Steve seem infantile. Tom had to have Steve choose a door to open. He picked the black one. And the live film began. Now came the hard part. Tom's personal filters for onscreen child abuse were porous and he could get upset. But he had to watch for a minute or two to make sure the content was sick enough. It was.

Tom set the live video feed playing on Steve's monitor. He didn't play it full screen. Only a rank idiot would watch hard core porn full screen in the workplace. The rape scene played out in the bottom right-hand corner. You could lean a book against it and hide it if somebody came along.

The guy in the livestream was fat, bald, naked, bearded, white. He might have been Hungarian, the live feed came from Hungary, but it might have been re-routed. The girl was white too, with long blond hair that looked like a wig, one that was too big for her tiny head. She clutched a pillow over her chest like that's what she could protect. Tom couldn't watch any more.

Tom looked out from Steve's webcam at the young ginger-headed guy across the way, willing him to turn around.

Tom jolted. There was a danger when you stared out through someone's webcam.

It had happened once, when Tom was starting out, when he was young, about six months ago. He had been practising. Could he go live on a teleprompter?

That was his game. For the attempt, Tom chose a news station in Hobart. *Breaking News*, he typed. *The coastguard was called out this afternoon to turn back a colony of king penguins approaching Tasmania's shores on a renegade ice floe.*

The newscaster leaned in close. That was to be expected. Tom's news item was surprising. She leaned in closer.

Tom leaned closer too, like her reflection.

She leaned back. Ignored the king-penguin news item and started a rambling monologue about having had to pull her car to the side of the road on the way to the studio, the rain was falling so fast. She thanked her lucky stars that it was her job to read the news and not predict it. Unlike the weather forecaster.

'And now' – she had spun enough time to alert the producer – 'to give us her best shot at whether tomorrow will be hot or frigid, it's over to Charlotte in the weather studio.'

The presenter paused to be sure the switch had been made then spoke into her mic. 'We've been hacked,' she said. No emotion in it, a statement of fact. 'A twelve-year-old fuckhead is gawping at me out of my screen.'

The quip about his age was unnecessary, but Tom accepted

he had it coming to him. He had to be more careful. He got black tape and covered the lens of his webcam. Sometimes lo-tech was the go-to tech.

He checked now. Fuck. The lens was clear. He had peeled the tape away. Did it yesterday, to surprise someone, got excited, didn't stick it back.

He went and got the roll, cut off three lengths to be sure and blacked out the lens afresh.

Nothing had happened. Ginger's head was bobbing a bit but he hadn't turned round. Maybe a techno beat was coming through his headset. Everybody used headsets and nobody used speakers. With speakers, Tom could have turned up the volume on Steve's computer. The Hungarian kiddie-fucker was grunting toward a long-thrust climax. That would have turned Ginger's head.

Although Tom blanked out his view into Hungary, the live soundtrack of the child rape continued in his headset. In some ways it was worse than the visuals because the sounds prompted Tom to come up with pictures that matched them. It triggered his imagination, like he was complicit. He had to listen to be sure the broadcast was still active, but it was hard to bear.

Couldn't someone stop it?

Tom thought about making the atrocity full screen after all. Turn your head, Ginger. See what's going on. Get in there somehow and save that little girl.

Tom worked to stay patient, but if this carried on much longer he'd have to rip off his headset and rush to the bathroom and throw up.

A woman went past, a brisk young thing in full stride, legs thrusting inside her grey wool skirt and a white blouse tight on her toned torso. She passed but returned, stepping backward. Her head cocked left to take in what she had just glimpsed. Was this for real?

The woman looked like a schoolteacher – specifically, Ms Bungay, Tom's PE teacher, with her blonde hair tugged tight into a ponytail, and yes, as the woman bent close, the same pale blue eyes that grew round and appalled whenever she looked your way.

Tom was never a star of PE. The whole group physicality of the thing was a torture.

He watched the woman's eyes and recalled that this wasn't school, he was home, safe, the ordeal of PE was no more, and he listened in to Hungarian grunts and the thin crying of the little girl and Tom knew that the shock in the woman's eyes was because she could see what he could only hear.

The young woman stepped across the walkway and tapped Ginger on the shoulder. He started at the touch and spun his chair round. The woman pointed at Steve's monitor. This was a waste of time, she should have called security, who would call the police, but maybe this woman wasn't as tough as she looked.

Tom felt it was always best to face things alone – other people only compounded whatever difficulty he was in – but not everyone's a loner. Some seek company. Tom didn't understand this aspect of human nature but he knew it was so.

The woman must have blinked when she saw Ginger face to face. The kid really was young. Maybe Tom's age, even. She must be wondering what she'd done, upsetting the intern and obliging him to witness a live broadcast of child abuse.

Ginger got to his feet and inched closer. The top two buttons of his white shirt were open. The skin that spread below the young man's neck was pallid. A gob of gold swung forward, attached to a short, thick chain. It took a moment, and then Tom recognized it as a rabbit. A bunny rabbit. This kid was not just an intern. He was adolescent.

The woman pressed her fingers on his shoulder, urging him to one side. They'd both seen enough. But Ginger held firm. He didn't look shocked so much as absorbed, like a science geek observing the mating of rare newts in an aquarium. His mouth dropped open in the shape of a word.

'Fuck.'

Tom couldn't hear Ginger's call, just the grunts of the Hungarian and the puffed-out shrieks of the child, but it must have been loud. Another man, the only one Tom saw regularly in a jacket and tie, a senior geezer, slid in screen left. He always looked affable, like the chubby kid at school who got bullied but stuck with the genial act till it finally paid off. Tom knew the man as a smiler, but there was no smile now. He looked briefly into the monitor, his eyes fixed there for a moment, and Tom could see the pink blanch from his cheeks.

Ginger reached forward, his index finger extended to press the power button. The manager gripped hold of his arm and pulled it back. He turned his head and shouted a command over the top of the carrels. Then he stood between Ginger and the woman, a hand on a shoulder of each, and shepherded them out of Tom's view.

The distant child rape ran live in Tom's headset. It was refined now, only the gasped cries of the child, a breathless bleating. Tom snatched the headset clear of his ears.

A woman came by, dressed in a grey security uniform, walking backward and wheeling a light blue display board in her hand. She left the board tight against the edge of Steve's desk.

The next thing Tom would see, he was sure, would be the police. They'd appear to look straight in at him, like the monitor was a sheet of glass, but they'd be noting the URL the manager had thought to leave live at the top of the screen. Nobody had hot-desked this space since Steve took his flight to Hanoi.

Tom guessed at the manager's thoughts. Is this what Steve had been doing? Was he such a sick shit that he'd stream child abuse to a fragment of his work screen? It wasn't likely, he'd be thinking, but who knew? They'd investigate.

For now, they had a live broadcast of an active crime scene on their hands. Deal with that first.

Tom imagined the scene. Two police officers would come. One was a woman who would take out her phone and snatch an image of the monitor. The other was a man who would peel on latex gloves. His fingers would whisk across the keyboard. He wouldn't look at them. He'd stare into the monitor while Tom stared back. The policeman would take a screenshot then dive one of two ways. He would search through the browsing history, or he would head straight into the system.

Tom bet on the latter.

He blanked the view from Steve's webcam. What was done was done. He'd never need to peer into that workspace again.

In place of the webcam view his screen filled with code.

It was time to give the police what help he could, All that cruising Tom had had Steve do, it did Tom's head in at times. At night, the cries of children pierced his brain and jolted him out of sleep. His dreams had become subterranean, stuck in scenes of torture where flesh writhed in distant cellars. He'd wake and find from toe to scalp that his body was slick with sweat.

Steve was the type who would claim innocence – he was only watching, no harm done. In fact Tom had never caught Steve watching porn but that was beside the point. Could the police stop these live porn transmissions? Tom doubted it, but he could help. He brought what was hidden, what was very, very private, to the fore. Not right to the fore, two layers back, just … there.

Now he had to cloak his work, to remove every trace, to wipe every fingerprint. He had to kill the worm.

Tom worked fast. And when he was done he cruised around and found a picture of a wildflower meadow. It was a speckle of colours in a wash of grass. At the rear were dark blue mountains beneath a pale blue sky. It was one of his favourite photos from the iPhone gallery of a sleeper of his who had spent two weeks hiking through Colorado.

Tom stood up and headed out. It was time for a stroll across his local scrap of park. He would seek out birdsong. When he came back the wildflower meadow would have cleansed his screen. He could take a break from his anti-Steve crusade. Till he resumed it.

Over to you, Steve. You had it coming.

Chapter 9

Steve trotted through Heathrow's customs hall. Inside his bag, a Maxwell-Scott Piazalle of black leather with brass trimming, was an olive-green cap with an embroidered hammer and sickle on it, yellow on red, a present for Colin, and a stringy doll in ethnic dress for Amy. For Karen, he no longer bought perfume – she'd decided they were all toxic – so he'd snapped up a Swarovski ballpoint pen from the plane's duty-free trolley. That was it. Nothing to declare there.

In the crowd beyond the barrier in Heathrow's arrivals hall Steve scanned for a sign. There it was, 'Stephen McInnes' hand-written on a wipe-clean board. The guy was big, the buttons straining on his purple shirt. Nigerian, Steve guessed. That could be good, or it could be bad. Steve had a notion about Nigerian drivers. They either succumbed to traffic, sat back, cracked jokes and cut the breeze, or they spun the wheel, treated bike lanes like taxi lanes, nothing held them back. Steve needed the latter.

'Hi,' Steve said, and raised his hand. The driver – his badge called him Kwame – gave Steve a broad smile. Steve didn't need it and his cheeks forgot to return it till he thought better of it and turned on a smile.

Too late. He saw the slight dilation in Kwame's eyes, a judgement form about the passenger he was set to share his car with. Kwame's hand reached forward and gripped the handle of Steve's bag. Steve wanted to resist, to hold on, but the bag was ripped away from him and Kwame was smiling again.

'I'm in a hurry,' Steve said. 'I want to see my kids before bedtime.'

'You've got kids?'

'Two. Colin and Amy.'

'That's great.' Kwame beamed. The man seemed delighted. 'I've got four. All boys.'

'What are the roads like? I'm wondering about a train. Straight to Paddington and a taxi from there.'

'You want to queue for a taxi at Paddington? At rush hour?'

'A Tube, then. I could go on from there by Tube.'

Kwame laughed, a sound from deep inside his chest, and strode on.

They got into an empty lift. The doors started to close but opened again. A young woman navigated her trolley in, talking Polish into her phone. Again the doors closed, one thin gap, then opened for an Asian man whose baggage labels had an address in Karachi and who shepherded his family into every free centimetre of the lift. Kwame kept smiling. Steve found he was holding his breath and let go.

Their car was on the first floor, thank God, and the lift opened on their side. Steve followed Kwame to a silver Mercedes, one of the mid-range hybrids, an E220. Steve sat in the back, his Maxwell-Scott Piazalle beside him and his briefcase on his lap, and the car shifted silently on its electric motor to join the cars belching diesel fumes as they queued for the exit.

'We're at a standstill already,' Steve said. He could still climb out and go back into the terminal and take the train.

'This part's quick,' Kwame said. 'We'll be out soon.'

Steve checked his watch. It took seven minutes.

'Here we go,' Kwame said. They were free of the car park, but the traffic ahead stopped and started even before they reached the airport tunnel. Yet Steve was stuck now.

'Could you lend me your phone?' he asked. 'I want to speak with my kids.'

'You need a charger? I can lend you a charger.'

'I don't need a charger. My phone's charged. I need your phone.'

'Why do you need mine if you've got your own?'

'Mine's been hacked.'

'It doesn't work?'

'I don't want people listening in.'

'You're telling secrets to your boy and girl? Kids don't need secrets. Tell them you love them. That's all they need. No harm anybody listening in to that.'

'It's just local. I'll pay.'

'Sorry, man. This phone does my navigating.'

Steve could see it, hooked into its stand, a map on display, showing no movement.

'We're at a near-standstill,' Steve tried. 'When the traffic moves, follow it to the M40. You don't need GPS to manage that. You scarcely need a brain.'

Silence. Kwame spoke again. 'Sorry, sir. Company policy.'

'It's company policy not to let clients use your phone in times of distress?'

Silence.

A silver cross hung on a string of multicoloured wooden beads from the rearview mirror. A small photo in a gold plastic frame, four grinning black boys in front of what must be their mother, was suckered to the dashboard. A fake pewter Jesus wobbled beside it.

'What's the company policy on filling the car with kitsch?' Steve asked. 'The bobbly beaded cross. The plastic Saviour. That your family? Your wife and kids?'

Silence.

'You wanted to speak to your wife and kids, I'd lend you my phone.'

Silence.

'You think all that gewgaw, the cross and the wobbly Christ, makes you a Christian? Corinthians, Kwame.' Steve had learned that technique. Use someone's name in conversation when you need to form a bond when you want something. 'The greatest of these is charity. That's what you Christians say, right? Why not show me a little Christian charity?'

They reached a roundabout. Traffic idled off it. 'We'll have you home soon as we can,' Kwame said.

'Who's this "we", Kwame? You and fucking God?'

Steve saw a little quiver at Kwame's temples, like the man's head flinched. Fair enough. You don't foul-mouth a man's god. Steve didn't always get it right. So what. You say what you feel. Steve could say sorry, but he didn't feel sorry. You talk how you feel and live with the consequences.

They filtered on to the M40 at something under thirty miles an hour. And stopped. Fuck it. Steve hooked on his earpiece and powered up his phone. He selected Facetime. He could talk to Karen then take a look at the kids, they could see he was back, they could all wave goodnight.

'Steve,' Karen said, a bit of a gasp, like she didn't trust it was him, she was checking on the caller ID. 'Don't use Facetime. Call me back. The landline.'

And she disconnected him.

What was that about? They never used the landline. Well, only to call their mobiles to locate them. Steve didn't know the number. He brought up his contacts and scrolled through. Home under H. It started 0207. That looked right. He called it.

Karen picked up. 'What is this, Steve? We live in a communication age and what is it now – twenty-five hours since we heard from you?'

'I've been …'

'You've been what, Steve? Busy? In Vietnam? Flying? Lost to the world? I don't care what you've been, Steve, you stay in touch. Do you know what we've been? Do you care what's happened to us?'

'The flight was late. I got stuck in cattle-class, sitting up all night, last off the plane. Immigration took forever. And now we're stuck in traffic. I'm not going to be back for the kids' bedtime. I thought you could show me the kids. Can I speak to them? Say goodnight?'

'The kids need a hug, Steve. They don't need a tinny speaker pressed to their ear. Some voice coming out of it.'

'What's happened, K?'

'Amy came in this morning, dead early, talking about a monster in her room. I thought it was a nightmare. I let her into our bed and held her, but you know Amy. She shrugged me off. She doesn't want comfort, she wants to know. I told her it was a bad dream, and she said it wasn't. It was a real monster, and it was in her room and it woke her up and it was groaning and screaming. I had to go and chase it away. We got up and I held her hand and we went to her room so she could see there was nothing there and we could all calm down. But she was right, Steve. We went into her room and there *was* a monster.'

'What—'

'Don't interrupt, Steve. Now I've got you, let me talk. It wasn't a monster, of course, it wasn't a Gruffalo or anything, but it was sick. It was coming out of the Nest Cam. Did you know it could do that? Did you know it had speakers? Those groans and screams and squeals of a monster? Well, Amy was right. That's what she was hearing. I could hear it, too, Steve. It was the audio of a porn channel – not in English, let's hallelujah that, Amy couldn't understand it, it was the grunts and words of sex, all in Hungarian, as it turns out. I recorded it on my phone and played it back for Hanga. She turned beetroot and stabbed at my phone to turn it off. Someone was streaming live porn from Hungary into our children's bedrooms.'

'Colin's too?'

'Yes. I checked. He was sleeping. He didn't hear it. I pulled the wires out. You know how you fixed those Nest Cams to the walls, angled down on the kids' beds? Well, someone's hacked them. Those things are two-way. You never thought of that. You never thought that you were letting strangers peer at our children while they sleep.'

'Those Nest Cams were your idea. You called them nanny cams. You wanted to check up on the nannies. You said trust was stupid and nanny cams were better.'

'Don't, Steve. Don't start getting at me. You weren't here. I was. I've had to deal with things. I put Amy in our bed. Told her it wasn't a monster, just a foreign radio channel and we'd turn it off and take it away. Took my phone and went back and recorded the whole sick feed for evidence then pulled out its wires. I'm going to redecorate both their rooms, Steve. A light yellow, maybe, something soothing.'

'I'm sorry, K. So sorry.' What else could he say? Start spilling his own shit all over her? He couldn't do that. 'Let's not talk now, love. Not over my phone. I'll get back as soon as I can. We can have dinner. Talk things through. Give the kids my love, OK? Love you, K. Love you.'

Steve broke the connection and stared out the window.

The car was moving at a crawl.

'You did what you could, man,' Kwame said from the front. 'You sent them your love.'

Steve didn't speak back. He had emotions and thoughts aplenty, lots he could say, but some feelings cluster round your heart and churn away and don't shape into words.

Chapter 10

Steve turned off mobile data, for whatever good that did, and opened his photo gallery. On his first night away Karen had sent him a photo. He had stored it in his gallery and needed to see it now.

There they were. Colin was in his Superman and Amy in her Wonder Woman pyjamas. And he knew he was way too tired because first there was the spasm of love for his little kids and then a flush of anger at what they were wearing. What sort of mythical world were they bringing their kids into, all dressed up in the DC superhero franchise? What was wrong with having them grow up as people?

There was Colin, with the bags under his eyes, and Amy with her scowl. Raising their hands bye-bye like they'd been told, like Daddy needed a salute. He should get home early one day and read them proper bedtime stories, Goldilocks and Little Red Riding Hood and all that stuff. He'd diarize it.

Steve had more photos of his kids in his phone. It was stuffed with them. Someday, he should sort them. Or stick them on a hard drive so they didn't get wiped. Or print them and have the children spend a weekend sticking photos into a family album. Now wouldn't that be retro? They could stay at home, watch *The Little Mermaid*, eat pizza and laugh and tell stories about family pictures. He'd love to do that. He would do it. He'd diarize it.

Fast lane of the M40 and the taxi had stopped again. These stop-starts were agony. Steve looked out the window then back at his phone. Memories were good. He could do with more of them right now. He scrolled down. Past the river and the men under the brollies working the oars of the boat with bare feet, the karst hills, that day out in Vietnam that was just two days ago but that was an age ago already. Past…

Steve didn't go past. An image flicked by in his run-through and he brought it back. The background was dark, but the girl was brightly lit. Her body was naked, her eyes were big and she was looking up, at a man, at some camera. She had his dick in her mouth.

Steve gagged. Kwame briefly turned his head, sensing the alarm, but space opened out ahead of the car and he drove into it. Steve swallowed his bile. He knew this girl. It was the one from yesterday, only yesterday, who had entered the hotel after his morning run in Hanoi, accosted him and run off with his headphones and Apple Watch. This photo was evidence.

But evidence of what? That Steve knew the girl? Could that dick in her mouth be mistaken for his? He checked the picture. The dick was thick and short and ugly with what looked like a red lesion on its side and grey hairs among the pubes. It looked no more like his than a donkey's would. Thank God.

But would this count as evidence of images of child sex abuse downloaded to his phone?

Fuck yes.

How could this have happened?

Steve scrolled down. Were any other sick surprises lurking?

He found the regular photos he could own to. Him and Koreans, laughing and brushing cement dust from their clothes. Views from his top-floor window, trying to catch the beauty of a Hanoi panorama without the smudge of smog. A series he took of scooters jammed across the highway, one with five family members riding pillion, others parked thick on the pavement, riders in smog masks, image after image snapped from cars, and then, oh my God no. Not that. They couldn't do that to a child. To do that, and then to take a picture with all that detail, like it was a trophy.

And then to download it to his phone. Who would do that? How could they do it? What else had they done?

Steve thought about opening the window and flinging the phone on to the hard shoulder. He wanted to do that, to get distance from the filth, but then someone could find it. Hand it in. They could find these pictures and come for him. OK, it wasn't him, he didn't do it, but already that sounded a weak defence because it was his, it was his phone, and he couldn't say how the pictures got there. I was hacked, he could say, and keep on saying it. Hacked hacked hacked – but what did that mean?

There were places you could go. You handed in your phone and your computer and they destroyed them for you, it was this century's version of shredding. But Steve didn't even know what such a place would be called. And he wasn't going to open his phone and put in a search string to find out. And, in any case, he wanted to get home.

He stuck the phone inside his bag.

He'd find a thick envelope, package up the phone and the laptop, call a courier and have the package biked over to 4tknox, the cybersecurity consultants. They could take a look at it on Hardbridge's paycheque. The items belonged to the firm, after all. They were no longer a company perk but a company problem. The company could fix it. And Steve would have got the child porn out of his house. Nobody guilty of downloading such stuff would hand their hardware with all its images over to their firm.

It was a plan. It felt like putting your head on the block because you needed a rest, but it was a plan.

Chapter II

A scooter with the Just Eat logo was pulling away from the space in front of Steve's house. Kwame indicated, paused and then turned in. Steve wondered about a tip and chose against. Kwame had his Christ, his happy-face family, he hadn't stirred to bring Steve home a minute sooner than he might, and he wouldn't loan his phone.

Steve felt sick, maybe from stress, but also because Kwame's hybrid Merc had tailgated diesel vehicles on a stuttering journey of hours. Steve's lungs and brain were choked.

He kept his wallet in his pocket. 'Thanks for the journey from hell,' Steve said, and got out.

Steve's father joked that their son lived in a two-up two-down terraced house. Well, yes, Dad, but those two-up two-downs are the house's four levels and you'd have to sell your semi in Pinner to scrape the down payment on my basement. It was Early Victorian, and Steve and Karen had had it gutted and architecturally remodelled before moving in. Even the four steps up from the roadway were hi-tech, weathered and tempered glass backlit. It was like stepping up through pools of turquoise water.

Steve pressed in the code on the security pad. It played out its song of pulse-like beats and the door clicked open. At least the locks weren't linked to the wi-fi. The basic structure of the house couldn't be hacked.

Steve didn't call out. He didn't want to wake the kids.

He didn't need to make a sound to bring on Millie. He heard the mouselike scratching of her claws as they scrabbled for purchase on the kitchen tiles then they dashed up speed on the light-grey engineered-oak planks of the hallway. It's like loving a bogbrush, Steve had said to Karen when she picked Millie out of the litter of Shih Tzu puppies, and it was true – that snout poking out through the ring of dark grey fur, the tiny teeth bared in her downturned mouth – and it was also true that he loved the scrubby thing. Loved her to bits.

Her paws were still sliding on the wooden flooring so Steve backed himself against the door. The mat was an oval of organic jute. Millie loved to stand there and bark at sounds from the outside world, a fierce yapping, because, tiny as she was, she'd always fight back. Steve crouched and reached around her snout to muzzle her. Her tongue stuck out and lapped at his hands, working to lick herself free, her feet pattering against his feet as she pressed into him. Steve laughed. God, that felt good, to laugh.

He looked up and saw Karen. She was coming along the corridor from the kitchen, her face showing above a festoon of yellow roses she had arranged in a plain crystal vase.

'You,' she said, and paused. It was as if she were telling him off, her lips pursed, but then she smiled. She was playing a game.

89

'I thought, "That was curt," when you cut off our call like that. We'd been hacked, I know, it made sense, but even so. Then how many calls did you go and make? You must have chased down every rose in west London. First one delivery, then another, then another.'

She set the vase down on the console table, adjusted the arrangement, turned to Steve, and gave in. Her bare feet with their shiny blue toenails scampered across the floorboards and she folded her body against his chest, her hands reaching for his shoulder blades as he wrapped his arms about her, her fingers curling hold. She trembled. Her tears wet the skin of his neck. And then he felt her grow calm. He relaxed his hold and she stepped back, tipped her chin and looked up at him.

'It's so sick, Steve,' she said. 'How anyone could do that to our children, feed porn into their rooms? But you're back. That's good.'

Karen took Steve's hands into hers, held them a while, squeezed them and let go.

'Look at those flowers. I can arrange them better than that, but they're beautiful. I've put a vase in the dining room. And the living room. And kept some back for the kitchen. That was truly sweet of you.'

'Did they come with any message?'

'Should they have done?'

Steve shrugged.

'You sent me my favourite flowers when I felt bad. Pink ones, red ones, and now these yellow. No need for any other message. And then you ordered in my favourite meal. It's just come. I've put it in the oven.'

The doorbell rang. Millie's body juddered as she exploded into a fierce sequence of yaps. So much for not waking the kids. Though they did tend to sleep soundly at the start of the night and Steve half hoped they'd wake and he could get to see them.

He checked the monitor. A young guy with a lime-green bike helmet. Another delivery, it looked like. Steve bent low, grabbed hold of Millie's collar and opened the door.

'Mrs McInnes?' The man looked at Steve then into the house at Karen. She stepped forward and he handed her a long box of parchment yellow bound in dark green ribbon. She lodged it under her arm and signed her name on his device with a fingernail. Steve let go of Millie who tried to squeeze through the closing door and yelped when it clipped her snout. It should have annoyed Steve, but everything Millie did he found funny. It was one of the mysteries of his life.

Karen pulled off the ribbon and opened the box. It held a bottle. She pulled at its neck.

'Steve!' His name came out in a little squeal and Karen bounced a couple of times on those bare toes. 'A Montrachet grand cru – 2013. It's amazing. How could you know? I was on Berry Brothers website and reading a review of this very bottle only yesterday. You've got everything so right. Come on, Steve. We've got those glasses Amanda and Caius gave us, the Riedel Sommeliers ones. And this bottle's chilled. Let's welcome you home.'

Steve forced a smile. Could he have named her favourite wine? If forced, he'd have guessed at a Meursault. Right region, too low a price bracket.

What was her favourite dinner, that one she said was in the oven? Thai lemon chicken? Again, just a guess. He didn't know.

The hallway was thickening with the scent of the roses she thought he'd sent her.

Should he tell her he hadn't sent them?

A drawer rattled in the kitchen then Steve heard the cork pop from its bottle.

'We've got some tapenade,' Karen called softly. 'Spread it on a few oat biscuits, will you?'

He had to tell her. They'd both been hacked. To Steve, out in Vietnam, they'd sent underage girls. To Karen, they'd shipped her favourite things. How long had they been cruising her to find out the things she most loved? And had they bought them on his card? He guessed so. When should he tell her?

Karen stood by the fridge, two glasses of white wine in her hands. It was a new thing for her, this wine connoisseurship. She'd taken a course. She held one glass out, looking both pleased and shy, her arm not fully stretched.

Later, Steve decided. He could tell her later. Karen had had a tough day.

The warm waft from the oven carried hints of lemon, lemongrass, garlic, coconut and something ill-defined but noxious. Could it be chicken? Was her favourite meal Thai lemon chicken after all?

'Anyhow, I left Amy playing with Colin,' Karen was saying. Steve had spread six biscuits with the tapenade. He'd eaten four and two remained on the plate. Karen made do with the wine, taking sips like a seal might take breaths, a quick gulp then plunging back into her story. 'I went to her room. That monster, as Amy called it, was still spewing out filth. All the come-ons and the grunts and the squeals and the shouts and that whole sex-rhythm banging thing. I wanted evidence. I took out my phone and brought up the app and pressed record. I pointed it at the Nest Cam. I know there was no need to point, but I did. It was like I had a remote control. I pointed the phone and the volume burst high. I was in Amy's bedroom and it was like I was at a rave turned orgy. Then there was this voice. It wasn't foreign, not Hungarian or anything, I think it was English, but it was strangled, like it was coming out of a tight throat, not a man or a woman, something in between. It laughed. Laughed because I jumped and dropped the phone when the noise burst loud. Then it spoke. "Nice to see you, Hots," it said. It was looking at me, Steve. That thing was looking out at me. It spoke to me. And it called me Hots. That's our secret thing. Only you get to call me Hots. But that monster called me Hots.'

Karen stared at him. Steve looked at her. He had to say something, but he didn't know what. Karen gulped down the last of her glass and refilled it.

'It wasn't me.'

'Jeeps, Steve.' Karen had these in-front-of-the-children words, her made-up swear words that had snuck into their adult time. 'I know it wasn't flickety you. This isn't about you. I called the police.'

'Nine-nine-nine?'

'Well, yes.' Karen's voice had flipped into a 'like, what other number did you expect me to flickety memorize?' singsong. 'Some freak's preying on my children. Isn't that an emergency? They kept telling me to calm down, to go slow, like I was losing it. "These are my kids," I told them. "Aged five and three. They're playing them sex sounds." Were there pictures? That's what they wanted to know. "Not pictures, not images of children, sex noises," I said, "like a monster, and a camera pointed at our kids." They asked if I'd put it there. "Of course I did," I said – Well, you did – "Steve did, my husband did," I said. "Your husband's filming your kids?" they asked. "Were they wearing any clothes?" "They're in pyjamas," I said. I think I shouted. "This isn't about us filming our kids. It's about sex noises. And the camera was watching me, talking to me. It called me by my secret name." I'd been passed on to a supervisor now. Do you know what she did? She asked if there was another adult in the house. She asked to speak to Hanga. Made me fetch her. Put me aside. I had to stand and listen as an emergency supervisor spoke to the nanny. Stood for ten minutes while Hanga gabbled her broken English. She said I was safe, just upset. I'd become the problem. The nanny vouched for my sanity, Steve. Said you were coming back today and that she'd stay with me. They said they'd send somebody round. That's what Hanga said they said. Who knows what she understood. We're still waiting.'

94

'Hanga's still here?'

'Now you too want to see Hanga? She's gone out. On a date.'

'Hanga's on a date?'

'Spiked her eyelashes. Painted her lips dark purple. Squeezed into a black body tube with a dark green shiny polyester top flung loose around it. The kids saw her and jumped in shock then giggled. I said she looked nice. That's been my shit day. It ended with me lying to the hideous nanny.'

Karen sipped at the wine, suddenly noticed the taste, sipped it again.

'Till you, Steve. You coming home. This Montrachet. All those roses. The dinner.' Karen took another sip. 'Time to eat?'

It was in fact Thai lemon chicken. Karen spooned it out of the foil containers on to china plates, arranging food and space with that finesse she had, and the whole thing was suddenly like a decent, chef-prepared meal.

How good it was, to watch Karen's deft moves of easy confidence. Steve wouldn't disturb her with his own stories, he decided. Not tonight. Call up a bike courier, that's what he had to do. Package up his laptop and phone and ship them to 4tknox for morning delivery. Get them out of the house. That's all he had to do tonight. Before bed. Someone had turned his laptop into a conduit for the global child-sex industry and had young sex workers beating down his hotel door in Hanoi. Who knew what images riddled the machine? Steve had a padded envelope in the desk drawer upstairs. He'd finish dinner and bike the whole mess far away from his home.

Karen took her first forkful, turned it around in her mouth before swallowing, sipped her wine and looked at Steve over the rim of her glass. 'That email you sent me from your room in Hanoi,' she said. 'It was filth. Like phone sex in print. What were you on, Steve? It made me miss you so bad.'

What email? Steve could have said. Like, what the fuck with all these roses around the house, this ultra-special wine, the oh-so-favourite food? I'm not the man who sent these things. I'm a sick fuck who doesn't know who he is right now. It wasn't me, Hots. I didn't do any of it. I barely gave you a thought. I might have done, once I might have done, but right now I've been hacked. It's not just you and the kids and the Nest Cam and this house. A little Viet girl stormed my breakfast table in Hanoi. She flashed a naked picture of me to all my clients. Demanded money, demanded sex, said I'd promised her God knows what. And it wasn't only her, there was another one. She nicked my Apple Watch and ran off with it. We've been screwed, Hots, and I don't know what to do. Tell me about this email. What did it say?

But the words didn't come. Instead, he watched the smile start to curve the edges of Karen's mouth. He saw her eyes start to shine again. She'd had a shitty day. He was back. She was recovering.

Karen speared a cube of chicken on her fork, leaned towards him and waved it before his mouth. Steve reached his lips forward, curved them round the meat and sucked till he felt it move off the tines and on to his tongue. He chewed as he watched her and gulped the morsel down. Karen laughed. This is what they had done at their wedding-day dinner. She had acted first, putting a forkful from her plate into his mouth. He had followed suit, fed her from his plate. Forkful by forkful, they had fed each other, till their mouths connected over a single spear of asparagus, she with the shaft and he with the tip, to the laughter and applause of their guests.

Steve pushed aside his glass and leaned across the table toward her. He needn't tell her yet, he decided, well almost decided. It wasn't only the Nest Cam that was hacked, Karen had to know the whole story, they must talk, but later. He would tell her later.

Chapter 12

Steve jerked awake. Two nights of sleeping in the tightness of a plane seat, two more adrift in an ultra-kingize high above Hanoi, time zones in one place and his body in another, so where the fuck was he now?

Step by step the answer came: London. Home. In bed. Karen beside him. Travel done. A workday.

Karen lay flat on her back, her arms above the sheet and at her sides, her palms upwards, her hair as if wind-pressed against the pillows. Her lips burred in a soft snore. Often she coasted through a night's sleep, in and out of consciousness, poked awake by small frets, but after sex she did this. Steve crooked himself on an elbow and smiled to see the pulsing of her eyes beneath her eyelids. He liked that Karen felt safe to dream.

As Steve's eyes took in his wife his mind clicked on to work. His company was into minerals but had never done limestone in a big way. Now Steve had signed them up as principal partners in a quarry. Coal was good still, he'd brought back a deal on that too, but cement was where it was at. No world got developed, no buildings rose without it. Look at those quarries chewing their way through Vietnamese mountains. You had to have a piece of that.

Was the deal sealed? That breakfast girl hadn't made it easy. At least his dick hung big in the photo on her phone. Any man would be impressed by a dick like that. When Steve had got to speak with his Korean opposite number, the talk was all about finance. Were funds ready for immediate release? Steven had blagged it. Said yes. Funds could always be found.

That was today's job. To make the lie come true.

Had his desk computer been hacked too? Safer to think so. His laptop, his phone. He'd have called the deal in from a hotel phone but they had checked him out of his room.

The blue dial on the bedside clock said 4.20. He'd had four hours' sleep. That would do.

It was warm enough to go naked, but he'd done that once and bumped into Hanga, who gave a yelp of surprise that woke Karen. Steve's toes found the red boxer shorts he had dropped to the carpet the night before. He hooked them up and slid them on.

Their door was open in case the kids needed them in the night. Millie had been trained not to come into the bedrooms – Karen's sense of hygiene – so she slept on the landing outside. She had sensed Steve's tread and was already up and sitting. Shih Tzus come with grumpy faces and Millie looked especially serious in the mornings. A slight wag of her tail, yes, there was that, but a grimace for a smile and she stood to do her duty. Which was to shadow Steve wherever he went. Karen called Millie Steve's 'blot', which Steve thought was a jealous term to use.

Coffee first. Steve led Millie downstairs. It was summer, but Steve didn't care, the underfloor heating was on a separate thermometer and the marble tiles in the kitchen were warm to his bare feet, which was one of the keenest pleasures in the world. Steve hauled open the trifold door into the garden and Millie paused in the doorway, looking outside then up at him, outside and up at him again. In her mind, she was signalling, this was too early or too cool for a doggie piss. Steve shut the door.

Steve's Nespresso spat out into a small bone-china mug, a bright green one from a range of primary colours lined up on their own mini shelf. Steve stood by the wall of window that faced the garden.

Dawn light washed the space with colour. They'd had terraces put in and xeriscaped them with a Japanese theme. The xeriscaping was Amy's idea. Five years old, and she was into gardening for climate change. Amy had the concept and, at that early age, the word. She even told her daddy how to spell it so Steve could look it up.

Steve blamed the school, but Karen said it was sweet that Amy cared about others and the planet, and not just herself. Amy had turned vegan. She demanded to be walked to school, because parents on the school run were poisoning the lungs of playground kids with their cars' diesel particulates. Such big words coming out of her small mouth.

Steve accused Karen of stoking the kids' heads with fears. 'Far from it,' she said. 'It's Amy, and even little Colin, who keep teaching me.' Well, Karen could walk them to school today.

Officially Steve could claim a day off to recover from the trip, but he didn't need it. His brain was already zinging.

Millie lay flat, her back legs splayed out to press her privates to the marble. She was fond of underfloor heating too. A blackbird sang outside. Steve listened to it. He used to curse blackbirds for waking him up but now that he rose before them he simply enjoyed their beauty.

He downed his coffee, set the mug in place for the next one, but it could wait; first, he'd get dressed. His travel bag, the Maxwell-Scott Piazalle, lay beside the front door where he'd left it last night. Steve bent and unzipped it.

On the top was a lightweight cashmere V-neck sweater in light blue in case the air conditioning in the hotel was too frigid. Steve hadn't needed it. He eased it aside now. Below it were the phone and the silver case of his laptop. Steve had meant to get these out of the house last night.

Maybe he could leave them on the steps outside the door. Give it ten minutes, someone would steal them. Let them wipe them clean. They would be off his hands. But then IT at work would complain, say they needed the laptop and iPhone to reverse-engineer the hacker's moves or some such drivel.

Steve leaned the laptop against the wall to get to the gifts beneath it: that doll for Amy, Colin's cap, and Karen's Swarovski pen now looking tawdry with its encrusted crystals. Steve could use it to write Karen a note so the note and the pen made a package. Some 'love you' thing, 'off to work but back early', hearts and kisses underneath.

Steve padded up the stairs, Millie the blot at his heels. Hanga was home. He could hear the rumble of her snores from the floor above.

Steve went to Amy's room first. The door was open the way Amy liked it. Steve took note of the wires sticking from the wall where Karen had ripped out the Nest Cam. Amy was flat on her back with her arms splayed wide, the mini-image of her mum. She, too, was dreaming, her eyes pulsing behind their eyelids.

Steve pulled the duvet up to her neck. She'd push it back down within five minutes even as she slept. Amy lived her own life. Steve lay the elongated doll at the foot of the bed. The embroidered dress had reflective sequins sewn into it. Last Christmas Amy had banned tinsel from the house for environmental reasons. Steve began to doubt the whole gift.

Across the hallway, Colin was sleeping on his side, his thumb in his mouth. Shouldn't he have stopped that habit? Steve wondered about shaking the boy awake. He made do with stroking his son's hair. Karen had booked to have Colin assessed. Special needs on the one side, gifted and talented on the other – who knew? Three was early, but in his nursery the boy didn't mix, and he had poor hand-eye co-ordination.

And then there was Amy, with such a babble of informed fear about the climate crisis it was like her head was stuck in a science lab. Were they bringing up two spectrum kids?

Steve set the cap down on the end of Colin's bed, with its hammer and sickle logo. To think kids had once been scared of communists. Now it was the climate crisis. Next it would be asteroids or AI downloading their brains or other made-up bullshit. What people feared would happen and what actually happened were never the same thing.

A model Typhoon and Tornado jet hung down on fishing line from Colin's ceiling. Steve had made them from a kit and painted them with miniature brushes. A futuristic Lego city filled a patch of hardboard near the window. Steve had put together every building. Amy then joined in and site-directed their placement according to a 'transport efficiency map' she'd designed with multicoloured marker pens.

Steve backed out of the room and, in the act of closing the door the way Colin liked, a new idea pricked his mind. He'd leave work early and pick the kids up from school. There'd be time to take them to Hamleys. Whatever outdoor game they wanted, he'd buy it for them.

On the way there Steve would talk Colin through the basic rules of croquet. He thought that might appeal. Then they'd head for Hyde Park and try the games out.

Steve didn't need more coffee, he decided. Shower off the sweat of the night, find fresh clothes, write the note to Karen and he'd be on his way. If he got to his desk before six, it would be fine to shoot off before three.

The dog had stopped shadowing him. Millie stood at the top of the stairs, facing down, ears erect. Steve heard her snuffle, that rush of air through squashed snout that she did when on the alert. Then she shot like a ferret down the stairs. Her feet slithered for purchase across the wooden floor to the jute mat, where she felt safe to jump. Millie's front paws scrabbled at the door while her back ones bounced. She tipped back her head and threw out high-pitched barks that jolted her head as if she was catching flies.

Steve bounded three steps at a time down to the hallway. He didn't need the dog waking the kids. He scooped her up, clamped her tight against his chest with his left arm and muzzled her with his right hand.

Frosted glass in the door showed movement on the other side, a cluster of people pressing close. The bell chimed. That triggered the display screen to the right.

The camera had a tight focus, but a crowd out there was jostling to be in view. Two men and a woman in police uniform at the front, two women in regular clothes behind, and more movement on the street in the margins of view behind them. The police officer in front held her warrant card up to the camera. The bell chimed again.

You see these things on TV. You don't see them on your own front-door screen at four thirty in the morning. Still, it was all too clear what was happening. An early-morning police raid. This didn't happen to Steve, but then, Steve didn't send naked selfies to Vietnamese girls either. He didn't fill his wife's house with roses and buy her favourite wine and dinner. He didn't do phone sex with his wife by email. Steve's life was getting filled with things Steve didn't do.

He looked down at his open travel bag. His laptop leaned against the wall beside it. He could zip the laptop inside the bag and fling the whole thing in the cupboard under the stairs.

As if that would confound a police raid.

Steve was right that he had to get rid of the laptop and phone, though, he had to be. His house had been hacked, his computer, the phone. Hanoi's underage sex industry had him tagged as a client. How does a foreigner worm his way inside the world of Vietnamese underage sex? Steve hadn't a clue, but if he had to start, he knew what tool he'd use. His laptop.

What trace records would a search like that show? Steve spoke no Vietnamese. Its script was no more than a pretty pattern. But would there be pictures of children and sex, like the ones that had shown up on his phone? That's what he feared. That's what he needed to get out of his house. A personal laptop stuffed with indecent images of children. He'd have got rid last night, couriered everything off to 4tknox like he planned, if only Karen hadn't got so turned on.

Steve could explain. Open the door, let the police in, hand over the hacked items, say he was worried that they were full of images of child sex, 'But honestly, Officer, it wasn't me.' He could do that if he had no wits about him.

Steve moved his right hand from Millie's snout. She started yapping. He lifted the flap of the letterbox. 'I'm going to put the dog out,' he said, not too loud, just at the voice level of a reasonable man. 'I'll be right back.'

He plucked the phone out of his bag, picked up the laptop and half ran down the hallway to the kitchen, across its warm tiles, and to the back door. Millie followed. Steve put down the laptop, slid the door open, flung Millie outside, shut the door.

What the fuck now?

The bottom drawer of the freezer was filled with frozen fillets of wild Alaskan salmon. He could slide the laptop beneath those. Or stick it in the Rayburn. Who'd think to look for a laptop in an oven?

A police raiding party with a warrant, that's who.

Steve had to get everything out of the house.

Millie's back paws were secure on the Portland Stone of the patio and her front feet were pattering against the glass of the door. She was still barking. She fell to the side as the door shifted and Steve stepped outside.

Fragments of tree bark were spread around the pale green leaves of the desert plants. Amy had done the job under Colin's direction, pointing the little fingers of his hand, to conserve moisture in the ground. 'Not too deep,' Colin kept telling her. Amy had told him she wanted total cover but not too deep, and Colin had picked up that phrase. 'Not too deep.' That put paid to Steve's notion of scattering bark chips over the laptop to bury it.

Millie was jumping up against Steve's leg now, yapping, scratching. What the fuck. Steve flung the phone over the fence and into next door's garden. He took a firm grip of the corner of the laptop, drew it back, then skimmed it like a Frisbee over the fence too. He'd been round to complain about the state of next door's garden, it was a wilderness and a disgrace, but an old woman lived there, waiting to die, and she hadn't even come to the door. So much the better, it turned out. The garden was choked with brambles and weeds. Before anyone ever came to clear it the laptop would be sealed in rust.

Millie raced away from his legs. She had watched him throw the phone, and now her head followed the angle of the laptop's flight. Even before Steve heard the laptop fall on the other side, Millie was up against the fence, scratching her claws against the wood. Playing fetch. Chasing a squirrel, that's what Steve would say if the police asked. She's chasing a squirrel.

Steve pulled the door back open. Its triple glazing kept the kitchen quiet from outside, even doused the roar of low-flying jets lining up for Heathrow, and now Steve learned it kept noise inside as well. A fist was smashing against the front door.

Sorry about that, that's what he would say, apologizing for the dog and for the delay. The police were shaking his household awake at 4.30 a.m., but best not be angry. Be submissive. Look like the sort of person the police want to protect. Naked but for your red boxers, rubbing sleep out of your eyes, asking them in, how you could help.

Chapter 13

Steve flipped the catch and pulled open the door. The porch was clear of the police he'd seen. Instead, four male officers stood with straps in their hand, a steel ram hung between them.

'What the fuck!' Steve yelled. 'You're about to beat my door down with that? I was putting the dog out. I told you I was taking care of the dog. It's early morning. We were asleep. My kids are asleep. You're ramming my door down. What the fuck is that about?'

At a quiet command that Steve barely registered the battering team drew back. A woman came up the steps to replace them, the same one who had flipped her ID into the security monitor. She stood feet from Steve, the same height as him, dark hair shaped close to her head, a face you'd call horsey if you were allowed. It was topped off by one of those chequered peaked caps policewomen wear. 'Stephen McInnes?' she said.

'Who the fuck are you?'

'You're Stephen McInnes?'

'And this is my house. And you've no fucking right—'

'Stephen McInnes.' She held up a sheet of folded A4. 'We

have a search warrant for this property. May we come in?'

She turned her head slightly to the side and nodded. Five police officers trotted up and somehow passed Steve and entered the house without touching his skin.

'What's going on?' It was Karen's voice.

Steve turned. Karen was at the bottom of the stairs. She looked ruffled, startled, gorgeous. Her bathrobe was white and her skin already golden brown from the summer. She raised a hand and hooked back her hair, first behind her left ear then her right, like her looks mattered, and they did. Steve locked the sight of her in his mind. It was a treasure.

'I called in the incident yesterday.' Karen faced the woman police officer and spoke out the only thread of logic she could come up with. 'My daughter was crying, said she could hear a monster in her room. She's five. Kids make things up. But I went with her to check, and she was right. Her Nest Cam had been hacked. Live sex was being soundtracked into her bedroom. I reported all this to you yesterday, and what did I hear? Nothing. Almost twenty-four hours, and nothing. And now this? A whole pre-dawn squad with the kids still asleep?'

'Stephen McInnes,' the officer said. Totally one track. 'I'm Superintendent Keans. I'm arresting you on suspicion of downloading indecent pictures of children.'

'Steve?' Karen stepped forward and pulled at the superintendent's sleeve. 'Jeeps. This isn't about flicking Steve. Steve was away. In Vietnam. This is about a twisted hacker spying on our kids and spewing filth.'

'Where are your children?' the superintendent asked. 'Are they in the house?'

'They're asleep. Or they were till you crashed in.'

The officer gave that nod of her head again. This whole scene had been drilled to run on nods of the head, it seemed. A woman stepped forward from outside. The thin yellow cardigan buttoned over a white blouse said she was a civilian, with baggy white cotton trousers and a round face framed in brown curls. Bright blue spectacles made her eyes too big for her face.

A woman like that comes to your door, you don't let her in. Steve moved to block her progress from the doorway. 'And who are you?' he said.

'Julie Monkton.' She wore a lanyard, and from it dangled her photo ID. She held it up and waved it, like a magic gesture that cleared the way. 'From Social Services. And this is Sarah Cooper.'

A girl scarce out of school stepped closer, pencil-thin skirt and jacket and long blonde hair pulled back and coiled on her head.

'We're here to take care of the children,' Julie Monkton dared to say. She stepped back as Karen jumped forward and slammed the door in her face.

'I take care of the children.' Karen's head angled to speak the words into the superintendent's face. 'And I take care of Steve, too. You're not arresting my husband. This has nothing to do with him. This is about some sick hacker.'

'It's not me,' Steve said. The words felt lame as he spoke them. 'I was hacked. We've all been hacked.'

'This isn't about a hacker,' the superintendent countered. 'It's about you, Stephen McInnes. About activities tracked on your accounts at work and at home. Transactions on your credit card.'

'Not me. I'm Steve McInnes, but that's not me. Someone's stolen my card details. Stolen my identity.' That was it. That's what had happened. It became clear to Steve the moment he spoke it out loud. He'd thought it before, but not said it. This wasn't just hacking. Someone had stolen his identity.

'See those roses? They came for my wife last night. I didn't send them. Someone found out what her favourite wine was and sent her a bottle. They had her favourite meal delivered. Karen thought it was me who did all that, but it wasn't. It was them. None of it was me.'

'What the flick, Steve,' Karen said. She was upset. No time to worry about that now. 'You didn't tell me this last night. You played along.'

'My wife said I sent her emails, sexy emails, but I didn't. I was working. In Hanoi. And underage girls kept coming to my hotel looking for sex. One had a picture of me on her phone. A naked picture. I don't send naked pictures. I don't even take them. Don't you see? That's proof. We've been hacked. None of this was me.'

It sounded utterly compelling as Steve spoke it out loud. Hard to take in, of course. He could see why Karen hung her mouth wide open and bulged her eyes wide. It takes time to understand a thing like that.

One of the male officers passed by. The superintendent raised an eyebrow. The officer shook his head.

'We'll need all your electronic devices,' the superintendent said. 'Phones, computers, laptops, Kindles, set-top boxes – everything. Most importantly, we need an iPhone and a Dell laptop registered in your name, Mr McInnes. Perhaps you can help us.'

'I lost the phone,' Steve said. 'Spoke with my wife when I landed and learned we'd been hacked. I didn't want to talk on the phone after that. I left it somewhere. I don't know where.'

'Try to remember. Was this at the airport? In a taxi?'

'I couldn't give a fuck about the phone. My wife was upset. I wanted to spend time with her.'

'And your computer?'

'It was hacked,' Steve said. 'I left it in Hanoi.'

'You just left your computer behind? In your room?'

'I discarded it.' It was funny how that word came up. A fancy word to cover his second lie. 'There was a skip behind the hotel. I chucked it in there. No point carrying it back. Who needs a hacked computer?'

'Is all this true, Steve?' Karen asked. 'You didn't say. Why didn't you say? We talked last night, but you never said.'

'You were upset. Why upset you even more?'

'But who sent me all the roses? Who sent the wine? And the Thai lemon chicken – who knows I love that, if not you?'

The superintendent looked between them, chasing their talk from side to side. And then she looked up. Steve looked, too. Amy and Colin had come down the stairs together. They stood five steps up, to stay above the heads of the adults in the hall. Amy had hold of her elongated doll in its ethnic dress. Colin held his communist hat by its peak.

'Why is Millie in the garden?' Amy asked. 'She's barking. It woke me up.'

Amy and Colin slept at the back of the house. The air pollution was not so bad away from the road. It meant they could sleep with their windows open and get some fresh air. It also meant there was no sound insulation from outside noises.

'I put Millie out to have a wee,' Steve explained. 'She saw a squirrel. That's why she's barking. It jumped over the fence. She's chasing a squirrel.'

The superintendent looked across to the officer who was standing with her in the hallway. She nodded. He nodded back. It looked like the whole force worked in silence. He moved down the corridor to the kitchen and the back yard.

'Stephen McInnes,' the superintendent repeated. 'I am arresting you …'

Steve watched the superintendent's mouth shaping words, cautioning him, but it was all senseless. Nothing – none of it, not one word – made any sense.

They said they didn't want to handcuff him, not with his kids watching. So long as he came quietly. Were they his clothes in the bag? Steve should put them on.

No way was Steve going to do that. Five minutes, he explained. He just needed five minutes to give his kids a hug, settle them, tell them everything would be all right, put on some clean clothes, then he'd come with them. He didn't want to cause any trouble. He strode forward, one step, and two male officers either side of him gripped his arms, dug fingers in deep, tugged him back. Steve was watching Colin and Amy. They were still standing on the stairs, staring down, mouths slightly open, and when Colin saw the police grab hold of his daddy the boy reached out his hand as if he could make them let go.

Within a fraction of a second Steve flexed, prepared to rip himself free. The policemen's grip tightened and the fight inside Steve swelled, but it was like a wave and it crashed and there was just a shallow nothing. He was emptied. 'OK,' he said, though no sound came out. The grip on his arms tightened further. Steve nodded, let the tension in his muscles melt. He looked down at his open travel bag. 'Let me get dressed,' he said.

That step forward Steve had taken opened the way to the front door. The men kept him in restraint and the superintendent moved and opened the door. The two social workers walked in.

'No way,' Karen said. 'I'm not having any social worker look after my kids.'

'We can take you to the station for questioning if you want,' the superintendent told her. 'Or Sergeant Sheddon can interview you here.'

The sergeant, twenty-something with wiry hair and a forced smile, tilted her head toward the door of their front room.

'Hanga,' Karen tried. 'The kids' nanny. Let me go and wake her. She can take care of the kids.'

'She lives here?'

'Her bedroom's on the top floor. It won't take me a minute.'

'Officers will fetch her down. We'll need to speak with her separately.'

'You're not going to interview my kids,' Karen said, disbelief in her voice now, rather than a challenge.

'There are two of us,' Julie Monkton said. The lead social worker had decided to take control. 'We'll follow the usual protocol. It's not exactly an interview, but we let the children talk if they want to. Some want to. Others express themselves in pictures or in play. We've got games, crayons, everything we need. Don't worry, Mrs McInnes. We know what we're doing. Colin, is it, and Amy? I'm Julie, and this is Sarah. Let's go upstairs, shall we? You can show us your rooms and we can get to know each other.'

Colin, who normally had a challenge to everything, turned first and held on to Amy's hand, which he never did, he didn't like touching, and the boy led the girl quietly up the stairs and away. Steve watched, thinking they would turn around and the kids and he could share a look, say goodbye that way, but the social workers made smart business of it, trotted up the stairs, and Steve's children were gone.

'Shall we go in here?' Sergeant Sheddon nodded toward the front room.

Karen simply complied. She didn't even look at Steve, just gave that toss of her head she did when she was upset and walked away. The door to the front room closed and Steve was left.

'Can we trust you to get dressed?' the superintendent asked.

Steve checked his body, noted the tension in every sinew, worked to relax a bit, nodded his head. One policeman let loose the grip on Steve's arm, then the other.

'There's nothing to wear in here,' Steve said.

'Your choice,' the superintendent said. 'We can take you as you are.'

Steve crouched and reached through his clothes. Two dirty shirts. Dirty underwear, dirty socks. The only trousers he'd taken to Vietnam were the ones he had been wearing, and they were draped on a chair in his bedroom. His jacket, too. His watch was on his bedside table.

'These clothes are dirty,' Steve said.

The superintendent shrugged her shoulders.

Well, fuck her. Steve wasn't the sort of man you could force to wear dirty clothes. The superintendent wasn't going to beat him that easily. He picked out the light blue cashmere sweater and pulled it over his head. It felt good against his skin. Then he picked out his running shorts and slid his legs into those. The shorts were skimpy. His boxers still showed as a band of red cotton beneath them. He pushed his bare feet into the trainers. Nothing to hide, that's what the skimpy outfit would tell them. He was a man with nothing to hide.

Chapter 14

The security gate drew back and let the car in to the rear of Shepherd's Bush station. Steve felt underdressed. They processed him quickly. He had no items to surrender. The door to the holding cell closed slowly but still it seemed to slam shut.

The room held a plywood chair. A thin bed with a white sheet and a rough woollen blanket was the only other furniture. Glazed white tiles covered the walls from floor to ceiling. A slot in the doorway opened on to the corridor. A naked bulb from a flex in the ceiling was the other source of light.

It was like being locked in a Victorian public toilet.

The locks on the cell's door shifted. A young guy came in, a constable probably, and led Steve out, along a corridor and through a plain wooden door into an interview room. This had a window, a green branch of a tree outside and other offices across a courtyard. Steve sat on a moulded plastic chair on one side of a laminate table. The junior officer stood with his back to the wall as the superintendent came in.

She settled herself on the chair that faced him. 'Superintendent Keans,' she reminded him. 'This isn't a formal interview, but we'll caution you once again. In case you weren't paying full attention before.'

From the wall the male officer read the words from a printout, though even Steve could have recited them, given a few prompts. 'You do not have to say anything,' he told Steve, not looking at him but at the printout. Steve felt like the perp in a crappy TV drama, only this wasn't TV. 'But it may harm your defence if you do not mention when questioned something which you later rely on in court. Anything you do say may be given in evidence.'

Keans took over. 'Do you want to call a solicitor?'

'Of course I want to call a fucking solicitor,' Steve said. He'd had time to ponder what attitude he should take. How do you address a senior policewoman? By her title? Ma'am? It was probably best to be deferential. But something in this woman goaded Steve. It was her clipped tones, maybe, the stare from those pale grey eyes that had no give in them when you stared back.

Steve changed tack. He wasn't going to go Zen-like to his doom. 'And that solicitor will wrap his fingers around the police authority's neck and shake it down for damages. You're hassling the victim. You've got me under arrest and in lockdown, but I'm the fucking victim here. It's me who's been hacked. My identity's been stolen. That's the crime. It's like I went away for the weekend, my house was invaded, teenagers partied and did drugs and smashed the place up, and then your crew waltz in and arrest me as a dealer. Call Nigel Fowler. Hardbridge's solicitor. He'll sort all this out. He'll sort *you* out.'

Keans poised her pen over the notes she was making on a pad, her lips pursed.

'Any alternatives?' She looked up. 'I believe that's the gent who reported you to us.'

'Nigel reported me? For what?'

The superintendent gave no answer. She finished making notes then looked up.

'You've just threatened legal action against the police,' she said. 'I can read your words back to you if you like. It seems we might both be needing legal advice. Can you name a solicitor other than Nigel Fowler, or would you like us to make a recommendation?'

Steve gave it some thought. The first face that came to mind was that of a friend – well, not a close friend and not a solicitor but an occasional drinking buddy he had placed some trades through. When he recalled the man's face – Leo, he was called – the cheeks were thick with a smirk and the man's face was flushed. He was passing round the third bottle of Margaux. 'We beat the bastards, Steve,' he was saying. Leo was fresh from the High Court, acquitted on a charge of insider trading, though he was guilty as fuck. He had won the case on a technicality. Steve wanted a solicitor with the balls to pull off that kind of thing.

'Can I make a call?' he asked.

'We'll do that for you.'

Steve gave her Leo's name: Leo Graus. He didn't know his number. 'Tell him I want the solicitor who did a job for him,' he said.

'Will his name be in your phone?' Keans asked.

What good will that do? Steve was going to say, but Keans's hand moved to her jacket pocket and she produced an iPhone and laid it on the desk.

'That's my phone?'

Steve reached forward to take it but Keans pulled it back. 'It's evidence,' she said. 'But I can look up the number for you. If you can give me your password.'

'Fuck you,' Steve said. 'That's the password.'

'A little cooperation might ease things.' Keans held the phone in her left hand, raised the index finger of her right, stared at Steve and waited.

Steve thought it through. 'You'll find images on there,' he said. 'Some really sick pictures. It wasn't me. I don't know how they got there.'

'Let's stop there. We need to move to formal interview.'

'One two one two one two,' Steve said.

'That's your password?'

'It's not a password. It's an access code.'

'A bit basic, isn't it? Give her ten minutes, my daughter could have cracked that.'

'It's the date we first met. A Christmas party. The twelfth of December, 2012. Karen's phone has that code too. Sometimes your phone needs a charge. When you can't find your phone you need another so you can make it ring.'

Keans keyed in the password, brought up Contacts and scrolled through. 'Leo Graus. This is his number?'

She held up the phone so Steve could see it. He nodded.

'We'll give him a call. See what we can do. While we're in the spirit of cooperation, would you mind giving us the access code to your laptop, too? That's another item we recovered from the neighbour's garden.'

'One two one two one two.'

Keans raised an eyebrow and tilted her head.

'We've got nothing to hide,' he said.

'We'll see, Mr McInnes. We'll see.'

Keans stood up. Her face showed nothing, no courtesy smile, no blink. It was as though Steve were a blank space in the room.

The constable led Steve back to the holding cell. The lock turned. Steve settled back on the plywood chair and faced the reflective tiles. But he couldn't settle. He paced. Did a few stretches. I'll beat this, he told himself, and jogged on the spot.

The trainers were great. They gave real lift. *I'll beat this, I'll beat this.* Every step gave hope, his soles thumping down on 'beat'.

I'll beat this, I'll beat this, I'll beat this.

They brought Steve what they called lunch, a cheese-and-tomato sandwich on processed white bread slimed with margarine.

He ate it.

Milky tea in a polystyrene cup was sugared. Steve asked for

some water so he could swill the taste away and they brought him another polystyrene cup, the water in it lukewarm. They walked him down the corridor so he could have a piss in the single toilet.

'Where's my solicitor?' he asked.

They said they were working on it and locked him up again.

An hour or so later they brought Steve his gym bag. It was Louis Vuitton but canvas with leather beading. Karen had bought it for him last Christmas as an upgrade on his Puma and had noticed his flash of disappointment when he opened it. 'That all-leather one you liked,' she'd said, 'black to match your jacket, it's a weekend bag, but this one's better for the locker room. It won't soak up the sweat.'

K was lying through her teeth. She liked the look of him in his leather jacket, he could tell, but hated to touch it, part of her new anti-leather love-the-cow-not-its-hide thing. Still, it was Christmas. Steve had smiled and agreed and used the bag. The canvas wasn't too bad.

'Did my wife pack this?' he asked, but the woman who had brought it in, a busty young officer in a tight white acrylic shirt, her long hair yanked back, said how did she know, get dressed.

The clothes were folded neatly, not stuffed in. That showed care. First, Steve felt through it for a piece of paper, just a scrap – 'Love you, Kx', something like that. It wasn't there. Then he pulled out the clothes.

His Tom Ford slim-fit washed denim jeans came out first. He checked the pockets. That would be a good place to hide a note.

Nothing.

He was glad to have the jeans but wondered if they were the right choice. A suit would give him authority, maybe his everyday black Apsley one. In movies they rustled up a suit and tie to spruce up drugged-out punks before they put them in the dock.

Then, because Steve had decided Karen did pack the bag – who else would know where his favourite things were? And Karen always knew what to wear – he knew she was right. These clothes would give him comfort and make him feel good.

Steve pushed down his red boxers and running shorts and pulled the black Zimmerli trunks out of the bag. Made in Switzerland of sea-island cotton, they were so snug he already felt better. Then the Zimmerli merino socks and the light pink sea-island V-neck.

Steve wasn't sure about the black Thom Browne sweatshirt. He didn't like logos on clothing – why pay to be an advertising hoarding, even if it was subtle – but it was another present from Karen, for his last birthday, and that made it dear to him.

And then Steve laughed to himself when he saw what she'd done. The four-bar white stripe on the left arm was more stripes than any police officer was likely to sport. You outrank them all, Steve. That was Karen's message.

The sweatshirt was damn comfortable, too. And here were the white Alexander McQueen trainers. Right choice! Heaps better than the shiny black Church formal crap she could have chosen. He put them on and started walking fresh circles around his cell.

This was all right. Steve felt almost good about himself.

Chapter 15

A middle-aged male officer with a prominent gut came in with an announcement. Steve's solicitor was there to see him. The officer led Steve to the interview room and left him there alone. Minutes later, the door opened.

The solicitor's suit was black pinstriped, doubtless Savile Row, and tailored to be comfortable with a waistline that could expand during meals. Such men didn't normally mix with the likes of Steve. They fed at clubs with men like them who they had known since they were boys.

'Rupert Hayes,' the man announced, and his hand encased Steve's and fleshed tight around it before letting go. Steve took in the signet ring on the man's wedding finger. It was gold and stamped with a crest that matched his cufflinks. Around the man's left wrist a grey crocodile band sported a vintage Rolex circa 1983.

'I'm corporate, not criminal,' Hayes said as he sat down. 'I don't take on charity cases. I've been in touch with Nigel. You can forget this year's bonus, Mr McInnes. You're suspended from all duties for three months, on half-pay till then, but Hardbridge will cover my fees. They recognize this as a work-based situation. That was their deal. My fees replace your bonus. I don't know what they pay you, but I know what I pay myself and you'll come out ahead. But then I get to the station here and I learn more. You've been a silly young pup, Mr McInnes.'

Hayes had curiously hazel eyes that matched the bronze of his half-moon glasses. He stared at Steve like a schoolmaster might at a schoolboy. Steve took in Hayes's hair. It was that colour that started out blond and then disappointed, became mousy brown. Did Hayes cut it himself? The hair wasn't layered but tufted. Perhaps he showered but never dried his hair. Steve's head dealt with the issue of Hayes's hair because his brain couldn't compute what Hayes was saying.

'I've been hacked,' Steve said. Was there much else to say? 'Some hacker's stolen my identity. That's what this is all about.'

'This is all about obscene materials streaming on your workplace computer while you were out of the country. About indecent images of children, minors, buried deep inside that computer's hard drive. Now I get to the station and I find things have changed. I learn it's all about lies you have told to the police. It's about a phone you lie about losing and a computer you throw over a garden fence. It's about a mix of threatening and cooperative behaviour while you've been held in this station. Bizarrely, the cooperative element involved surrendering a password which allowed the police to unlock your phone and laptop and discover a further rack of indecent images. It's hard to parlay all that into a convincing case for bail. Have you and your wife got separate accounts? She'll be seeking her own legal advice.'

'Karen?'

'That your wife?'

Steve nodded. He was used to instructing lawyers to close deals. They listen closely and do what he says. This was a different kind of lawyer. Hayes did the talking and turned Steve mute.

'Well, that was yesterday, Mr McInnes. Today, she's your children's mother. Her lawyer won't be on Hardbridge's ticket, I'm afraid. The harder we push, the steeper her fees will be. Hopefully, we're hours ahead. No one's found paw prints on your kids yet. We're just talking computers. We need to get you out on bail before things get worse.'

'Worse?'

'You're still classed as human, Mr McInnes. You're set to be dirt.'

'I've done nothing.'

'That's what you say. And that's fine, Mr McInnes, fine. Now let me tell you what I've learned these past two hours.'

Rupert Hayes would clearly have preferred to settle back into a leather club chair. He leaned back against the plastic one, hands folded on his stomach, but it didn't work. He came forward, steepled his arms on the table, clasped his hands but soon freed them. They became like puppets, dancing a story of Steve's fate. Steve watched them, looked up at the glare of Hayes's eyes, then back at the play of his hands.

'I've known Nigel since school,' Hayes started. 'He's a tough nut. Always has been. Hardbridge took twenty-four hours before calling him in. They hoped it wasn't a case for Legal. Gave it to Tech. The outsourced analysts. 4tknox. It took them minutes to discount the obvious. This wasn't a few random links out of pornhub.com and, whoops, didn't mean to go there and what the fuck but boy how do people even do that kind of thing? This wasn't a quick wank-search by some Bengali or Estonian cleaner in the dark hours between emptying litter bins and giving your desk a wipe. Searches logged from your computer reached into the dark web. They were skilled, literate and calibrated to the time you were logged into your workstation.

'And they are sick. One analyst, their most skilful and, sadly, their most tender and youngest, was the first to convert the data capture into live images. He spewed up and his vomit just missed the keyboard. And that was just one URL near the beginning of the search. Trouble is, the deeper they went, the more liable to prosecution the analysts became. They were doing nothing more than chasing down your activity ...'

Steve didn't speak, he couldn't, but a part of him wanted to resist. His eyes widened, he raised a hand, his mouth opened.

'OK, sorry, Mr McInnes, not *your* activity, let's not go there, your *computer's* activity – but their work was open, they were a team, nothing covert about it. The server was riddled from multiple entry points. Once they clicked on a URL they became culprits themselves. OK, they were just investigating, but Pete

Townsend got banged up for "just investigating". It was time to get Legal in.

'They called in Nigel. I've not seen those images on your computer, I've only seen Nigel's face. It's a poker face, he never gives anything away, but his neck to his forehead blushed crimson and he couldn't face me while speaking. He looked down, he looked to the side. He was shocked.'

Hayes left a silence. Steve used it to find words. 'It wasn't me,' he said.

'You've seen some of these images. You must have. You threw away your laptop and hid your phone because you knew they were there. Were you shocked, like Nigel was shocked?'

'I was shocked to find them there. They were nothing to do with me.'

'They were nothing to do with Nigel either, but they upset him. Deeply.'

'They were sick images. Terrible.'

'How many did you see? Did you scroll down for more?'

'Just a few on my phone. I didn't open the laptop after I learned it was hacked. It sounds like Nigel's seen more than I have.'

Hayes tucked in his chin and stared at Steve over his half-moon specs. He raised his right eyebrow.

'I'm happily married,' Steve tried. 'I've got kids. I don't do porn.'

'This isn't about you, Mr McInnes.' Hayes spread his hands wide, then clasped them. 'You've been set up, or you're a really sick and foolish puppy, and either way, Nigel's sorry for you – that's why he spoke to me – but his advice to Hardbridge was immediate and they had no choice. This is about the company, not the employee. Has to be. They have to protect themselves. "Now," Nigel told them. "Take this to the police before you're raided." That's what they asked Nigel to do on Hardbridge's behalf.

'There's a lucky side to this. Well, two lucky sides. First up, Nigel was prepared to speak to me. Off the record, he might – just might – get us a copy of the analysts' report. Once the police get their hands on a hard drive it can be months before we hear anything else. Months while you're on remand. With this, we're ahead of the game.

'Our real luck here, though, is the fact that the call to the police came from your workplace. Women aren't fingered much in child-porn cases, but we're talking children here, we protect them at all costs. Your wife, your Karen, she's never been to your office. Whatever they find on your home computers, well, it's not likely to be hers. She's been questioned, I'm sure it wasn't sweet, but it shouldn't be too long before she gets her children back. Remove the woman from her children and she gets vicious. Karen gets her children back and she'll be stunned, but not vicious.'

'My children,' Steve said. It was a small point, but he had to make it. 'You keep saying "her children". They're my children. Our children.'

'Well, let's hope this doesn't get to be a custody battle any time soon.' Hayes sucked his lips against his teeth and made a kissing sound. He pulled back his hands. He was set for a change of direction.

'Let me be frank, Mr McInnes. You're not here on a rumour. Whatever you did or didn't have to do with it, your office computer's guilty as fuck. I've seen nothing, I've only heard, and when we met, Nigel was too upset to tell me details. He phoned when I was already here at the station and read me sections of the report. People who do that to kids should hang in hell. There is no defence. I told Nigel I'd heard quite enough. I was walking off the case. Like I say, I'm being frank. Nigel talked me down. Told me to meet with you and now I'm here. I'm like you, Mr McInnes. I've got young children. And now that I am here, and you're across the table, I find that my flesh doesn't creep, and I trust my flesh. Looking at you, first take, I'd let my children play with your children. But I'd stay in the room.

'Weeks down the line, Mr McInnes, that's what we'll shoot for. I'll put my associate on to this aspect. Have her aim for a supervised visit in a safe space, you and your children and a welfare officer. If the children want it. For now, Mr McInnes, you and the children, you and Karen, you and home, you and friends, you and work, park it all in a safe place, because we're not going there for a while. All you've got is you and me. I'm ready to go that far. It's a gut thing, not a head thing, but I advise you to sign before my head takes over.'

Rupert Hayes pulled out of his briefcase an agreement marked with pencilled crosses for signatures and laid it on the table. He produced a pen out of his jacket pocket. It was a Mont

Blanc, not showy, dark matte blue with palladium trim. When Steve took it into his hand, he simply held it a while. He wasn't weighing up his options, he was always going to sign. It was simply a beautiful pen. It calmed Steve somehow, holding it. Its weight was so real and perfectly balanced.

Chapter 16

Father and son had never been touchy-feely. In Steve's life, his dad gave him just the one hug, and that was on the morning of Steve's wedding. One brief clash of tense bodies, chest to chest, the father's fingers curled to press into the son's back, and then they pulled apart again.

The father had built up the insurance surveyor wing of a property group. He was used to entering strange rooms in awkward situations and assuming control. It was his job to assess damage. In this square room of painted plaster and stark light, the only damage to assess was to his son.

The father was in his M&S suit and white easy-iron shirt, eyes magnified by black rectangular glasses, angular face and wiry grey hair. 'Thank God you got your looks from your mother,' Karen said till she met the woman, and then: 'Who did she hump?' she whispered.

The father checked the room first. It was habit: people lie but rooms give counter-evidence. Then he sat down with his hands on his knees and managed one direct glance at his boy.

'Your mother sends her love,' he said, and looked away.

They had let him bring in a piece of paper clipped to a plastic board and a pen. He wrote the date at the top of the paper.

'It's my things-to-do list,' he explained. 'We'll find the ways I can be useful and I'll get on with it. You've got a solicitor?'

Steve explained the situation while his father took notes. The solicitor was arranging bail.

'Well, that's good,' the father said, and Steve noted the little dance of the man's pupils that showed he was already calculating.

'I can't simply walk out of here, Dad,' Steve then said. 'I need somewhere to go. A secure address. And I can't go home. I thought I'd come back if that's OK. To yours and Mum's.'

His father's calculations were complete. 'We've got twin beds in your old room now. For when the children come to stay.'

'When did they last do that?'

'It's not just your kids, Steven. It's your sister's. Sheila's rebuilding her life. We help out quite a bit.'

'I could sleep in Sheila's old bed.'

'Your mother uses that room now. It's her office.'

'Then I'll sleep on the sofa. I need an address to give to the police. Come on, Dad …'

'Your mother sends her love, like I said. She's sure there's a mistake.'

'Of course there's a mistake …'

'Even as a kid you spent hours in your room, staring into that computer of yours. She never did think it was healthy.'

'I was playing games.'

'It wasn't only games, Steven.'

'This is what you and Mum have been talking about?'

'We put a parental lock on your computer. You found your way around it. We caught you watching porn.'

'I was fifteen. It's what fifteen-year-olds do.'

'You were a child, Steve. Too young to be watching that sort of thing.'

'What was it in your day, Dad – page three of *The Sun*? A *Playboy* centrefold passed round school?'

'This is different. This is the internet. It sucks you in. You started looking, Steven. You put in search terms. You showed an interest. It's like knocking on the door of hell. A whole team of devils and minions do the rest. They open the door and in you go. At first you're shocked. Do people really do this kind of thing? But you don't back out. You get excited. One room leads to another. Things get more depraved. And there you are, watching. You can't get up and stop it. Sure, you can turn off the screen. But turn on the screen again and there they are, still at it. You try another room. It's an addiction. That's what your mother says, and I think she's right.'

'Mum said that?'

'She read a feature on it. In the *Daily Mail*.'

'The police came for me this morning. When did you get to hear, Dad, a few hours ago? And you and Mum have come up with this addiction crap since then?'

'We've talked about this for years. Worried about it.'

'This isn't about addiction. It's about me.'

'It's about far more than you, Steven.' Steve's father took

off his glasses and pressed the heels of his hands into his eye. When he pulled his hands away his eyes were still dry. 'This is destroying your mother.'

'You mean her identity was stolen and her phone was hacked and filled with sick pictures and she was pulled from home in her bathrobe at dawn and slammed in a prison cell? Sorry, I didn't know.'

His father stared at him. No, he glared at him.

'I'm sorry Mum's upset, Dad. Really I am. But I don't need that right now. Can't you get her to do anger instead? That could do us both some good. She could be out there giving people a piece of her mind. Telling them I'm innocent.'

'How can we do that, Steven? What do we know?'

'You know me. You know I'd never do the things I'm accused of.'

'Parents are the last to know. That's what they say.'

'Christ.' Steve stood up, a hand pulling at his hair. He backed away from the table. 'You're believing the lies. You're giving up. You're giving me up.'

'We love you, Steven. That's your mother's message. Even if you did it, we love you. She can't give you more than that. Not yet. Not now.'

'Have you spoken to Karen?'

'I haven't. Your mother took the call. She's round there now, helping out. Karen's upset.'

'Mum's calming her down? When did that last work, with anyone? Mum freaks Karen out. You know that, Dad. You know what the atmosphere's like when Mum and Karen are put together.'

'This isn't about Karen and your mother. It's not about us. It's not about you. It's about the children.'

'*My* children. Karen's and my children.'

'Yes, well …' Steve's father blinked, looked his son in the eye for a moment, showed the twinge of a smile, and managed to keep on looking.

'Yes, well what?'

The father broke the look and shifted his attention to the room, as though it were interesting. 'I've never been behind the scenes in a police station before. They called this an interview room. That must mean you don't get to stay here. They lock you in a cell? What's the cell like?'

'I'll be getting out. I need somewhere to go. If Mum wants to make Karen feel better, she'll let me come home. Till this is sorted. Karen needs to know where I am. The kids need to know where I am. If I'm somewhere they know, then they can imagine me there. That will be good for them. Things need to settle down.'

'The children are used to you being away. You're just back from Vietnam, Karen says. How did things go there? It sounds as though things got awkward.'

'It's a matter of identity theft, Dad. All of it.'

'Karen said something about young girls. About films. And this morning you threw your phone and computer over the fence into the neighbour's garden, apparently. I'm only reporting what's been said, Steven.'

'They were hacked. Both the phone and computer were hacked.'

'You didn't say anything last night. Karen was overwhelmed by how you treated her, she said. Roses, fine wine, dinner. You had dinner together, and you never told her any of this. Yet it was on your mind. It must have been. You got out of bed and threw the computer over the fence.'

'She was upset. The kids' Nest Cams had been hacked. I didn't want to make things worse. I wanted to make things better.'

'Well.' Steve's father looked at him again, briefly, no smile at all this time. 'You took her to bed, she says. Got her drunk and took her to bed. You had sex, it seems, she went out like a light, and then you got up and roamed the house. You did that, she said. Went in to check on the kids. That home-help you've got, she found you walking around naked once. Those cameras – Nest Cams, is it? – they were filming through the night but it's you who always checked them.'

'What is this, Dad? Where are you going with this?'

'Karen put her head against your mother's shoulder and she cried, Steven. Her whole body was shaking. Your mother wrapped her arms around her and held Karen till the shaking stopped. Even your mother recognized that was unusual, that Karen would let her that close.'

'Karen's worried about me and the kids? That they weren't safe with me?'

'She's a mother, Steven. That's what mothers do.'

Steve strode toward his father. The man flinched, but

Steve walked straight by and banged his fist twice on the door. It opened.

'We're done here,' Steve said.

A woman officer stepped in. Steve's father stood up. 'I'll do what I can,' he said.

'You'll do what you choose, and that's fuck all. You've made that very clear. Thanks a lot, Dad. Be seeing you.'

The father held his clipboard. Steve crossed his arms. The man nodded, not quite at Steve, and stepped out. The door slammed shut.

Chapter 17

This was Karen's own hallway yet it was like being next in line to see the headmistress. The dining room door opened and Hanga emerged. Her moon of a face was grey, her black hair frazzled, and a tiny silver cross hung from its chain on the outside of her sweatshirt. Without looking at Karen she stomped past and up the stairs.

Karen loved the dining room. It was elegant and airy, especially when early afternoon light slanted in. Her and Steve's interior designer had the tables and chairs made by a friend of his, with matching light oak frames for the four Elizabeth Merriman flower portraits that were spaced around the walls. The painted flowers added vivid rectangles of colour to the egg-blue walls. The cornices were deep and original and bright white.

This was their adult room for when friends came round; the children always ate in the kitchen. Now her solicitor 'Call me Rachel' sat at one side of the table behind her two slim stacks of papers.

Rachel's hair was blonde and straight and expensive and her makeup highlighted high cheekbones. She could have looked like one of Karen's friends but instead she wore grey, charcoal for the jacket and mouse grey for the silk blouse and grey-framed spectacles. Karen's friend Eleanor had recommended her. Eleanor lost custody of her child but even so was considered to have been the winner of her divorce.

'Do you have a PayPal account?' Rachel started.

Karen nodded.

Rachel directed her eyes at the opposite chair and slid a scrap of paper across the table. 'Hanga's packing. We've reached an agreement. Three months' wages paid direct to avoid the agency cut, which she's always found to be intolerably steep. She's been clinging on to the UK since Brexit but it turns out she's sick of the country. A night's stay at an airport hotel. A British Airways flight to Budapest first thing in the morning. A new Apple phone. It's all on this paper. Hanga's PayPal details are on the top.'

Karen sat and looked at the paper with its accounting and then up at Rachel.

'She wanted six months. Cash. I talked her down. Told her she was redundant with immediate effect. As of this morning you're effectively a single mother with no direct income.'

'Then why should I pay her at all?'

'So far Hanga's only had a cursory interview with the police. They searched her room and demanded her laptop and she had to explain she doesn't own one. She does everything on her phone. So they took away her phone. We don't want them to come and interview her more formally.'

'Why would they bother?'

'They might or they might not but Hanga feels she has a lot to say. When I showed an interest she was very forthcoming.'

'She's generally silent as a cow.'

'Well she mooed. Apparently she's very concerned for your children. It seems you and your husband have a healthy sex life. It's your cries especially that wake her in the night. She did an impression of you. You might have heard it through the door. It was loud. When you wake her like that she waits a while then goes down to check on the children, to see if they were also "made awake". Three times she has found a bed empty and when she looks in through your door the child is in your bed. She fears the children are being drawn into your sex life.'

'That's jeeping disgusting.' Karen noted Rachel's left eyebrow lift a little. 'Jeeping' was her in-front-of-the-children word and she could see it was not needed. 'A disgusting thought.'

'She says your husband roams the house naked at night.'

'Once. She saw him once. And in any case why shouldn't he?'

'And you watch dirty movies.'

'We do not!'

'In bed. In German and in French.'

'Oh that. Why does she know that? We have seasons. We've been watching films from Michel Houellebecq novels. And Michael Haneke movies.'

'They're sick, Hanga says. And violent. She borrowed them. Watched them. It put her on the alert.'

'The alert for what?'

'Colin won't let you hug him, she says.'

'What's got into her? He's never liked touch. That's just who he is. We respect it.'

'Not always. Not at bathtime.'

'What are you implying?'

'This isn't me, Karen. This morning's events have rattled Hanga. She needs to talk. Let her do so in Hungary.'

'I just pay her off?'

'She's much cheaper than I am. This could save you days of my time. Currently the police are focusing their investigations on your husband. They're inclined not to see you as complicit in his actions. Let's keep it that way.'

'But Steven's innocent.'

'You pay me to protect you. My first task is to present you as the injured party.'

'I know you did Eleanor's divorce but this isn't about divorce.'

'It is what it is. Last night you were happily married and possibly "in love". This morning you called me in to act for you, not for your husband. You acted early. That's good. Wait for emotions to settle and these things get expensive.' Rachel pressed her index finger on her phone's sensor to unlock its screen and brought up the PayPal screen. 'Soon this conversation will have cost you more than Hanga is demanding. Use my phone. Please pay her, Karen, and we can move on.'

Karen logged in, typed the payment details into the keyboard, and pressed send.

'I know that was tough.' Rachel took back the phone and set it in precise alignment with the two stacks of paper. 'But you're well shot of her to be honest. She had fixated on her story. When someone does that you have to accept you're dealing with a pathology and not a rational mind. Hanga's packing. She'll wait with her bags in the hall. When I show her that the payment has gone through she'll leave.'

'Good. I want her out. And I want my children back. Have you got children?'

Rachel picked up the phone, pressed in her finger to power it up, and held it for Karen to see. Two dark-haired girls sat on a swing, one in the lap of the other, their tiny brown hands wrapped around the string's ropes.

'Rana and Amrita.' Rachel noted the question on Karen's face. 'My husband is from India. These are his sister's children. Their parents died. We've adopted them.'

Karen's mind played with condolences and platitudes. For a moment the comeback in her head was 'so you're not a birth mother' but that was nasty. 'They look happy,' is what she came up with.

'The girls were very young. We are their memories now. They know where their home is. It's good for your two children that their grandparents could take them in.'

'Is it?'

'Let this storm pass. We'll work with the police to ensure you're cleared of all suspicion. We'll have the children back with you soon. In the meantime social services can arrange supervised visits.'

'I don't need supervision to be with my own children.'

'That's not for me to assess. But I will give you my assessment in any case. Your children are safe with their grandparents. Your husband is in police custody and you have never asked how soon you can get him back. You keep asking about your children. That's as it should be. In these situations I always listen for the parent who asks after the children. That's the parent I trust. Usually it's the mother, sometimes it's the father, seldom is it both.'

'Steven loves the kids.'

'Yes. Well.' Rachel lifted her head. 'That's Hanga on the stairs. Is it OK if I go out and show her the payment has gone through? You don't want to talk to her yourself?'

Karen stared back at Rachel and her body shivered. Rachel nodded and stood up. Karen heard the click of the door closing behind her. Rachel spoke but Karen couldn't make out the sense. Then the front door opened and closed. When Rachel came back to the dining room Karen stood up. 'I'll make you a coffee,' she said.

Rachel checked her watch. Karen had read of these George Jensen watches in an *FT* 'How to Spend It' feature and wondered if one might suit her. Its silver dial displayed hands on an otherwise blank face, and instead of a watch strap it had a steel clasp like a bangle. On Rachel it looked good. Could she try it on?

Karen stopped herself asking. 'For Jeep's sake it's just a coffee. Even solicitors must get a break now and then.'

Karen marched down the corridor leaving Rachel to follow. The long kitchen countertop was of veined white marble and lined with paper bags of flour and spices in pestles and packs of eggs and butter and tubs of spread and dried fruit that Karen had measured into stainless steel bowls. The word 'organic' was emblazoned on each product.

'This is a big day,' Karen explained as she walked past. 'It's my business. We make party cakes that cater for food intolerances. No child should miss out is my motto. This is for our first wedding cake. It's for a lesbian couple whose little girl is at Colin's pre-school. Wheat and nut free throughout, vegan on top, dairy for the bottom layer. Suzie should have been here to help by now.'

Millie was out on the patio, scrabbling her paws against the glass of the door to be let in.

'Do you mind dogs?' Karen paused with her hand on the handle.

'That's what that is? A dog?'

Karen gusted half a laugh. 'She's Steve's really. He's besotted with her.'

'Perhaps make the coffee and we go out? It would be good to feel the sun for a moment.'

The triple glazing made Millie's yapping tolerable. Karen moved to the Nespresso machine. 'Eleanor said you became like a friend,' she said.

Rachel checked her watch again. 'I can give you ten minutes. Without billing. That's the length of a break. Let me be clear. I took you on because of Eleanor's recommendation. You two went to the same school, is that right?'

'She was in the year ahead. I ran around for her, delivering messages, fetching anything she wanted. She let me.'

'Her husband was older. A billionaire. He desperately wanted a son. She gave him one. That baby was her trump card. She played it. The husband paid her legal fees. Our firm was paid well for me to be "like a friend" to Eleanor. To be frank, Eleanor's led us both astray here. The firm presumed that you and she were both in the same super-wealth bracket. Now you and I have both looked through your bank statements and discussed your finances. You and your husband are young. You've both chosen to pile everything into your pensions to max them out. You've relied on the annual bonus for your spending money. Failing that bonus, to access any significant funds you'd have to strip your ISA. Your best hope is that your husband really was hacked, that he isn't a paedophile, that he doesn't download child porn, and you can sidestep the expense and agony of seeking a divorce. If that doesn't work, if he's guilty, then you don't need me as your divorce lawyer. It will be a slam dunk case with automatic custody, no visiting rights for your husband, and minimal assets to fight over. Any bog standard solicitor could do it. Your husband is a broker. He is in no position to pay my firm's fees for me to act "like a friend" to you. You need a real friend.'

Karen finished making the coffees and poured cream into a plain white Wedgwood jug and set it on a tray beside the two coffees and two silver spoons. 'Sugar?'

Rachel shook her head.

'Open the door, would you?' Karen stood with the tray in

her hands and waited. Millie's yapping became frenzied. 'She should just speed past and slither on the tiling. If she starts scrabbling at your leg just kick her. As hard as you like.'

Both women sipped. Their cups chinked in unison as they set them down on the saucers. They closed their eyes a moment and steered their faces to feel the warmth of the sun.

'Thanks for being honest,' Karen said. 'It's something.'

'You'll be all right,' Rachel said. 'You've got no choice. You will have to be all right. You've got the children to take care of. But do you have a friend you can call on?'

'Perhaps. Who knows. Who knows what I've got any more.'

'Siblings?'

'A sister. She's not available right now.'

'Parents?'

'They never cared for Steve. They felt I could do much better. I'm not telling them. Not yet. I can't bear them thinking they were right all along.'

'Steve's parents?'

'They'd do anything for the children. Kill me if they had to.'

'I've got a printout I can give you. Of helplines you can ring.'

'You know where you can stick your printout.' Karen saw the slight jar of shock on Rachel's face and smiled. 'Sorry. But I'm not helpless. I do have a friend. A very bestest friend. He's Steven.

I don't know what he's done, he can be stupid and careless and not think things through, but he's not bad. He's not a wicked man. And I do want him back. Till then I'll make do.'

She had been staring out into the foliage of the garden as she spoke but now turned to Rachel. 'Your watch.'

Rachel checked it. 'Don't worry. I've got a few more minutes yet'

'No, I mean your watch. It's a George Jensen, isn't it? It's lovely. I wondered what they feel like to wear.'

Rachel unclasped it and reached it across. With one hand she turned Karen's wrist and with the other she slipped the watch in place.

Its metal still held warmth from Rachel's skin. It looked stylish, its blank face almost floating above the skin of Karen's arm. She studied the watch, looked up at Rachel, and tears smarted her eyes. She clipped the watch free, handed it back, then rubbed the heels of her hands into her eyes to make them dry.

'Thanks,' she said. 'The watch looks great. It feels great. I've got a birthday coming up. I'll tell Steve.'

'I really should go,' Rachel said. 'You'll be OK.'

Karen sucked her lips against her teeth, blinked to dry her eyes, and nodded. 'When in doubt, bake a cake. I wonder where Suzie's go to. Could I just borrow your phone again for a second and check my emails?'

It didn't take long. There were twelve new messages but Karen only opened the one from Suzie. Her eyes widened, she gasped a little and handed the phone back. 'Suzie's not coming.'

'You can bake that cake on your own?'

'There is no cake. The wedding couple's cancelled. We had two birthday cake orders for next week and they've both cancelled as well. News of Steve's downloading kiddie porn has gone wild on the school's WhatsApp group, apparently. It's just killed my business.'

'Social services will have informed the schools. Do you think the leak came from there? Do you want us to send a letter demanding a correction?'

'Oh yes, sure, the school says they were perhaps a little hasty about calling Steve a paedo and the parents will be immediately mollified and content to send their children round for sleepovers at Steve and Karen's because Steve is of course innocent until proven guilty. You think? We're fucked, Rachel. And I believe our time's up, you and me. Thanks for keeping it brief, for Lord knows I can't afford to pay you. Don't worry about me. I'll get used to being alone, I guess.'

Karen bit her lips, stared up at the strip of sky between the houses, and let tears stream her face.

Chapter 18

Mel's pronouns were ze/hir/hirs. Ze despised all the
societal assumptions stuck to female gender assignation
and couldn't abide the lumpen otherness of they/their/theirs.
Hirs was a fourth-floor unit whose balcony overflowed with
greenery, ferns inside the railing and three species of ivy that
trailed over the sides.

It was early morning but, being summer, it had been light
for hours. Ze clipped along the concrete walkways at a speed that
incised hir way through other early commuters, feet in black
polished pumps, skinny grey trousers, pinstriped waistcoat over
a white cotton collarless shirt buttoned up to the neck. Its sleeves
were down over Mel's slim wrists, the double cuffs bound tight
by cufflinks that looked to be of the yin-yang coupling, only the
black-and-white sperm-like figures had sprouted little grap-
pling hands.

It wasn't so long a walk, a tight matrix of streets beyond St
Paul's. Mel entered the atrium that fronted an office building.
In London, a display of space was a fuck-off show of wealth. In
hir head, Mel retaliated. Ze bumped up hir consultancy rate by

thirty-seven per cent. When your skills are unique, you name your own price.

Of course, in this instance ze was peculiarly well placed to succeed. They were about to pay hir to track down Tom Snelling who ze had been secretly tracking for months.

A guard in a dull peaked cap and buttoned-up uniform asked Mel to stare into a camera so he could prepare hir visitor's ID. Mel stepped aside from the camera's range, repeated hir name and that of the man ze was visiting, said ze would give it five minutes then leave.

The guard made a call and spoke through his headset. He stated the problem, nodded, and with a 'Will do' clicked the call to a close. 'Mr Hayes is coming down,' he announced, and nodded toward a line of five yellow-and-red fabric chairs across the marble floor, their backs reflecting on the plate glass. 'You can wait over there.'

Mel stayed where Mel was. In the breast pocket of hir shirt ze kept several blank rectangles of paper which could serve as hir business card. In biro, ze jotted down the revised terms of this deal then tucked the paper away again.

Mel followed the digital display above the lifts and tracked one down from the seventh to the ground floor, where it pinged. Its doors opened and the man inside looked Mel's way as he came out and cocked a finger at hir. He turned on a smile that made Mel think of a toad.

Mel watched the man flick his card at the security gate to gain exit, slide the card into the breast pocket of his pinstripe suit and reach out his hand, the toad smile still holding.

Mel kept hir hands by hir sides and tilted hir head slightly, as a question. The man tucked a cardboard file he was holding under his arm, wiped the palm of his raised right hand against his left and stared at his guest. His smile was gone.

'Rupert Hayes,' he said. 'We can't give you access to the building without a visitor ID. There's a Starbucks round the corner?'

Mel nodded. Starbucks was corporate but at least its doors kept opening to let air in and out. Office complexes, with their blizzards of renovation, new carpets new chairs flame-retardant fabrics fresh paint, discharged toxic gases that saw Mel's glands swell and temporarily crippled hir short-term memory.

'Ms …' Rupert Hayes tried.

'Just Mel.'

'Call me Rupert.'

As if. Mel led the way out the door of the building and turned left. Starbucks was down the street on the right. Five people waited by the counter and only another five were sitting, in groupings of a three and a two.

There were two low chair-and-table options but Mel parked hirself on a stool by a counter. Ze doubted Hayes had ever sat on a stool. That suited Mel. Ze liked all aspects of a meeting to be on hir terms.

Hayes stared at the seat. His toad smile pushed back against his cheeks then faded again. 'What are you having?'

'White tea,' Mel said. 'Citrus Defender.'

'That exists?'

Stupid question. Why would ze order it if it didn't exist? Mel simply stared. Hayes went away. Mel sat, slightly swivelled on hir stool to face his, and lay hir hands on hir kneecaps. It was a posture of waiting, of patience. Hayes brought back the two drinks – Mel's in a thick rounded teacup, his a large latte in a mug.

'You've got a delicate constitution?' Hayes said. 'That why you choose Citrus Defender?' He settled himself on the vacant stool.

'I've got my skillset. I presume that's what we're here to discuss.'

'We're here. Face to face. Human stuff. And that's got me thinking. This job, it may not be up your street.'

'Because I drink white tea?'

'We need someone robust. My client's been hacked. We need to chase down the how, who and why. But the hacking leads to deep dark web stuff. Kiddie porn and the like. An analyst who viewed it threw up.'

'It's data. That's all it is.'

Hayes took a sip of his latte and curled the top of his tongue around his upper lip to lick off the foam that stuck there. He put down the mug and reached his hand inside his breast pocket. In pinched fingers he pulled out a thin silver tube. Its top unscrewed. Attached to it was what looked like a broad silver needle.

'My wife gave me this last Christmas. One of those presents for the man who has everything. It's a toothpick,' he said. 'I find pork's the worst, the way it sticks between my teeth. This lets me poke and scrape any meat shreds away, decorously, before the plates are even cleared. It's just a toothpick. That's all it is. Only, if I stabbed it into the jugular of someone's bare throat …' Hayes performed a few neat stabs against the air. 'It's like data. My silver toothpick is what it is. Only it can also kill. You know this, Mel. My client is learning this. Data kills.'

'I don't meet with clients. Not live. Not as a rule,' Mel said. 'For you, I've made this exception. Because you spoke with Sam.'

'Ah yes, Samuel and I, we go way back. Preschool. We've got a primal relationship. He's the man I trust.'

'I don't trust.'

'Too right. You shouldn't. What's Samuel to you? Just a boss.'

'I'm freelance.'

'Of course. But you've been vetted. You signed up. Samuel says you're the best he can offer. You fight injustice, he says. That's what makes you tick. That's what we've got here. Injustice.' Hayes patted his hand on the file of printouts. 'My client's office hard drive was heavily compromised. This is the analysts' report, made before they contacted the police. Early yesterday morning the police raided my client's home. They have his phone and laptop, which compromise him further. He's banned from returning home and visiting his kids. A little boy and a little girl. We can try to get you the computers when the police have finished with them, before anything goes to the courts, but you know how long that takes. Months. And months. Meanwhile, my client's professional life and loving wife and home and little kids all swirl and spiral down the plughole. Who hacked him, Mel? And why? These reports are your clues. You can do something with these?'

'You have anything else? His wife's phone?'

'The police took it. They say they'll return it.'

'Social media accounts?'

'They exist. In his name. Though he swears he neither set them up nor uses them. Doesn't trust them.'

'Personal email?'

'That's all in the file. Username and password are on a cover sheet.'

'His financials?'

'They show odd spending patterns. Calls he says he didn't make for goods that were delivered to his house. Server fees. Deposits for services overseas. Charitable donations. Nothing that doesn't trace back to him somehow.'

'I'll need a full financial record.'

'We're working on it. My client's somewhat detained right now.'

'You're sure he was hacked?'

'I know what guilt looks like when it gets dressed up and goes out to dinner. When my clients tell me they're innocent, that's the look I expect to see. This one's different. My regular clients are the type who hunt this one down. I know his type. Cornered, lost, angry, lashing out. The hunted.'

'May I?'

Mel put hir hand on top of the file. Hayes nodded. Mel opened it.

The first printouts were familiar. Some material was months old, a record of the gradual accruing of details from Steve McInnes's life. Such was normative behaviour, an operative insinuating themself into all aspects of a target's business on track to assuming their identity. What wasn't normal was the choice of McInnes. The standard target worked directly in the energy industry. McInnes was simply a commodities trader. What was the use in holding such a person as your sleeper? He had no direct access to the grid, no fingers on the running of a coal-fired power station. What was such a sleeper meant to do when you triggered him into action?

Looking through Tom's live feed when he was first targeting McInnes, hir initial sighting of McInnes was a shock. Ze recognized him. This was the man from the train, whose seat ze stole, who created such a scene.

Ze reported the matter to Glyph. They considered the matter for twenty-four hours and then told hir to carry on. Tom Snelling is getting creative rather than going rogue, they decided, but keep close tabs on him.

And ze had failed.

Here was a bundle of sheets stapled together that showed the workflow from McInnes's workplace computer. It absorbed hir. Though it was just day to day stuff from McInnes's trading life at Hardbridge, ze kept turning the pages. Aah, here it was. Could this be Tom at work? It had to be.

Ze was meant to know everything about Tom, so how had the little nerd done this? Kept all this stuff hidden.

'This is a regular workflow,' Mel reported to Hayes, as though hir scrutiny of the data had been purely objective. 'Analysis your client was studying, trading patterns, screens he pulled up that likely contained pertinent business data. Then here, for example,' – Mel pointed a finger at one point a third of a way down a page – 'to here. This details action in totally separate territory. We've spun away from regular URLs and into dark web territory. This section?' Ze pointed at a passage of dense coding. 'You say there was a hacker? Well, the hacker's at work. All goes still for a time, just here, as though they've reached the page they were seeking. Then here,' – Mel's finger moved again – 'we're back at the screen we jumped from. As a hacker, whoever you're hacking, you want them to find the screen the way they left it.'

Hayes pulled the sheet toward him and studied it a moment. 'You're saying this is evidence?'

'It points toward evidence. There's no time stamp on the printouts, but that should be retrievable. Set that against any CCTV footage. If we can show your client was snatching an unrecorded break elsewhere while his workstation was recorded as active, that would be evidence. I can keep this?'

'It's a copy. It's yours.'

Mel took a square of paper out of hir pocket and handed it across to Hayes. 'My terms,' Mel said. 'And payment details.'

Hayes looked and blew out a gust of laughter. 'Steep. You don't present ID. Do you present invoices?'

'If required.'

'Half payment seven days after invoicing. We'll call it thirty-five hours a week, so invoice us for seventy hours. We'll pay that second week on your retrieval of the hacker's identity.'

'Done.'

So far as Mel knew, only one person knew of Mel's shadowing of Tom's online activities these past months: Hayes's preschool buddy Samuel. Why had Sam selected Mel, unbriefed, for this meeting with Hayes? What game was Sam playing?

Mel stood to leave.

'You've not drunk your tea,' Hayes said, and took a glug of his coffee.

'Smell it,' Mel said. Hir nose had worked to distinguish the constituent ingredients that wafted in the cup's cloud of steam. The effect was sensory overload. 'Cardamom, carob, black pepper, amaranth, cloves. They use that many layers the real taste gets hidden. Sometimes people try too hard.'

Chapter 19

Steve's body was too long for the bed in his cell. Eventually he pulled up his knees and held himself in a foetal position. He shivered under the thin blanket. His mind raced. The holding cell had no windows.

An officer opened the door and declared it morning. Steve wanted coffee and they brought him tea with two sugars. They brought him a plastic bowl of cornflakes that swam in milk and were also sugared.

Steve lifted the bowl to his mouth to drain off the last of the milk, but drops escaped and dribbled down on to his Thom Browne sweatshirt and left a stain he couldn't rub out. He had no opportunity to shower. He had no clean clothes. He felt grubby.

This trip down the corridor was the big break of the morning so far.

They had settled him into the interview room. Now its door opened slowly. Rupert Hayes pushed his head around it, smeared his face with a smile when he caught sight of Steve, and stepped fully in.

'Rough night, Steven?' he asked, and closed the door. 'I don't expect my clients to overnight in a cell, but then *their* sex offences are legitimate. They claim you were voluntarily helping with their enquiries for some hours before they formally detained you. I'm not going to argue. That leaves us five hours. After that they charge you or let you go. No way will they let you go. You're guilty. You possess indecent images on both your phone and your laptop and your workplace hard drive is sick with the stuff. We might get the Category A offences downgraded to B – it's hard to prove pain to a child without chains and spikes and blood and, thankfully, we have none of those. Just grossly distorted faces. Kids pull that sort of face if you make them suck lemons. Kids can be whiney. We can throw in shreds of reasonable doubt. That could bring a custodial sentence down from years to months.

'Then there are further factors. You threw the laptop and phone into the neighbour's garden. Both locked with a ludicrously simple password. Knowing that they were filled with indecent images. Did that amount to distribution? That would be a viable claim from the prosecution. There's no obvious reason, Steven, for the police to have kept you here. The simplest action for them by far would be to have charged you and shipped you out to Wormwood Scrubs, pending trial. But we've done what we can. We've insinuated mitigating circumstances. Namely, that you're innocent. To get you bail, we have five hours to come up with scraps of supporting evidence for that palpable untruth.

'We've got a lead on the workplace. We've got a full record of those times that your hard drive recorded Steven McInnes burrowing into dark cellars of the world in pursuit of live and penetrative kiddie porn. Now we need to line those times up with another possibility. Perhaps you simply didn't have the wit to log off when you went off for a slash, chatted up a colleague in the corridor, grabbed a coffee, ran off to impromptu meetings, hit the street to buy a birthday card or take a private call. Perhaps CCTV footage captured you off-piste like that and we can match that footage with periods of frenzied kiddie-snatch action at your workstation. A hacker could have been viewing a feed to spot when you were on your way back.

'Of course, a hacker could be working behind your screen even while you're staring at it, but if the hacker keeps working like that, it could slow things down. You might suspect a virus. Make a call to IT. A hacker wouldn't want that. Our best shot is to prove how totally you were hacked. In a while, Steven, I'm going to ask you to come up with all those places you wandered off to while you were logged in at your keyboard. There may be cameras we've missed. In the meantime ...'

Rupert Hayes unfolded a sheath of bank statements and laid them flat upon the table. Black-and-white photocopies, they were marked up with stripes of different coloured highlighters.

'This part of the case, you can imagine, Steven, gives me some relief. With these bank statements, I'm back in a corporate world. These are domestic matters, of course, but finance is finance.

'We have a catalogue of activity on your and Karen's joint accounts, savings, deposits and credit cards that goes back a year. We opened a line of communication with Karen's solicitor. This came through. These here are your wife's biggest concerns. The items in yellow.'

Hayes turned the papers the right way round for Steve to read and slid them toward him.

P. Edgerton. Marked in yellow, a payment of £2,878.92.

Steve lifted one sheet from the other, then the next. Regular yellow stripes.

Steve checked the dates. On the twenty-eighth of every month. 'What's this?'

'That was exactly your wife's question. She made inquiries. The P stands for Pamela. She lives in Walthamstow. A single mother. She has a son. A little boy. Called Blake. It's an unusual name. The name you wanted for your little boy Colin.'

Steve was studying the statements. Hayes stopped speaking and left a silence to hang. Suddenly Steve connected. He looked up.

'Karen's suggesting that the kid's mine? That I'm paying child maintenance?'

'To Pamela Edgerton.'

'For fuck's sake. I don't know any Pamela Edger—' Steve broke off. 'Screwy Pam? I forgot her last name. My PA.'

'You have a PA?'

'I share one. Five of us pool one executive assistant. Pam was my hire. She tarted up well for the interview. Was currently holding down a job. We got glowing references. It was a sham. She was no sooner in the door than bleating. Needed time off for this, time off for that. Her son's a fucking runt.'

'Not yours, then?'

'How old's Screwy Pam? Forty? Older? Have you seen her? Would you poke her? Women who squeeze out a last-gasp baby, their kids are often sickly. They have it coming.'

'Her boy's got leukaemia.'

That paused Steve. You wouldn't wish that on a kid. Not even Pam's. 'She never said.'

'You sacked her. She gave up another job to come to you. Her son got diagnosed soon after. Then you kicked her out. During her three-month trial period. She was distraught. Her word. Thought you were an arrogant, self-centred prick. Her words again. And then her salary kept getting paid into her account. Pam let it slide for the first month. Thought it might be the company's kindness rather than error. After the second month she got in touch with the accounting team. They assured her the payment had nothing to do with them. She checked with her bank. You were paying her. You must have heard about her son. That's what she figures. After you fired her you learnt her son was sick. You took it on yourself to pay her salary. You think you know people and then you have to think again, she says. She wonders how to thank you. If her son makes it to his next birthday she's going to hold a birthday party. She'll send you an invitation.'

'What the fuck? I hate kids' parties.'

'Don't worry. The way things are panning out, you won't

be allowed near children for a long while yet. But that was kind, taking on Pamela Edgerton's salary.'

'You think I'd do that?'

'Frankly? As I come to know you? No, I don't.'

'Too fucking right.'

'It does you no harm, though. Character references such as one from a grateful mother can swing a judge toward leniency. You appear to be a very generous man, Steven. Close to being a philanthropist. Look at those other lines. For instance, the ones in green.'

The green lines marked another series of repeat outgoings, each for the same amount on the same day of the month, every month. The recipients were Greenpeace; Fauna and Flora; Bug Life; Pond Life; The Woodland Trust; Friends of the Earth; RSPB; World Wildlife Fund; ClientEarth.

'What the fuck?' Steve said. He ran his finger down the right-hand side of a page, totting up figures in his head. 'This comes to thousands.'

'You have an epiphany? Watch a re-run of *Blue Planet* or something? Your outgoings don't betray a whiff of charity. Then *bang*. You're scattering money to every environmental group in the country.'

'This must be Karen. She's been getting broody. She's green and all that. This is the sort of thing she might do.'

'She says not.'

'She thinks I did it?'

'Maybe. To please her. She's not sure. Not that bothered.

Those items marked in red? They bother her more.'

Steve took his focus back to the statements. The reds were one-off payments from the credit card, one or two per page, and none of them ran to three figures. Steve put his finger on one.

'Ninety-seven pounds seventy-three. To XXX-Holdings. That's a meaningless name. Who is this?'

'We've been working that out. That payment is a sterling conversion from Bulgarian lev. All the payments we've highlighted relate to porn sites. Pretty hard-core. Not stuff you'd get banged up for. Not the sort of stuff found on your laptop. Titillate you, does it?'

'I don't do porn. I don't need it.'

'Then why subscribe to porn sites?'

'I don't. I don't do any of this.' Steve was mostly curious now. He scrutinized the pages. Waitrose. Yes, that was his. A jar of organic capers and a bottle of walnut oil. Karen had texted him and asked him to pick them up on the way home. He paid contactless. And the same for this, a duck wrap for a quick lunch from Pret a Manger. But this?

Steve lay his finger beneath a line marked in light blue. A payment of £6,200 to Coinbase. Steve checked the line again then looked up at Hayes. 'Coinbase?'

'Bitcoin. Ethereum. Litecoin,' Hayes explained. 'Coinbase sells cryptocurrencies. You made a purchase nine days ago, with money transferred from your deposit to your current account.'

'Like fuck I did. Screwy Pam. All those green groups. Triple X Holdings. Coinbase. None of these payments are mine.'

'Then whose are they, Steven?'

'A hacker. Isn't that fucking obvious? I've been hacked.'

'But why? Where's that cryptocurrency gone? Outside what you've sent to Pamela Edgerton, that's the largest outgoing. Is that what bought you access to the extreme kiddie pornstream at work? Is that what paid for girls to come to your Hanoi hotel? Did you use it all? Is there any left? Where's the account held, Steven? Do you keep all the numbers in your head?'

This guy was deliberately trying to get up Steve's nose. Steve stayed calm. He slid his chair back with his legs as he stood up and walked round to the door. He turned the handle and pulled at it. The door wouldn't budge. Steve moved toward the intercom.

'Call an end to this interview, Steven, and I won't come back.' Hayes had stayed seated but bothered to turn his head. 'Suits me if I don't.'

Steve tensed his shoulders. Boy, the muscles were tight. He relaxed them. 'Will you quit role-playing?' Steve said. 'Stop implying I did all this shit. You know I'm innocent.'

'Whatever you say.'

Hayes's reply irked Steve as much as it calmed him, but he paced back to his chair.

'Those payments to Pamela Edgerton,' Hayes continued. 'They go back months. Now your wife knows about it, she's really pissed off. It's funny neither of you noticed before.'

Steve settled himself back at the table and studied the statements, looking for the Pamela Edgerton lines marked in yellow. 'These were direct transfers out of our savings account,' he said.

'Saving is Karen's job. We go through the actual figures together at the end of the year. Till then, Karen's focus is to make sure the account doesn't top 80k. That's the limit that's guaranteed if a bank goes under. Before that happens, Karen shifts any likely surplus into an investment account.' Steve pulled up the sheets to reveal the most recent. 'There's 53k in there just now. Karen's on track.'

'You had fine wine, roses and dinner delivered to your wife the night you came back from Hanoi, Steven,' Hayes continued. 'As I understand it, you say you didn't order them. You say your card was hacked. But who benefits from all these payments you say you didn't make? That's my big question.'

'Screwy Pam.'

'Presents for your wife? This is because Ms Edgerton decided she likes you after all? OK, let's examine it. As your PA, Ms Edgerton had access to all your personal information, including your email. You sacked her, so she had reason to hate you. She clearly took direct benefit from these payments. That's why we had her interviewed. Ms Edgerton is genuinely grateful to you, Steven. That doesn't put her out of the frame, but her little boy's got leukaemia. It's not likely she spent her time staring out of your webcam, spotting the moment you wandered off, cruising the dark web to pay for direct live footage of child sexploitation, to get revenge. Perhaps she has a nephew aggrieved on her behalf, something like that. We're checking it out, Steven. But let's say you were hacked, so this wasn't someone out to use your bank details and head off on a personal shopping spree. You're either a random target, or this is an act of revenge. Of those two, I like revenge. It gives us a motive. Who apart from Ms Edgerton hates you enough to tear your life apart, Steven? Any ideas?'

Steve blinked fast while his brain clicked through possibilities.

That cowboy builder who demanded payment even though the mortar job on the patio wall was so crap the coping stone fell off and nearly crushed Millie the dog.

Phyllis Carter, who blabbed her best trading ideas around the coffeemaker and then put in a formal complaint when Steve put one of the ideas to use and it worked out. Steve was able to prove that he could have come up with the idea himself. Phyllis Carter was made to quit. Served her fucking right. But women like that, they carry hurt.

His sister-in-law, that titless wonder Michaela 'call-me-Mikey' who thinks her little sister Karen's in the marriage for the money, or maybe Steve's big dick, but Karen used to have real values and whatever happened to them? 'Call-me-Mikey' would think it funny to give Steve's money to green causes. She was the best bet so Steve told Hayes about her.

'She quit her comms job with an NGO to campaign for Extinction Rebellion,' Steve concluded, but kept on thinking out loud. 'But she's been locked up for the past ten days. Flew a drone inside the departures hall at Heathrow's Terminal 5. Stupid fucking thing to do. Kids could have got hurt. But that means she was out of action when this currency exchange was made. When I was in Hanoi. When Karen got all those roses.'

'Think it through.' Hayes peered above his half-moon specs to give Steve the full bland force of his hazel eyes. 'Your sister-in-law could have had an accomplice. What about your job? Could an eco-activist hate you for that?'

'Who the fuck knows? Mikey could hate anyone for anything.'

Steve slapped his hands against the table and looked up at the ceiling, to where a panel light was buzzing. He hated this whole crazy box of a room. The conversation was swirling around it, getting nowhere.

'People like me. I'm not a do-goodie guy, but I'm not bad. I'm not Shell. I'm not Rio Tinto. OK, I'm in the corporate world, but I'm a cog. Take me out and nothing crumbles. We xeriscaped the garden. We feed Millie vegan dog chews. Our closet's stuffed with tote bags – we don't let single-use plastic into the house. I refuse bottled water in restaurants. I've even got a Tesla on order. There's plenty worse than me.'

'Did your sister-in-law know Pamela Edgerton?'

What the fuck did that have to do with it? Steven cocked his head.

'When you sacked Pamela Edgerton, did you talk to Karen about it? Might she have told her sister?'

'We don't talk about work at home. Karen's not interested.'

'Ms Edgerton's dismissal is key. The first unauthorized payment starts with her. What did she do wrong, Steven? Why did you sack her?'

Steve thought back.

She let her hair go lank. She was beginning to smell. Once she got a car to pick him up at the wrong airport and when Steve made his own way to the address on the printout she'd given him the hotel was fully booked and didn't recognize his name. He had them phone around. It turned out the hotel had two branches in the city and Screwy Pam had sent him to the wrong one. She kept taking days off.

'It wasn't one thing,' he said. 'It was a whole catalogue.'

'What was the last thing? What triggered it?'

Steve thought again. 'She got me the wrong train ticket,' he said.

'Wrong train? Wrong destination?'

'Wrong class,' Steve said. 'I always travel first class. That way, I can get my work done. She booked me into second. The coach was full.'

'You didn't have a seat.'

'Someone was in it. I had to sort it out myself. Then someone stole my ticket. This bitch of a conductor made me pay. The whole thing was a right fucking mess.'

'That's it?' Hayes said. 'You had a train trip and Ms Edgerton booked you into second rather than first class.' Hayes blew air out of his cheeks so that his fat lips fluttered. He looked like a puffer fish. 'Let's start from there, shall we? Let's reimagine the scene on the train.'

It took questioning, but Hayes was good at that.

Steve recalled the daft old woman with the painted lips and the big red bow in her hair.

That timorous Muslim girl mouthing along to her phone.

The young bitch in the corner who sat in his seat and answered back.

And that thin little teenager, black curly hair, black T-shirt and thin, pale face. Thought he was clever, started back-chatting, claimed insane stuff like Steve's watch and phone belonged to him. Steve's spine started to chill.

That runt. He was the hacker. Steve suddenly knew it.

Hayes was looking into Steve's eyes. He saw them lose focus a moment, and the focus returned. 'What could he have learned about you?' Hayes asked.

'About as much as I knew about him. What he looked like, where he sat.'

'You didn't make calls he could overhear?'

'I just wanted my seat.' Steve went quiet and thought a while. 'I called the office.'

'Pamela Edgerton.'

'She was off. Her kid was sick. It was someone new.'

'Which meant you had to identify yourself?'

Steve nodded.

'This Pamela Edgerton. You spoke about her?'

'Probably.' It was such a nothing conversation it didn't seem to matter. 'You're saying that little kid decided to hack me because of what I said on the phone?'

'What you said. What he saw. What he felt. He had your name. Your seat number. Your workplace. Did you hook your phone up to the onboard wi-fi?'

'I was on a train. The signal cuts out otherwise.'

'Which means your data was flowing through an open, unsecured system?'

'This was all quick. The scene took mere minutes. The kid was getting off. He gave me his seat.'

'You saw him get off?'

Steve gave it some thought. 'I nearly trod on him,' he remembered. 'The coach was packed. I went to the loo. He was crouched near the luggage racks, working his phone. He didn't even see me.'

'Do you think, maybe, that we've found Pamela Edgerton's white knight?'

'White knight?' Steve echoed. He looked so bemused at the concept that Hayes had to smile.

'The little fucker,' Steve said. 'I'll wring his fucking neck.'

'Before you wring his neck, take his picture, will you? This kid steals identities, but he's stuck with the same face. It would help to have a record of it.'

'It's a scraggy little face,' Steve said.

'How clearly do you remember it?' Hayes asked. 'You can draw this boy for us?'

Steve was crap at drawing. He could give it a go, though. Start with that black mess of curls on the boy's head. Paint in the dark glasses. The thin sneer of a mouth. 'Draw him?' he said. 'I'll hang, draw and quarter him.'

Chapter 20

M el's walking technique was to focus on the ground five metres ahead. Don't catch their eye, and other walkers allow you to walk where you want.

A camera strung high above the Millennium Bridge would show this, the Thames flowing beneath and people on the bridge like corpuscles, each on their own A-to-B route and each with their own speed but never colliding.

We aren't our bodies. That's what Mel thinks it shows. We crowd into cities but try not to touch. We carry our own worlds within ourselves. Cities are a context, but the landscape in our brains does not match the place we see. We walk inside a bubble of memories, grief, loss, threat, fear, pleasure, guilt and hope and what we see is a trigger to a neurological response.

That's what Mel found hirself thinking as ze crossed the bridge. Mel snuck a look at approaching faces. Some were blank and most looked grim and none were smiling. They were going to work or with nowhere to go.

Also on his way to work was Samuel Blunkett.

He took the 7.23 from Milford for his daily transition from

country life to London. His train pulled into Waterloo at 8.10. Mel imagined him in his first-class seat at that moment, his head turned toward its reflection in the window, and beyond it the green shift of hedges, fields and hills.

Sam's hair still had ginger in it, trimmed to a fringe. His spectacles were rimless slides of glass that magnified his grey eyes, but not by much. His eyebrows were near invisible their hairs were so fine. Freckles touched the flesh that padded his cheekbones and stopped his face from being scrawny. His nose was trim, just enough to support the bridge of the specs.

Sam was short and slight and the whole effect of the man was boyish but in that odd sense of the boy who was bullied, whose voice often squeaked yet he put up his hand and knew every answer. Not boyish in an appealing way. He studied group and individual behaviour, and years passed and at Oxford he wooed and married the hottest and brightest girl in the college and every man saw too late that he had the advantage over them.

Before leaving to take the train Sam had walked the family's golden retriever on a leash along a path then released it to chase around his wife's paddock. Back in his house outside Milford the couple's two children, a girl and a boy, were eating their breakfast cereal before school when he kissed them on their heads and left. Family formed the settled order of Sam's life and so he did not give home a thought as he stared through the train window. The pupils of his eyes shifted fractionally and fast side to side while his brain spanned the panorama of possibilities and fixed on strategies.

Mel had considered whether ze fixated on hir 'boss' and decided that ze did and that it didn't matter. Though the two of them met irregularly, Sam was Mel's only regular in-person human contact. He was different. With others, conversation lagged so far behind the speed of Mel's brain that words became burdensome, like straining to explore Kantian philosophy with a toddler. With Sam, though, his first words began where Mel's last thought had left off. He had what Mel called a quantum intelligence.

Mel checked hir watch.

It was a small-faced Timex hir father had given Mel. Hir father's father had given it to him and now, with this pass-on, a cheap wind-up hand-me-down was supposed to become an heirloom. 'It's a man-to-man thing,' hir father said when he handed it over, 'but you're my girl and that will do. Maybe you can have a son and pass it on.'

Mel's wrist was still slim as bone, its pale skin covered in invisible down. Ze liked that the watch still fit hir.

Mel had about thirteen minutes to spare and so stepped from the pedestrian thoroughfare of the South Bank and through the gap in its wall. The Thames was tidal and its waters were low. Mel took the stone stairs down to the pebbles that still shone in riverwet.

Even when low, this river was mighty. Mel loved that it surged through the city. Ze had visited the tidal barrier but only to let hir mind blink out at the future.

Temperatures would climb, sea levels rise, and a wave would push against this barrier and roar above it. Each incoming tide would be its own tsunami, ripping the Thames Barrier into loose steel. Now, from the mud bed of the Thames, Mel looked up and imagined the days when the river's banks would be meaningless. The upper decks of the tallest buildings would stare emptied windows out on floodwaters, foundations would crumble and London would settle down beneath an inland sea.

Usually, that thought was a comfort. People fucked up the planet. Let them be swept away.

Mel looked around and waited.

Come on, comfort.

Ze tried to force it. Focused on the fourth floor of a building that ze happened to know housed a private-equity firm.

The regular water level would lie at the third floor, Mel decided, but when the tides came in waves would gush from those fourth-floor windows till waters rose and the whole floor was submerged. Barnacles would stud the cement of its walls. Mel imagined the scene in action.

Still no comfort.

Did ze feel distress? No, it wasn't that.

Ze felt flat.

This file in hir hand was the problem, with its record of Tom's activities and Mel's failure to spot a good whack of them.

Presume Sam's train was punctual. His regular walking pace was steady rather than fast, he would come out of Waterloo

Station inside the stream of commuters, down along the side of the Royal Festival Hall, then turn left and join the walkway by the river.

It was known that the boss made himself available in this way. He was headed to Thames House, where people in offices stared across the river to see who had joined him today. Twice before, Mel had arrived at this time to take this walk with Sam. On neither of those times had Mel booked hirself in.

How did that happen, that only one person showed up, and always one?

Because each day, Mel reckoned, Samuel Blunkett engineered the need for one conversation.

That's the only way Mel could see it working. Sam knew of hir pre-breakfast meeting with his buddy Rupert Hayes. Mel had left that meeting and known what ze wanted to do next: speak with Sam. The fucker must seed these walk-along meetings in people's brains. Sam had a viral mind. You thought you had a thought and all along it was Sam's thought.

And yes, Mel didn't even have to retreat inside the shadow of Hungerford Bridge. Ze walked from beneath it as Sam trod his way down. He was wearing a light green sweater ze hadn't seen before. Cashmere, as ever.

It was nice.

Mel adjusted hir pace a little, slowing down, and their paths merged. Sam's head nodded, just slightly, to acknowledge ze was there.

'I've come from meeting Rupert Hayes,' Mel said.

Sam nodded. He already knew this.

'What's the game, Sam?'

'Sam?' he said, and glanced at hir.

Mel felt heat stream to hir face. When ze blushed, it tended to show most vividly in hir neck. It never lasted long. Ze felt the flush subsiding. Maybe Sam didn't notice.

And what was wrong with hir saying Sam? It was better than Blaster. His family called him Blaster, after a fart he let off at the dinner table aged four when the visiting bishop had them all bow their heads and he was saying grace. Mel knew about that pet name yet chose Sam.

'You want me to call you sir?'

'Did Rupert call me Sam?'

'Samuel.'

'As I'd expect. He's known me almost all my life. Yet you choose to use Sam and not Samuel. It degenders me, Mel. I simply note it.'

They had a file on Mel. And now this would be added. A psycho profiler would grab this new chance to objectify hir. Insecure of hir own identity, a note would say, ze seeks to degender others. Some such crap. Or it could get more personal than that. Like: 'Tendency to render male colleagues in senior positions gender neutral, perhaps to avoid paternal power patterns from childhood.'

Mel had searched for hir digital file. And failed. For the likes of Mel, people who prise apart security walls like kids do a box of chocolates, maybe they keep such files on paper.

Or maybe it's all retained in Samuel Blunkett's brain.

Mel stuck a dam on the thoughts that Samuel's comment had triggered. These walks didn't last long. Ze wanted to keep on track.

'Hayes showed me these printouts.' Mel lifted the file a little then lowered it again. Samuel either knew or he didn't know what the file contained, and of course he knew. 'It's the data flow from Steven McInnes's workstation. With Tom Snelling's interventions.'

Mel could have said more, but the great thing about talking with Sam was that not much had to be said.

'Rupert's a workhorse,' Samuel said. 'Decent bloke, clever, always was, doesn't like boats to be rocked. He won't like Steven McInnes. A man like Rupert doesn't take the likes of McInnes for a client. McInnes works for Hardbridge. Hardbridge is run by Oliver Zumak. Zumak's a couple of years junior to us, but he's done well. Hardbridge runs five billion in global capital. It's a strain to keep Hardbridge in London, but Zumak does so. London *felt* secure.'

Mel caught the past tense, its inflection. 'Now McInnes has changed that,' ze said.

Samuel turned his head to stare at Mel for a couple of steps, then away again. It was an instruction for Mel to try again. Try harder.

'Tom,' Mel said. 'Tom Snelling has changed that.'

'Of course, Zumak doesn't know of the boy Snelling. He knows what doesn't fit. McInnes as an extreme kiddie-porn fanatic doesn't fit. McInnes is no world-beater, Zumak is told, he needs spots knocking off, but he's a stand-up guy.'

'What have they worked out?'

'McInnes's digital identity was hacked. Through McInnes, someone unknown gained access to Hardbridge's system. For all Hardbridge knows, a hacker has set trading algorithms in place that could plunge their five managed billions into chaos. Automatic trades were suspended, pending full security checks. Those checks are showing clean, Zumak's set to resume trading, but not on my advice. Is your Tom Snelling better than Hardbridge's cybersecurity consultants? Likely as not he is. MI5 could live with it when Snelling was focused overseas. This is different. This is London. Hardbridge is a British company. No more free rein for Snelling.'

'You're delivering him up?'

Sam turned his head, looked at Mel, two more paces, and turned away. Mel had to try again.

'We give Tom Snelling to the police?'

Sam blew air from his cheeks, his head rocked back a fraction, a pantomime of shock. 'This is the twenty-first century. We don't do public sacrifice. We don't want narrative. Zumak doesn't need a name. Doesn't need a person. He needs Snelling's methods. You can deliver those.'

'And Tom?'

'Another abbreviated first name, I note, without use of the surname. Has this case become personal?'

'Maybe.'

Ze gave it a moment's thought, about the time it took to stride a step and a half.

'That time we met, on the train, I made up stuff about him being like my brother. He has kid brother qualities. Annoying as hell but so sparky. I'm good, I second guess him, I shadow him, but he's a cluster of surprises. Tom took over Steven McInnes. That was his way into Hardbridge. Could he have taken over your Zumak? Without his knowing?'

Mel let the question hang for a few steps. Ze had Sam thinking, but he didn't respond.

'See? You don't know. I guess Tom didn't do that but I don't know. He could have. He's that good. If he didn't, why not? If he did, why? And why did he target McInnes? You can't reduce the likes of Tom to their skillset. What's his identity? What drives him? Is it this primal urge to kill coal or is there more? Do we know yet? Should we care? Handle Tom, take him out, and you'll never know what he could have done. Let me find out.'

Samuel turned to look at Mel again, not with the fixed glare this time, something more open.

'We're going in for Snelling's hardware. Tomorrow morning. If he happens to be there too, we take him.'

Then he did what Mel had never known him do before. He increased his pace. Mel knew not to keep up but paused and followed him from a distance, then stopped by the stone balustrade that edged the river and watched Sam climb the steps to the roadway. His ginger head sped above the railings of Lambeth Bridge till it became a speck and was gone.

Chapter 21

Tom had a wooden box on his shelf. He'd bought it in the same auction where he bought his chair. He imagined the same craftsman who made the chair sawing and chiselling and planing the box into being, polishing its walnut so the knots shone. Tom kept his treasures inside it.

They were few.

Now Steve was out of the picture he could turn his attention to them. He took the box into his hand and pulled off its lid.

There on top was the scrap of paper that girl gave him on the train. Mel, she said her name was. Melissa. In Mel's block capitals, DILL PICKLE was spelt out in childish biro.

The note refreshed the memory of his train ride back from Edinburgh. And the interview with Glyph. He'd left behind his voice patterns and fingerprints and a deep scan of his retina and whatever profile they put together from his multiple-choice responses. Was the whole thing just an exercise in data capture?

His data.

He'd been busy since, creating his sleepers. And handing them over. Did Glyph really expect everyone to do as told?

Of course they fucking didn't. He was a spectrum teenager. Teenagers don't do as told.

So what if he jumped the gun? What if he activated one of his sleepers, to see if it worked?

He knew at what time one of his Indian sleepers in the small town of Kaniha took her lunch break. She could think she had signed out but Tom would be in control. In just twenty minutes he could screw up operations at the Talcher Super Thermal Power Station so that its chimneys would stop belching for a week or two.

He gave it a go.

Thought so. It didn't work. Tom was given free rein to set up his sleepers but Glyph retained an override. Glyph's agents couldn't activate their sleepers. They got them in place and then Glyph assumed control.

Tom was happy to have his work-around in place.

For fun, Tom liked to log in to computer simulations that tracked the evolution of galaxies.

A science lesson at school had taught him that his body placidly absorbed heavy elements that were left over from the Big Bang, but Tom had learned more since. Half the material in the Milky Way blows in from other galaxies on intergalactic winds. Our galaxy grows by absorbing starbursts that can blow for a million light years before they reach us.

Imagine a wind that can blow as hard and steady as that.

Tom kept learning.

Astronomers might never see a particular exoplanet, but they watch its star. The star moves, spinning an ellipsis, or a little circle. It comes closer and its colour shifts into blue, or it moves further off and the spectrum switches into red. Astronomers keep watching. These shifts form a pattern.

What would make a star wobble like that?

The gravitational pull of an orbiting planet. There you have it. You don't see the planet, but you spot its effects. You know it's there.

The simulations were interactive – this was science, not fiction; you couldn't affect what would happen, but you could pick your perspective. Click at an expand button and you could bring a distant star close, for example, so the screen blazed with its whiteness.

Tom picked his star, just a prick in spangled blackness, but he didn't want to bring this one close. Not yet. First he wanted to slide the star centre screen and bring the cosmos to its left into view.

Tom clicked and held down the mouse. That should grip hold of the star so he could move it.

It didn't.

Tom moved the mouse toward his body in the way he wanted the star to move on screen.

The mouse moved, but the cursor didn't.

Tom shifted the mouse again, looking to reconnect. Instead, the cursor sailed its own course to the right and locked on a separate star. That star pulled closer then held to the centre of the screen while the galaxy around it moved.

Tom puzzled a moment and then guessed. His perspective was orbiting the star from light years away. Tom was journeying inside the galaxy.

For a while, it was thrilling. And then Tom thought to move the mouse again. It brought no response. The galactic journey carried on but it was not in Tom's control.

This wasn't some star wobble. Tom was sitting at his console, but someone else had taken control.

And because, like a galaxy, Tom's mind was also a swirling vortex, a giant maelstrom of thoughts funnelled through his brain.

Tom kept a paperless house. His flat's door contained no letterbox. Tom didn't need letters and couldn't stand junk. Any mail was junk mail. The one paper exception in his whole place was the scrap with the words DILL PICKLE written on it in biro.

Tom brought it from his wooden treasure box to sit on his desk. No logic could link that paper scrap to the hijack of Tom's onscreen galaxy. Yet with Tom's mind in associative hyperdrive, where everything is linked, the girl's note became a fulcrum.

Tom turned from the screen to the note and away, stared up at the pale-yellow ceiling, then plunged his head forward into the enfolding bowl of his hands. He drew the hands back and pressed the heels of his palms against his closed eyelids and rubbed hard against the eyeballs. He opened his eyes, blinked three times, settled his fingers back on the keyboard and got to work.

The reverse hack was easy. Too easy. Like hide and seek but with Post-it notes and arrows and lots of shouts of 'Colder!' and 'Warmer!'

Tom took a break.

He had half a lemon left. He squeezed it, boiled water to sixty degrees, mixed the water and lemon in his white china mug and sipped at it. He welcomed its warmth and tartness. Sour was good when you needed taste to bring you out of your head and back into your body.

Tom swallowed. That was good, too, water pouring down his throat.

Tom knew the danger of losing touch with his body. Online, you can get so caught in the chase you'll chase anything anywhere. You forget why. You forget to come back. Tom made it a habit to come back. At least once each day he shut down his computer and rebooted himself. He sat still, his back erect and not touching the spindles of his Windsor chair, his hands cupped in front of his groin, his feet flat on the floor, and traced a flow of energy from each of his large toes up through his body to the crown of his head then back down and through the feet to the toes once again.

Tom didn't shut down now, but the lemon and water worked something of the same job. It cleared his mind.

His reverse hack had led him to a screen that at first looked like Tom's own. It was locked into the same simulation of an evolving galaxy that had begun Tom's night. Then, of course, he saw that the screen was a conscious mirror of his own. It was like an open door, an invitation to come inside. Whoever had hacked him was expecting him.

Tom drank the last of his drink, and with his tongue pressed lemon pulp from the dregs against his teeth. The hacker's webcam was accessible. Tom had found that much. As Tom swallowed the lemon pulp, he made up his mind.

He would access that camera. See who was staring back at him.

The galaxy blanked on Tom's screen. Instead, he looked out into a room.

It was dark, so likely not far out of Tom's time zone. The computer screen shed blue light into the room, but only to give some sense of space, no detail. A separate light source burned on a table in front of the webcam. It was the orange light of a candle. A beeswax candle, a sheet of honeycomb wrapped around a wick. It stood next to a tall cactus in a terracotta pot. Pinned on two spines of the cactus was a square of paper.

Tom had no control to focus closer in so he screwed up his eyes. A message was inked on the paper in blue capital letters.

> BE OUTSIDE 21.30 4 PHONE DELIVERY
> PASSWORD l0dL0d!
> LONDON TICKET 2MORROW LOADED
> EXIT

Tom's flat had no bell. Tom didn't want deliveries. He didn't buy off the internet. He bought second-hand. Whoever had sent the phone knew that. That's why they said to be out there when the phone came. And if they knew that much about him, Tom reckoned, they'd know he didn't care to wait outside.

Why this weird approach, tempting Tom to track down this note stuck on to a cactus, to be read by the light of a yellow beeswax flame?

Tom sat and watched the candle and thought it through. He didn't trust candles, didn't want the toxins from their flames drifting up his nasal cavities and fogging his brain, but it looked pretty. Tom could see the point of deploying the note on paper. Unless someone was flashing stills from the webcam, it left no digital record. But couldn't you simply turn on a light and make the note easier to read?

The candle was for aesthetics, Tom decided. It formed a stage set, and the beeswax melting into a stub added a touch of drama.

The note was clear. The password made things urgent and told him the ultimate source of the message.

On Tom's interview day in Edinburgh, they had alerted him to two acronyms. See those, and act. One was FOF. Tom's first guess was that it was short for fuck off, but they said no, it was Fight or Flight. They were on to you, but when FOF came through you still had the choice. You didn't have to run.

The second acronym was LOD. Tom was already tuning in because that first time the letters popped on to his screen he guessed it. Life or Death. They're coming for you. Don't stay. There's no way you can win. And there it was, LOD encrypted in the password. l0dL0d!

With that, there's only one thing to do.

EXIT.

It was written in block letters, like his DILL PICKLE note. But the writing on that was shakier, more cramped, in biro.

Tom left the candle burning on his screen – you never knew, someone could think Tom gone and walk by to snuff the candle out and he might spot them – and switched a few cables around to power up a separate monitor. It connected to a separate router. Tom hadn't touched that router for a while so was glad to see it power up and the flashing amber light settle to a steady green.

It was time to turn off the candle shot after all.

Chapter 22

'Shouldn't my solicitor be here?' Steve asked.

Twelve minutes in and this was the first full sentence he'd managed to speak. Superintendent Keans – she used that full title, like she called him Mr McInnes, and others called her ma'am, but Steve was fucked if he'd sink to that – stared at him, pale grey eyes that seemed to probe clean through Steve's skull and take apart his mind.

'You've charged me.' Steve broke the superintendent's stare and nodded at the papers spread across the table. 'Now you want me to sign away my rights.'

He wanted to sound angry, but somehow anger got stoked up when he was locked on his own in his cell yet seeped out of him when he was brought to the interview room. His voice was a bleat.

Keans slid the papers into a bundle and tapped the edges into neatness. She looked at the constable to her left. Was the minimum height for the police force lower for women than for men? Steve guessed so. This constable was short and stubby. Her torso looked normal, but her legs were stumpy and she'd never grown a neck. Her head sat squat on her starched collar.

'Take Mr McInnes back to his cell,' Keans instructed. 'He chooses to refuse bail and remain in custody.'

The constable moved to the doorway and her chin bobbed down over the knot of her tie and back up again. She was nodding to Steve to follow. Well, fuck that.

'Those conditions,' Steve said. 'They should be open to negotiation. A solicitor would help with that.'

'I don't know you,' Keans said, 'but here's what I do know. Your office computer, your personal computer and your phone are choked with Category A pornography. During your recent stay in Hanoi, we have reports of frequent visits to your room by child sex workers. You admitted to trying to dispose of your phone because of the images it contained. So, presumably, you understand that downloading obscene images of children is not one of your rights?'

'I didn't download them.'

'So you say, Mr McInnes, but stay with me. Imagine a man, fresh from reports of likely abuse of minors in Asia, referred to the police by his workplace, a call to the police from this man's wife speaking of pornography channelled through the children's Nest Cam, and this man subsequently seeking to hide personal devices that prove to be stuffed with child porn. Would you leave such a man alone with your children?'

'This is not an imagined man. This is me. And these are my children.'

'That makes them ripe for abuse? Because they're yours?

Are you aware of the proportion of indecent acts against children that happen within the home?'

'Nothing's happened to my children. Nothing's going to happen to them.'

'Indeed. That's our primary concern. Hence the bail condition that allows you nowhere near them. We'll consider limited supervised access in the future, in a neutral venue with a member of social services present. If reports of the children's welfare permit it. As their father, you must appreciate that your children's welfare must be our primary concern. What other conditions would you like to negotiate?'

'The surrender of my passport. My job requires frequent travel.'

'Your job?' Keans raised a thin eyebrow. 'After your exploits in Hanoi, you think your company wants you anytime soon? If so, have them write to us. Have them state their case.'

'The police station,' Steve tried. 'You say I have to report in weekly. Why make it the station on Bishopsgate? It's nowhere near home.'

Keans slid a page from the back of the sheaf of papers in her hand and laid it in front of him.

'Your temporary address,' she said. 'Somehow, your solicitors have arranged it for you. Your solicitor will meet you in the lobby there at midday. Bail is discretionary. Your solicitor built a plausible narrative of stolen identity and possible hacking, which we will investigate. Frankly, the evidence for such a hack evaporated the moment your solicitor left the room. If you want your solicitor to meet you here rather than in the lobby of your new residence, we can pass that message on.'

Steve turned his head. He faced one wall of the interview room, then the other. This room was the one interruption to life in his cell, but it was like getting stuck on a merry-go-round. Others got to choose the music. You went up and down and round and round without a chance of ever breaking free. Steve wanted out.

'I'll sign,' he said.

Keans set the sheets back in front of Steve and passed across a black biro. Steve pressed his signature hard against each sheet. The 'S' was the only stroke recognizable as a letter. The rest of his name was like a flatlining hospital graph topped by a dot.

Steve was proud of his signature. He had practised it lots. At university, friends had tried to forge each other's signature, for a laugh, and no one got close to his. Steve tapped the sheets back into a thin and tidy block and handed them over the table to Keans. He stood up.

'Now I can go?' he asked.

Keans looked across to the constable and nodded. The constable opened the door. Steve walked toward it, without a goodbye.

It felt like a win.

Yes, he decided. A win.

*

One more signature, scored into the paper, and they gave Steve back his Louis Vuitton bag. 'Canvas bag' was all it said on the form. Steve stuck in the dirty boxers, the cashmere sweater and the trainers he'd picked up from his cell, and his stack of papers on top of that.

They'd brought him in the back way, through a high-security blue gate. They were letting him out the front. A door buzzed as Steve approached it, and he was in a lobby and then outdoors.

Fuck. Steve's trainers rooted to the ground. The street was packed with people out walking, squirming and twisting around each other, both left and right. Past them, in the road, traffic clogged.

There are two ways to stay still on a street. Hug the wall, maybe crouched under a blanket, and wag a paper cup at whoever works their way around you. Or stand on the road-side and hail a cab.

Cabs were Steve's default mode. What's freedom? Freedom means you can go home. Back home, Steve had his Colnago road bike. Handmade in Italy. You don't fit a kiddie seat on a Colnago, so for now Steve kept it in the cellar. That problem was dead; they wouldn't let him take his kids for a ride even if he wanted to. Give him thirty minutes and Steve could be home, mounted on his Colnago and on his way again. Who would know?

Steve scanned the street. There was nobody obviously lurking. But who saw police on the street any more? London was a world leader in terms of CCTV coverage. You want to catch someone when they go home though you've told them not to? Track them when you let them go. They're on auto-pilot. You'll catch them out. That's what Steve would do if he were the police. He started to scan higher and wider, looking for cameras.

Out in the road, caught between two buses but heading Steve's way, a black cab. It was one of those new electric ones with fancy bubble lighting round its headlamps. That would do.

Steve raised a hand. It was a reflex action. The cab indicated right and pulled in against the kerb so Steve could walk past the stationary bus and climb in. Its door clicked and Steve pulled it open.

'North Kensington,' he said. The driver was a bruised white, in her thirties, dull brown hair pushed back behind her ears and a tired smile. Steve settled into the seat. 'Do you know Highlever Road?' he started to ask, but tailed off. 'Fuck,' he said instead. 'I've got no money.'

'Can someone pay the other end?' the driver asked. 'Are you going home?'

'No,' Steve said. 'No no no no.' It was the most he could say. I've got no money. No cards. I'm not allowed home. I'm in shit and I don't know what to do. No no no no no.

'You know Heron Tower, on Bishopsgate?' he asked instead. That was the address written down by Keans. Where he had to meet his solicitor at twelve. 'How would you get there from here?'

'Keep on down the Uxbridge Road,' she said. 'Stay north of Hyde Park. Round Marble Arch and along Wigmore Street. Keep on along the A40 from there.' Thank fuck for black-cab drivers, Steve thought. They still had the Knowledge. Even spoke English. None of that Uber crap of tapping an address letter by letter into their phone. 'Fifty minutes, if we're lucky. Though this traffic doesn't look lucky.'

So what would that be? Three hours on foot? 'What's the time?' Steve asked.

'Ten twenty.'

OK. Ninety minutes on foot. He'd have to run.

Steve got out of the cab and closed the door.

The cab driver didn't give Steve the finger or anything, she just shrugged her shoulders and pulled out to follow the bus, and Steve was left alone.

Get to Heron Tower for twelve and he had a place to be and someone to see. Fail to get there and he had fuck all.

Steve crossed the road to a church. Low stone walls linked its doorway to the street. It was about the size of a changing cubicle. Steve backed up to the door and prised off the Alexander McQueens. He'd run in his Adidas. The change into his running kit meant standing for a moment in his Zimmerli trunks. So what are they going to do, arrest him?

Chapter 23

Maybe Glyph was better than Tom thought. Maybe they knew he had kept control of his sleepers. He could activate them whenever he chose. The way to stop him was to remove him.

And so Tom worked a way around that. Taking him out would not stop the meltdown. It would guarantee it. Because he had already triggered it to happen.

He picked 20.00 and set a timer. At that time on any day, unless he stopped it, his first algorithm would shoot into action.

And then he entered Hardbridge's system. He no longer needed access through Steve McInnes to manage that. Algorithms were already in place and he triggered each to let loose at 14.00 British Summer Time the next day.

Tom stepped outdoors at 9.30. A girl on an electric scooter glided to a stop beside him thirty seconds later, a snood pulled up to her nose. She handed him a padded envelope and sped off. He had his phone.

His sleeves down over his hands, Tom set to wiping his place clean of fingerprints. He went through his wooden box of treasures. Each thing inside had a memory stuck to it but he didn't need memories any more. He didn't want strangers looking through the box and making up stories about what they found. What would he take with him?

Tom tipped the box's contents into one of his compostable bags and sealed it with a double knot. He would find a bin and chuck the bag away.

What else would he take with him?

A wad of banknotes.

A bank's Visa debit card.

Was that it?

The phone they had sent him.

It had come in a padded envelope so Tom would drop that into a recycle bin along with the scrap of DILL PICKLE paper.

There weren't many compostable bags left and they folded up easily. Tom slipped the roll into his back pocket.

That was it.

✈

Tom's flat had two doors. Tom locked the one on the top of the stairs and went down the bare linoleum steps to the street door below. He left the keys on the third step and walked out without locking the door. It was a crap PVC door, but it did its job. It would be a shame to make them break it down.

Tom's new phone showed two tickets. One was for a bus to Northampton and the other a train ticket from there to London. He had taken a bus to Northampton once and hadn't even got to Dodford when he yelled at the driver to stop because he was going to throw up.

Tom had felt the churn in his guts and bile was burning his throat. He pushed through a hedge and ran across a ploughed field till he heard the bus pull away, and he fell to his knees and choked and choked but no sick came out. He got up and stuck with the fields and found a way home. That was it for Tom and buses. True, he'd never actually been travel sick but the past didn't predict what was happening right now. He was terrified of throwing up or shitting himself in public.

Tom would catch a train from Long Buckby, like he did once before. It meant a little roadside walking, but Tom found a route across fields that made it OK.

When Tom learned to hack the school's attendance register he used to come to these fields instead of school. He couldn't go home before four and have his parents find him so he was out here in all weathers. Three times he had seen a hare. Five times in summers he had heard a lark and traced its song high into the sky.

There were always rabbits. They bred in the copse. Then, one early summer, a posh guy in a green jacket and flat cap kept coming by for a walk and the dogs rampaged through the copse, dug into the burrows, grabbed the baby rabbits in their mouths, shaking them to death, and flung their bodies aside. Tom was hiding in the copse so he couldn't cry out.

The countryside was dying. Tom hadn't even seen a rabbit for two years.

A boy had once tracked Tom to these fields. Josh, his name was. Tom was in the copse, on his knees beside a hole he thought might be the entrance to a badger sett, when Josh came up. Tom hadn't heard him.

'What are you doing?' Josh said, not loud but even so Tom jumped. Josh laughed.

They spent the day together. Tom saw a yellowhammer. Josh had brought a cheese-and-tomato sandwich which they shared. At the end Tom offered to add Josh's name to that day's register when he hacked his way into it. No need, Josh said. Josh would tell his dad he took the day off to help a friend. His dad would think that was a fair thing to do and sign a sick note.

Josh wasn't made for school but he kept trying. He had a flop of dark hair and pale skin and thin cheeks, and his eyes always looked bruised. Both Josh and Tom were always picked last for teams in games. Josh's dad, a half-bald head on him and a bit of a belly, was a man who tried to make everything he said sound like a joke. He ran a pub, and Josh's mum was gone.

Tom wasn't at school the day the news broke. 'Isn't that kid who topped himself the runt who hung about outside the house sometimes?' his mum said when Tom got home. The news had stirred Tom's mum up a bit, so he was able to keep her talking till he had pieced the story together. Josh had been found dead in the bathroom of their rooms above the pub.

The next day Tom went to school. A group of girls was bunched together in the corridor talking. Tom pretended to have something stuck on the bottom of his shoe, which gave him time to listen in.

Josh had been found hanged, the girls said. But it wasn't, like, suicide. He had been naked and using the pressure of his school tie on his neck to help him get off. He had tied it to the cable that held the light fitting. Stood on the edge of the bath and placed his head inside the noose. The bath was slippery. Of course it was, the edge was wet, it was such an idiotic thing to do. So it was a mistake that he died. Stupid fucker, one girl said, he could never do anything right.

Boards were now nailed over the windows of Josh's Dad's pub. Tom thought of the abandoned pub, and of Josh, as he walked the fields away from the town he had grown up in.

This wasn't a proper path, just that strip you can find between crop and field, but it was grassed and even. The soles of Tom's trainers were cheap rubber. At each step he felt small stones press into his feet.

◢

The station was a shed and two platforms. Tom pulled his hood over his head so his face couldn't be captured by cameras. He reached the platform as the southbound train roared in. He picked an empty section and sat by the window.

Over the speakers, the guard started her prattle and Tom tried not to listen.

Chapter 24

Mel learned something about Samuel Blunkett from general hearsay. He had a blonde wife, a boy aged twelve and a girl aged ten, a golden retriever, lived in Milford, sang in a choir, that kind of thing. But ze didn't mix much so to learn more ze took a train to Surrey.

Samuel's choir was holding a concert in a church in Guildford, all proceeds to Save the Children. Mel lingered outside among the graves and watched the audience appear and sat in a pew at the back of the church. Ze wore a charity-shop shirt of faded grey and yellow stripes. Ze wanted to be disregarded and felt it worked.

Samuel and all the men of the choir were wearing dark suits and drab ties. Ze had never seen him in a suit.

It turned out he was a counter tenor. It took study, matching the sound to the movement of his lips, to convince hirself that the voice was his. The choir was singing Bruckner's 'Christus Factus Est' and he had a treble line that carried clear to where ze sat. When he was singing he followed the score. Occasionally his eyes looked toward the church's ceiling but never toward his wife and two kids sat in a pew near the front.

When the music finished and the audience was applauding the first move of his eyes was toward a young woman in the choir. They shared a quick smile. She was a bit plump with a round face and hairstyle and glasses. Mel deduced the two were having an affair.

This was a Tuesday and Samuel's day for taking his daughter to school. They would have gone on foot, and then Samuel took the footpath that led him to the station. That's what Mel imagined from hir study of a map. His train stopped at all intermediate stations and arrived at Waterloo at 10.05. Mel stood with hir back to the Thames so ze could watch the people coming down the steps from the Hungerford Bridge.

He wore a cashmere sweater that Mel had seen twice before, pastel as ever but this one was pink. His desert boots brought him down the steps. He was wearing a backpack of black and beige canvas. Mel had never before seen Samuel carrying anything.

'Here,' he said as Mel drew alongside. Just that 'here', no 'hello'. He barely looked hir way but kept his route along the Thames. He pulled off the backpack and Mel took it and shrugged it onto hir shoulders.

'It's a picnic,' he said. 'For you and your Tom Snelling. Take him back to the Barbican but not to your flat. Head to the forecourt. There's a new patch of artificial grass. The benches will be full but a couple will get up to leave as you approach. Sit there.'

Mel nodded. There was something curt about Sam this morning. He left no opening for questions.

'We swept Snelling's flat this morning. All the hardware was wiped. You know he had two routers?'

Ah. Ze didn't.

'Snelling is playing you, Mel. Everybody plays you. For someone so smart, you're highly gullible.'

'I …'

Samuel raised a finger. 'No time for that Mel. But here's proof of your gullibility. You think we planted you in what's become known as Glyph. So who runs Glyph?'

'You've others examining that for you, Samuel, but from what I've learned …'

'You've learned nothing. We run Glyph. I run Glyph.'

Mel's breath caught in hir throat.

'We profiled you before we recruited you. The opportunity to sign up for Glyph passed through chatrooms while you were present. You passed up the chance. You live an impeccable eco life but at core you're an observer. You're more interested in watching people than changing them. Glyph's a honeypot. It drew scores and scores of cyber wackoes who we track, and a few demonically talented eco activists who we've trained and sheltered as cyber terrorists. They've been very useful. They've engineered for us a handle on global power supplies that Putin would kill for. You've observed this as our monitor of Tom Snelling. You've been dutiful. And frankly, you've failed.'

'Because he had a second router …'

'Because he was better than you. Not to worry. That's a good thing. We hold your skills in high esteem. And since he has outwitted you and outwitted us, that shines a light on Snelling. He's worth our full attention. Glyph's other recruits are remarkably conformist. They think they have the world's power grid in their control. And yet they wait for us to tell them what to do, when to act. Snelling, on the other hand…'

He left an opening for Mel to speak.

'He's a quantum kid,' ze tried, back to pacing hir thoughts with Samuel. 'You think he's at work in one place, and he is, but at the same time he's active somewhere else. And that's what you find tough. You can handle what you can guess at but you can't guess at Tom.'

'Oh I can guess.'

He stopped so suddenly that Mel took two steps ahead of him. He moved behind hir and placed his hands on the concrete balustrade and stood to face the Thames. He was headed for Thames House and its vast block filled the North Bank of the river.

'I take it there's no collusion?' Samuel asked. 'That you didn't know about Snelling's second router?'

Mel stood beside him. Ze shook hir head.

'That's what we decided. You'll find dill pickle in that backpack. Snelling's favourite. He'll be pleased you remembered. There's a bulgur wheat salad. All in glass containers. Two forks. No need to return them. We took them from your kitchen. Unbleached paper napkins. All organic and environmentally correct. You keep a clean house. You sent Snelling a phone?'

Mel nodded. Samuel had just thrown in the fact that they'd raided hir home and ze didn't even have time to feel violated.

Ze was back in a scenario that had reduced hir to yes and no. Ze hated the fact.

'I presume you're fully linked in to the phone?'

Ze nodded again.

'We need to take Snelling out. You'll appreciate that. And we can't. You can guess why?'

'We lack information.'

Samuel didn't nod. He stayed silent, staring across the water. He waited. Mel spoke on.

'He got out of Daventry ahead of your raid. He could be grateful to me for pulling him out. In fact you're using me to bring him under surveillance. If he's smarter than us, like you say, perhaps he knows he's walking into a trap. Perhaps he's gaming us. He's happy to be taken.'

'And why might that be?'

'It's no longer about what he does. Because he's already done it.'

Samuel nodded. It was only slight, but it was a nod. 'What do we call someone who administers poison?' he asked.

'A poisoner.'

'And someone who administers the antidote?'

Mel gave it thought. Ze had no answer.

'We have no term,' Samuel agreed. 'It's symptomatic of how we see things. We're threat orientated. We fixate on agents of harm not agents of remedy. But what happens if they're the same person? What if it's the poisoner who has the antidote? And then we take out the poisoner before we even know what they've poisoned and how?'

'There's no antidote for cyber chaos,' Mel said. The sky above the Thames was clear but hir mind had been hazy. It was getting crisper. 'No antidote. If Tom has set a chain of actions and reactions in place, it could be on a timer. That's what you mean. Everything is triggered unless he chooses to stop it. But why would he do that? He targets coal. For Tom, coal is the poison. If he can stop coal burning, why wait? Why put it on hold?'

'Find out,' Samuel said. 'For some in my community, eco terrorism is our current greatest threat. If you believe that humans cause climate change, then it's no bother if you kill humans. Tom Snelling is the anarchist who won't stick with the group. The disruptor. We've found him and brought him out of his bedroom. He's on the loose. The challenge now is to handle him. You're right, Snelling has a quantum nature. While we watch him doing one thing, he's equally busy elsewhere. Out of sight, doing Lord knows what. There's a microphone in the handle of the bag. We will be listening. Win him round. Keep him talking.'

Samuel raised his hands off the balustrade, turned to leave, but paused a while.

'Can you do human, Mel?' he asked. 'Not just the full-on stare but something softer?

Ze stared at him. Is this how he saw hir? Something alien?

'Tom Snelling's on his way to London. He's coming to see you. That's all that's here for him. Why should he bother? Is he curious? Is he lonely? That's our hope. That he thinks you and he are on the same side and wants to share. And what's our fear?'

'That Tom and I are on the same side.'

'True. But convince him, Mel. Forget about us.' Samuel faced the MI5 building across the water, raised his right hand in the air, and then dropped it. 'Your microphone has just been turned on.'

He gave hir a tight smile. It was Samuel's way of saying goodbye. Mel stood with hir back against the balustrade and watched him walk up the steps from the embankment. Ze noticed ze had stopped breathing, and gasped air into hir lungs.

Chapter 25

Steve had done five-kilometre fun runs with Karen, holding himself back so as to keep pace. It was a love thing. Normally he hated to run in a pack.

Not that Karen was a slack runner. She could go like a whippet. Make Steve pick a dog that he ran like and he would say an Afghan hound. Afghans lollop but manage to keep some real grace when they kick up speed, their heads held high.

What made a fun run fun was when it was over and he and Karen headed back to the finish line to watch the stragglers. Best were the fatties, heaving their way through the final steps, Nike flashes on their trainers, chests and headbands, cheeks tight with strain, pushing for that extra stretch in their legs that would count as more than a walk.

Steve would laugh out loud to see them and their effort and Karen's eyes would moisten in compassion, and that was sweet to see, too.

And now here he was, a plonker near naked in his running kit, adrift in the city. Men looked, women looked, even a little girl stared at him till her mother yanked her forward.

Steve wasn't a stickler for time. He got to work early, he came away late, that was hardly clock-watching. Yet now he kept looking at his wrist and feeling for his phone. If the Viet bitch hadn't run off with his Apple Watch it would have been on his wrist now, he wore it at night to record his heartbeats. How close to twelve was it?

Close. It had to be close.

And how near was this Heron Tower?

A woman, her hair long and straight and brown, clad in a green wool jacket and skirt, confident enough, you would think, but all Steve said was 'Excuse me'. He was set to ask for directions. She jumped like he'd groped her. And like he stank, her nose screwed up and her plucked eyebrows screwed down. She turned and in her solid ugly shoes walked back the way she had come.

A taxi pulled up, so close to Steve he had to step away to let its door open, and two girls got out, students or something. They were young, why get a taxi, couldn't they walk? And Steve got in. It was like fate had gaped wide in front of him, this open door of the taxi, and Steve pulled it shut and settled into the seat.

'Heron Tower?' he asked. The driver clearly knew where it was. The taxi pulled out and sped off.

And arrived.

'That's it?' Steve said. It was a white guy driving the cab. Thick neck and creases in his shaved scalp. 'It was round the fucking corner? Why didn't you say?'

'You didn't ask, mate. That'll be three pound eighty. And mind your language.'

'But it took less than a minute.'

'Three eighty. Minimum fare.'

'I haven't got it.' Steve pulled at the door handle. It was locked.

'You what?'

'I came out without my wallet.'

'You climb into my cab with no money. And now you tell me.'

'You didn't ask, mate.' Using the cabbie's words back at him like that, to Steve it felt for a moment like he was winning.

'I'm recording this.' The cabbie reached forward to press a button.

'It's three quid. Does it matter?'

'You're refusing to pay?'

'I can't pay. Let me out. I'll get it. I'm meeting someone in the lobby. They'll give me the money and I'll bring it straight back.'

'Who says you won't scarper?'

'We're talking three quid. It's nothing. Why would I run away and not pay it?'

'You think it doesn't happen? It happens all the time. But not again. Not to me. What's that in your lap?'

Steve looked down. He was clutching his bag. 'Louis Vuitton,' he said. 'A bag.'

'OK. Put it on the floor. No funny games now. No grabbing at it. Get out, get your money, come back, get your bag, and we're done.'

'You're holding my bag hostage?'

'It's a deposit.'

'But it's worth hundreds.'

'Yours for three pound eighty, mate. That's all I want from you. Are you ready?'

Steve set the bag on the floor.

'Off you go.' The door clicked. 'I'm waiting. But not for long, mind.'

Steve opened the door and jumped out. He left the door ajar so the driver couldn't drive off.

A woman got in.

One of those thin, older types, grey hair smartly cut into the nape, open-necked silk shirt and beige linen jacket. She could almost have been Steve's mother, except she was groomed and confident and successful and smart.

Steve turned and took hold of the door as she tried to close it. 'This taxi's mine,' he said.

She raised an eyebrow.

'You can't go. Not yet. I've got to pay. I've got to get some money so I can pay.'

The woman didn't pull at the door. She just stared at him. For a second Steve stared back and then let go of the taxi door. He heard the woman talk but it wasn't to him, it was to the taxi driver.

'How much does he owe?' she said. Her tone made Steve furious, but he couldn't work out why and didn't have time to take issue. He ran across the pavement.

This was the right building, at least: silver letters on black glass spelt out 'The Heron'. The glass reflected Steve as he ran toward it. His blond hair had spiked into a quiff. He pressed it down. Not much more he could do to make himself look smart. The entrance was a narrow door angled on the corner of the building. Do you push at it or press in a code?

As Steve looked for the answer the door opened. A short, narrow man in a light grey suit, a beardless Asian in his twenties, looked at Steve and nodded his head, just slightly. He had opened the door but was barring the way.

'I'm here to meet my lawyer,' Steve said. He leaned forward to peer over the short man's head. The reception desk lay straight ahead and the reception was to the right. It was triple room height but no larger than Steve's own entrance hall. No room for anyone to hide. No sight of Rupert Hayes.

'There's no lawyer here, sir.'

'There has to be. We're meeting at twelve.'

The man checked his watch. It was a Longines. Steel case and a steel band. About three grand new. How come the guy who guards the door gets to own such a watch?

'It's three minutes to twelve, sir. Perhaps you'd care to wait outside?'

'I need money. For my taxi. Four quid. Can you loan it me? From reception? My lawyer will pay you back.'

'I'm sorry, sir. We keep no cash on the premises.'

'But it's only four quid. Not even that. Three eighty. What about you? Have you got a card I can borrow?'

The man smiled, like he was kind, and stepped back. The door shut. Steve went to pull at it. Locked.

Behind him, Steve heard a car door slam. He looked to his right, at a reflection caught in the glass. It was his cab. Driving off.

'Hey!' Steve shouted. One thing about London; you could outrun traffic if you had to. In two bounds Steve had crossed the pavement. With the third...

The third stride never landed. It hung weightless, the foot carried beyond Steve's body, and his right leg stretched to follow it, and then the foot turned. Your foot turns, you turn. It was aerial ballet, without any skill or charm.

Steve twisted his arms so his hands took the first blow against the ground. His arms crumpled. The soft weight of a body folded around him; the press of a rib cage across Steve's side, a Lycra-skinned arm pushing Steve's cheek against the roadway.

'Fucker.' A man's voice, and the weight was removed from Steve's face and body, limb by limb.

Steve was free to move. He sat up, his knees out in front of him. A thin man in a yellow helmet crouched low to tend his bike. It was a Colnago. Not the same as Steve's, not quite as good, but still beautiful.

'You ran into it,' the man said. A Welsh accent. 'You fucking idiot. You slammed your foot straight through its spokes. Look!'

The front wheel was buckled. Steve would be angry, too, if it was his bike.

'Did you see it?' The cyclist was talking over Steve's head now, to someone else. 'You saw it happen, didn't you? You saw it all. You're a witness.'

'Reckless cycling.' Steve recognized the voice. He turned his head, paused when it hurt and turned more slowly. It was his lawyer. Rupert Hayes. Still in his pinstripe suit with its buttoned vest, but he'd left behind his tie as a sop to summer heat and lunchtime. In one hand he held trays of food. In the other, his mobile.

Hayes addressed the driver: 'I caught it all. On my phone's camera. You were cycling with your head down, like this was a racetrack. Paying no attention to where you were going. I've got film of this gentleman crossing the road. The collision. You slamming into this gentleman then rushing to check on your bike.'

Hayes looked down at Steve. 'Are you all right, sir? Can you move? Can you stand?'

Steve tried. It felt like balancing on a cloud. Aches, he felt aches, but nothing broken. He stayed upright.

'Shall I call an ambulance?' Hayes held out his phone, to make the offer real.

Steve shook his head. Gently. It hurt.

'Do you want me to collect this man's details?' Hayes asked. 'I'm a lawyer. This isn't my field, but I have contacts.'

'It's me who should sue,' the cyclist said. 'The fucker wasn't watching where he was going. You know that. You saw it. He leapt straight into me.'

'I have the evidence.' Hayes waved his phone again. 'The court can review it. Read my witness statement. A doctor's report. We can call the police. They can impound your bike – unless you've seen sense and carried it away. Perhaps that's the smartest thing you can do. Carry yourself and your bike away. Excuse me one moment while I tend to this man. To the victim.'

Hayes placed the trays of food on the ground, his phone in his pocket, and took hold of Steve's arm. 'Let's find you somewhere to sit till you recover,' he said.

'I needed four quid,' Steve said. Even to him it sounded crazy, like a man in shock. 'To pay a taxi. It's driven off. With my bag inside it. A cab driver's stolen my bag.'

'See if you can walk.' Hayes turned his head for moment to check on the street. He spoke on, his voice lower. 'The cyclist has picked up his bike. He's carrying it away. I think he bought it.'

'Bought what?'

'That line about our suing. What got into you? You're standing still one moment, the next you've leapt from the pavement and straight into a cyclist.'

'You saw it. You caught it on your camera.'

'Why would I be taking pictures of the street? My hands were full. I'd got us lunch.' Hayes nodded back at a store slotted into the black glass walls a few steps along the road. 'You like sushi?'

No. Not particularly. Sushi did nothing that a sandwich couldn't do better. But that wasn't the point. Steve nodded.

Hayes bent down to pick up the plastic cartons.

'You really can walk? You're not too injured? That leg looks a bit rough.'

Steve looked down. His right leg was streaked with blood,

running from its kneecap. 'It's a graze.' He moved his leg, and winced.

The man in grey opened the door to Heron Tower. Hayes turned on his smile and reeled off his litany of persuasion. The man at the door stepped back and opened it wide.

'Welcome home,' Hayes turned and said to Steve. His smile had slipped. A jerk of his head urged Steve to hurry before the door could close against him. Steve moved his body through all the aches it felt. Hayes let him come past, in through the door, and clenched his hand on Steve's shoulder.

'Get used to seeing this man in his running gear,' Hayes said to a to a dress-a-like man-in-grey at the reception desk. 'He runs six marathons every year, all for charity. One of our finest.'

Hayes locked his hand on Steve's shoulder till they reached the lifts. Hayes stepped in first, flashed a card to gain access to the controls and pressed 28. The lift surged upward.

'I've never run any marathons,' Steve said.

'Totally fucking obvious,' Hayes said.

Chapter 26

'There. Sit down. Look at the view.' Hayes pulled out a chair, steel ribbed with a grey padded seat and back, and set it to face the window.

Steve did as told. He looked at his right arm. It felt like it was shaking, but it didn't show. The shock of the accident, he guessed.

Hayes came back with a white facecloth he had soaked in warm water. He bent and wiped at the blood on Steve's leg, The cloth came away streaked pink. It was a graze, like Steve said, and a welter of bruise. 'Try not to bleed over the apartment, will you? We've paid a sizeable deposit.'

Hayes took the cloth away to drop it in the sink. When he got back, Steve was staring out of the window.

'Impressive,' Hayes said.

'The view?' Steve presumed Hayes must mean the view. The sky was haze, like a dirty grey, and this high flat was in it. Beyond and largely below was the concrete cityscape of London. Steve had spent his time counting the cranes. Thirteen, all but two of them busy.

'Makes a change from a cell,' Hayes said.

The cell had had no window. This window was plate glass, floor to ceiling and wall to wall. Steve turned his head, then his shoulder to make the act less painful. Was this place bigger than the cell? A tad. He returned to the view.

'You hungry?' Hayes asked. A café-style table, its top of black glass, was set by the window. Hayes moved to the chair on its far side, sat down and opened one of the boxes of sushi. He shoved the other across the table to Steve. 'Excuse my eating. It's a luxury. Time was, we used to have lunch. That got shifted to having lunch meetings. Now it's nothing but meetings. I've got ten minutes. A cab stole your bag, you say?'

The question gave Hayes a slot to pop a slice of sushi in his mouth. Steve gave no answer. He watched the sushi churn in Hayes's mouth. Two gulps of the gullet and it was gone.

'With your clothes inside it, by the looks of you. A word of advice, Steven. Wear clothes. The naked look is odd. It draws attention. We don't need attention. From what you say, you took a cab ride without having the fare. From what I saw, you then sprang an assault on a passing cyclist. You're on bail, Steven. Scamming cab drivers and assaulting cyclists are not explicit violations of bail conditions, but they're implicit. You need to work harder to seem like a decent human being.'

Hayes put a fresh slice of sushi into his mouth. Then another.

'What am I supposed to do?' Steve asked. 'I've no money. No cards. No clothes. Can't go home. Can't go to work.'

'Think what to say to Karen. That should keep you busy.'

Hayes popped another slice of sushi and stared at Steve while he ate it. 'Find a reason why pictures of your two children are posted in global chatrooms.'

'Amy and Colin?'

'Naked. In the bath. In your bathroom.'

'With bubbles? Bubbles in their hair and in the air? Splashing and laughing?'

'I've not seen it. It fits the description.'

'Karen knows that picture. I took it for her. She loves it.'

'She presumed it was private.'

'It is. It was.' Steve pushed his hands up through his hair so it stuck up from his head like a cabbage for a while, then let it go. 'So some fucker's hacked my photos, pictures of my kids, and posted them online? This is so sick.'

'Karen's on her way. She's bringing new clothes. And a little cash, I understand. We offered to have things couriered, but she wanted to see you. In a public space. That was her one condition. She expected you to be able to dress for it. To wear clothes. We could divert her here.'

'I don't want her to see me here,' Steve said. 'I hate here. I belong at home.'

'We rent this place so as to sublet it.' Hayes spread out an arm, as though proud of what he was displaying. 'I've got friends beg me for its use. By the week, by the day, by the hour. Behind that partition there's a bed that folds down. It's well used.'

'Great. I'm wanted for sex offences and you've put me up in a fuckpad.'

'Multiuse residential is how the owner sees it. Be grateful, Steven. You don't exactly come with references.'

Hayes had brought wooden chopsticks but had been picking up the sushi with his fingers. He wiped them clean on a paper napkin and shifted on his seat to reach into his pocket. 'Here,' he said.

It was an iPhone 14 Pro Max in grey. Steve picked it up.

'Am I allowed?' he asked.

'It's from your firm,' Hayes said, while chewing. 'New number. New ID. Your username is Plonker.'

Steve glared across at Hayes. The anger made Hayes laugh. Grains of rice spat from his mouth and stuck to the black marble table. He swallowed what was left.

'It's a joke,' he said. 'Be glad they're joking. Hardbridge spends seventeen per cent of its annual revenue on cybersecurity. After your little shenanigans, they foresee that going up to twenty-one per cent. Yet all the cybersecurity in the world won't secure the weak spot. That weak spot is the person who clicks a link in an email. The person who shares their password. Who walks away from their computer without logging off. That weak spot right now, Steven, is you. If it amuses them to call you plonker, let them be amused.'

It was all so unfair. 'Ask around the office. Have they done that? Make them do it. Check who logs off when they go for a piss. Nobody does that.'

'And nobody got hacked. Only you, Steven. I've spoken with Nigel, he's put in a good word, we've managed to change the office narrative. Your colleagues are no longer saying "Steve the paedo, who knew?" It's more like "There but for the grace of God." I say "more like", we're not there yet, a couple of women have filed complaints about remarks you've made, but you're a lone wolf, Steven. That's got its good and bad aspects, but right now we're focused on the good. You've investigated your own areas and run your own trades. The company has no one with Asian expertise to match yours. The whole Vietnamese coal stake with its cement side deal was your baby. It feels orphaned. It needs you back.'

Hayes pushed the second tray foward. Steve popped one into his mouth. It was slime, a cold fish slime, and rice that glued itself to his palate, and he worked his tongue to clean his mouth and gulped the mess down his throat. 'What the fuck is that?'

'Yellow-fin tuna,' Hayes said. 'Raw. Special. You don't like it?'

'Karen won't let it in the house. Yellow-fin tuna's not sustainable, she says. It's going extinct. No loss, I'd say. It's disgusting.'

'You don't mind?' Hayes didn't look for an answer but nabbed a couple of Steve's slices. 'What's dead's dead. A shame to let it go to waste.'

Two more of Steve's sushi slices shot into Hayes's mouth and he ate them.

'Turn on your phone,' he said when he was done, 'and a screen will come up. It'll run you through a cybersecurity-awareness program. Each section is followed by multiple-choice questions. You need an eighty per cent pass rate to obtain your clearance certificate. Take your time. Get it right. Fail, and you're diverted to a more basic training program. And a twenty-four-hour lock-out to advance from that. You'll need your certificate to activate your new account. Once that's set up, they'll ship you a new computer. It's best that you work from home for now, they say.'

'I can go home?'

'This is your home. Be glad of it. Your case has been referred to Interpol. They're gathering in reports from the police in Hanoi, but web connections see you linked to the global child-porn industry.'

Hayes sucked his fingers clean then wiped them dry on his napkin. One slice of sushi was still stuck to the bottom of the plastic tray. Hayes nodded at it. 'I'll leave you that. In case you get peckish. Now, if you'll excuse me ...'

Hayes slid his chair beneath the table, taking care to leave it straight.

'You're going?'

'I've overstayed. We've got you installed. You're safe here for a while. To be frank, Steven, you're a bit spooky. It's understandable. Arrest is a trauma. Do what you need to do to sort yourself out. Take a shower. Hot, then cold. Towels and basic toiletries are supplied. See how normal you can look for your wife. She could do with you being steady. You know the Barbican courtyard, those tables in front of the theatre and by the ponds? She says you do. You shared a picnic there once before a Necks concert. She'll be there at one thirty. Be there and waiting.'

Hayes turned on his smile. Who had it ever charmed?

'No need to see me out,' he said, and was gone.

Chapter 27

Study a wolf in its enclosure for years and you can call yourself a wolf expert. Then you let the wolf out. Suddenly, you're no expert at all. The wayward wolf does what it wants. It's in charge.

Mel had seen wolves in an enclosure once. It was on a school trip to Whipsnade Zoo. Ze stood by the railing and let rip a howl, and a wolf howled back. That cry of response thrilled hir spine and changed hir. It was the first time ze ever felt known for who ze was.

That encounter is what gave wolves to Mel as a reference point.

Ze had watched Tom in his enclosure, in his room, and tracked his reach in the cyberworld. Mel's studies made hir an expert. Anyone who wanted to know about Tom came to hir.

Now Tom was set free. Out in the world, here in the city, where he had no known habits.

Mel was stationed against the dark grey wall of a house, one of the street's few eighteenth-century remnants. This was a narrow street of shadow. Mel's plan was not to be seen.

Mel saw him. It was the first time ze had seen Tom walk. His legs in their black jeans jutted out a bit, like his kneecaps knew the way and he followed. And his left foot was turned inward. Was he born that way? Or was his leg broken and left to set wrong?

A hood was pulled up to hide his curls and his head was bent to his phone. Mel had programmed in this route and Tom was following it. Hir spine thrilled like that time in the zoo. It was a wolf buzz. Energy charged Mel's legs and hir rubber-soled feet connected and flexed on the stone path like a wolf's pads. Tom was ahead of hir, the road narrowing to a thin strip between two rows of double-yellow lines. To Tom's right, black iron railings and beyond that was the greenery of St James churchyard. Tom's hood shielded his eyes and his head stayed tucked toward his phone.

Mel drew alongside Tom and slowed hir pace to match his. Tom glanced at hir then away.

'It is you, then,' he said. 'You've got the same eyes you had on the train. You're the same height and build. Is your voice the same?'

'Hello, Tom,' Mel said.

Tom nodded. 'It's the same.'

He lifted his phone and stared at it. 'We're almost there. Except the there on this phone is a nowhere place to be. Are we headed somewhere different?'

'You can just follow me now.'

'You're worried we're being tracked?'

'I don't carry a phone.'

'You had one on the train.'

'It was a prop. You could ditch that one of yours if you want.'

'Later.' Tom slipped it into his jeans pocket. 'I might need it, might not. I've not decided.'

So Tom had something to decide. Mel had to find out but wouldn't ask questions. Questions suggest a need to know. Ze couldn't let on that ze needed to know.

'I compared the handwriting on your note to the one about dill pickle,' Tom said. 'The result was inconclusive. I take it that cactus is in your home. Is that where we're going?'

'It's sunny,' ze said. 'I thought we'd have a picnic. I've made us some food. Here, you carry it.'

Ze pulled the backpack off hir shoulders and handed it to Tom. They did the switch while walking, but the move got Tom to look Mel's way. Tom's fingernails were chewed, ze noticed. The knuckles of his right hand were raw, like he had punched a wall or something. His fingers were thin and long. Tom's eyes looked past hir, expanded a fraction when he took in the greenery of the last stretch of churchyard, and he was looking ahead again and shrugged the pack on to his back.

'Will there be other people?'

'A picnic for two,' Mel said.

It wasn't a full answer.

Mel led them both across a street. The route did its best to avoid main roads, but you can't always avoid traffic. Mel turned them right, down a pedestrian lane. Jerusalem Passage. Buildings pressed together aside a tight alley. Tom walked a little closer to Mel's side.

'I bet this place used to stink of shit and piss,' he said. 'And horse dung. And smoke. I've read old books set in London, but they don't mention it. I guess when you live in filth you get used to it. It's not worth writing about.'

'They wrote about smog,' Mel countered.

'The smog was full of sulphur. From sulphurous coal. What's sulphur taste like? I bet they didn't write that. Did people in those days smell soot, like the air was on fire? Sodium chloride's another constituent of fog. What's your tongue's response when sodium chloride hits it? Writers wrote about pea-soupers. They wrote about smog like it was a conscious force, swirling and gripping and choking. They never wrote about its composition. They never wrote about the interaction between smog in all its elements and people's sense organs. Nobody wrote about smog.'

Mel had expected Tom to be quiet.

'Do you know Hogarth?' ze asked.

'William Hogarth?' Tom turned his head toward Mel a little, to catch the nod of hir head. 'Of course I do. He wasn't a writer. He was an artist.'

'He lived there,' Mel said. They had stepped out of Jerusalem Passage, into a merging of roads. Ze pointed ahead, to a turreted archway that sealed the road beyond but allowed people to walk through its arch. 'That's where the route on your phone ends.'

'You've brought me from Daventry to here? Why?'

'A gate of some kind has been here for a thousand years. This one's six hundred years old.'

'No way. It's a Victorian mock-up.'

This little guy was sharper than he needed to be, Mel thought. 'Victorians added stuff,' ze said. 'Like the towers and the turrets. It was simpler before that. The entrance to an old priory. In 1704 Hogarth's father set up a coffeeshop there. It was a place for gentlemen to speak Latin. Nobody spoke Latin. It folded.'

'*Sic transit gloria mundi,*' Tom said.

Mel gave him a quick stare. 'He spent five years in debtors' prison. That's the world William Hogarth grew up in. You can't say he didn't depict London in all its filth.'

The moment ze spoke Mel realized that Tom could say exactly that, that there was more filth to depict than Hogarth dared look at, but they took silent time to cross the road and avoid the traffic.

'Art can't show filth,' Tom said. 'Filth sticks to you. It coats your mouth and tars your lungs and stuffs your nose. Hogarth drew debauchery. London was a stage set and he filled it with cartoons of mad and distorted and bloated people. They've cleaned London up, but it's still full of mad people. They're all intense. They all walk fast, like they're frightened. Their faces are grim. Nobody looks at you.'

'You're the same,' Mel said. 'You don't look at anybody.'

'Why should I?' Tom suddenly stopped. And turned his whole body to face Mel, full on. 'Are we going to talk? If so, can we cut the chat and actually talk? Yesterday I had a life. Last night you sent me a message and snatched that life away. Fine. No big deal. I'm moving on. But right now I'm stuck here and I've not much time. If you've got something to say, can you please say it?'

Mel stared back. Tom meant to look mean, ze guessed, and he put that meanness into his frown. Then there was the pale face and the puckered grey skin under his eyes that showed someone worn out. He was crabby, a kid on edge. Mel was young, but Tom was younger. He wasn't made to grow up. His thick eyelashes were like a calf's.

Something changed in Tom's eyes while Mel watched them. It was hard to tell what – did the pupils dilate or something? The big thing was that Tom didn't blink or look to the side. He let hir gaze in. Tom's eyes had a point of black at their centre and veins shot through them, but the main ocean of each eye was a warm brown. Look into an eye and there's a cosmos there somehow.

Mel felt hir own eyes start to water.

'Fair enough,' ze said. 'We'll have our picnic and talk. Follow me.'

Mel took the lead. Ze set off fast, Tom slotting into the space two steps behind and a little to hir left. Ahead of Mel a man in a suit switched course. He had taken note of Tom, not hir, and seen something to avoid. It was Tom's way of walking, Mel guessed. He kept straight, but that in-turned foot, the kneecap-led stride, made his walk look haphazard, like he might veer off course. Mel slowed hirself down a bit.

This was Mel's territory. Stepping out this way to meet Tom, ze had been on hir own. Now that the two of them were walking back, Mel was not the lone wolf. This was something like a pack. Protect those in your pack. That had to be wolf-pack lore, right?

This was a new concept. Old concepts such as loyalty and trust and habit were no use to Mel. Ze couldn't be duped by those. But wolf-pack lore? Mel pondered it as ze walked and Tom loped and padded along beside hir.

Chapter 28

Stark naked but for the iPhone in his hand, Steve stood in front of the floor-to-ceiling window. Maybe he reckoned that from outside he could be no more than a pale speck on the twenty-eighth floor. Maybe he thought the black sheen that mirrored the walls of Heron Tower would shield him. Perhaps he gave it no thought at all, but after a night in a windowless lock-up his body was drawn to the light.

He was staring into the phone. Anyone looking out through the phone's camera would have seen Steve tip back his head in a laugh of triumph and punch the air with his left fist. That cybersecurity awareness program? He had aced it!

And they would have seen Steve stare out in surprise. All London. Wow. Out there and higher than him was the concrete-and-glass spike of the Shard. Closer and lower was the classical dome of St Paul's Cathedral. His home in Holland Park had a London postcode, but from up here Steve could see forever and there was nothing but London to see. Mighty!

Back to his phone. He would try and get into his work account. The screen had turned to black and showed only the time.

13.24.

Across in the galley kitchen the clock on the microwave read 13.21. Steve hated it when his timers were out of sync. He'd fix it. He walked over, watching his phone for the second it clocked on to 13.25. There!

And at that second Steve's heart lurched. Karen. He was due to see her in five minutes.

Quick. Get ready.

Steve bent to the reflection in the microwave door. He had ruffed up his hair when drying it and now patted it into shape. The bathroom had no razor, but that was OK. Blond wasn't best for a day's beard, it barely showed up as soft fuzz; he always shaved, but Karen liked to run the palm of her hand across it, so it wasn't so bad.

Clothes. He had to get dressed.

Steve was clean from his shower. The bathroom had no deodorant, but there was lavender-scented soap in a pump jar. Steve smeared two dabs of that under his armpits. His running gear was puddled on the bathroom floor. He had meant to bung it in a twenty-minute wash and quick dry but the thought of his iPhone had distracted him.

At the touch of his damp top his fingers felt so sullied he wanted to wash them. No time. The damp was his own sweat. No harm in that. He fitted his body back into it.

He dared to sniff the crotch of his underwear. My God. Was it better to go naked under the shorts? He picked up the shorts. No way. The last thing he needed today was his dick swinging

233

loose in public. He pulled on the clothes, the socks, went into the front room and pushed his feet into his trainers, and checked his phone.

13.28. Fuck.

Steve hit the contact icon. Let Karen be listed! She wasn't. Contacts: zero. He didn't know her number. Why bother? You just press her little photo. But did Karen even have a phone any more? Had the police taken it away?

13.29.

Steve opened the door into the corridor. It was hooked up to a self-closing mechanism. He tugged to speed it shut then gave up. What did it matter? He had nothing to steal.

Which way was the lift? Left? Right? Steve settled for right. And then span round. His key card to get back in through the door was on the tiny side table inside the flat. He reached the door as its closing mechanism clicked it shut. Steve tried the handle. It wouldn't even turn. Great, just great. Locked out.

No time for that now.

One lift counter showed its lift at floor 17. Then 16, 15. Going down.

The other lift was at the ground floor. Steve pressed the up button and the down. Again and again. Up it came, and paused at floor 7. Steve jumped from foot to foot, limbering up. How long would it take to run down twenty-eight flights of stairs? He checked his phone.

13.32.

Oh, Karen, please wait. Please be kind.

✎

He took time to breathe. Called up Google Maps on his phone. Keyed in the Barbican Centre. B-A-R, and the phone worked it out for him.

It took three minutes, two; he was fast, he was breathless. In through the door of the concert hall and that Necks concert from years ago came to him as a flashback, the only time he'd been here, up and down staircases that led nowhere, level after level, searching for the loo, for the bar, for Karen.

And now here he was, back in the carpeted maze when all he needed was to be outside. Upstairs, down more stairs, he chased the bank of daylight ahead and was out through the doors.

13.39. Karen?

He saw her, more stooped than she should be, wearing that dark blue Dior summer dress of hers, walking away toward the flight of steps in the distance.

'Karen!' he shouted.

The shout came out with the last of his breath. His voice carried.

The woman didn't turn around.

Instead a different woman stood up from a bench on a patch of artificial grass twenty feet away. She had been facing away from him, looking toward a lake, but now turned and Steve saw this was Karen.

She was in jeans and a cream cashmere top with a V-neck that showed her bare throat. No necklace and only studs in her ears. Karen never wanted pearls and diamonds – jewellery for her needn't be high end but a chance for designer playfulness. Make-up was for play, too, putting on the glamour for a special evening out, but the day-to-day Karen felt no need of it.

Today she wore it. It was a mask to cover the overnight wreck of her face.

Steve went up to her.

'I thought that was you,' he said, and pointed at the woman he had taken to be Karen but he saw now was a woman, a blonde Bulgarian or Pole or whatever, returning from her cleaning job most likely, and she wasn't dressed in Karen's Dior summer dress but in a blue smock nylon coat, and while her hair was basically blonde and the same length as Karen's it had frizz to it and was streaked with grey.

Karen looked toward the woman, a faint adjustment of her eyes as she took in the woman's stout legs and flat shoes, and she looked back at Steve.

'She's nothing like you, I know, I was crazy scared you couldn't wait and were going.'

Steve watched a complex of emotions wash across Karen's face. She was judging how he looked. It didn't go well. She turned from Steve and sat back down.

'I'm sorry I'm late,' Steve said. 'People gave me the wrong instructions. I got lost.'

Karen lifted her wrist, checked her watch, a simple Swatch with a band patterned in red love hearts Steve had bought her last Valentine's, and she brought her hand to fold its fingers inside the other one on her lap. Karen didn't look at Steve.

He sat down beside her.

'Hayes told me you were bringing my things,' Steve said. 'That them?'

Steve's Puma Gym Duffel, Porsche design, black, lay on the ground by Karen's right foot. She didn't move.

'You're a lifesaver,' Steve said. 'You see what I'm wearing? That's all I've got. A taxi drove away with the Vuitton bag and everything in it.'

Karen stared at him. To spare the silence Steve kept on talking.

'It was shit in the station. They locked me up. In a cell. Picture a Victorian prison and it was like that but without the bars, just a little hatch with a cover on it. Glaze-tiled walls and no windows and a hard narrow bed with a rough blanket and you couldn't turn off the light. I'm the victim, I've been hacked, my identity's been stolen, and they treated me like I was the criminal. They let me out this morning and I just ran and ran. I ran all the way here. They've put me in a flat. It's narrow as fuck but not bad. It's got a great view. Come back with me. I'll show you.'

'I've been out to your parents,' Karen said. 'I walked.'

Steve blinked at her. Her words didn't compute. 'To Pinner?'

'I couldn't sleep. I took Millie.'

'You took Millie? You know they don't let dogs in their house.'

'The children need their dog.'

Steve gave her a blank stare.

'You've not asked about the children,' Karen said. 'You've

told me about you, lots of poor-me stuff about you, but not one word about the children.'

'They're at my parents?'

'It was better than foster care. Just. When I insisted, social services allowed me a supervised visit. Your mother stayed in the kitchen with the door open so she could watch, and a social worker sat and waited while I hugged our children.'

'How are they doing?'

'Now you ask.' Trust the parent who asks about their children, Rachel had said. It had taken Steve a while. Karen thought of the children's faces as they watched her leave the room. Amy held Millie in her arms. Colin just stood, his little shoulders drooping, his mouth open.

Karen reached into her bag and took out her phone. 'I've brought you your things,' she said to Steve without looking at him. 'If you don't mind I'll leave you now. I've got some calls I need to make.'

'Wait,' Steve said, and reached out, took hold of Karen's left arm, but she snatched it away from him as if his touch gave her an electric shock.

'You got a Google Pixel?' he said. It just struck him, the sight of this phone in her hand.

'They took my phone. They took my laptop, all the phones.'

'But why go Android?'

'You think I'd want an Apple? Like yours? You had a phone stuffed with photos of little girls. You think I want reminding of that?'

'They've got good cameras, those Pixels,' Steve admitted.

'Jeeps, you think I give a fuck about cameras just now? They've taken our children. You get that? Our children are in your parents' custody because they don't think we're safe to have them. Does that mean nothing to you?'

'I'm sorry, Karen.' He stared at her till she looked back into his eyes. 'So sorry. You really don't deserve this. OK, this has been bad for me. It's bad for the kids, really horrible. But it's worse for you,' and from the slight widening of her eyes he knew it was a good thing to have said and while he couldn't see how it was in fact worse for her than him it was worth repeating. 'So much worse for you.'

It worked. She turned her head away and then back to him. They were best friends. That's what their marriage was like. They shared stuff.

'That big wedding cake order,' Karen said, and Steve blinked as he tried to compute what she was saying. 'My first ever. It's gone. They cancelled. The two birthday cakes on my books have cancelled too. Messages have gone round our mothers' group on WhatsApp. They know about you. Everyone's talking. They know our children have been taken away. They think their own kids aren't safe with us. They don't want cakes from the house of a paedo. I've no business. And my friends have all got young children so they won't want to know me. I've no friends. I've nothing.'

'This will be over soon,' Steve tried. 'They'll clear me. They have to.'

'I see you've got a new Apple.' Karen nodded down at Steve's hand. 'The police took mine. Hanga's too. She broke down this morning. Said it was all her fault. Said she guessed what was going on when she found you roaming the house naked at night. Says she should have said something, but who wants to believe it, a father with his own kids? I told her it was nothing like that, but she won't have it. She spoke with my solicitor. I had to wait in the hall while they had an interview. You can't believe what she's been saying. What she's been thinking. She's been lying in her room at night listening to us, judging us. Getting off on the sounds from our bedroom when we made love and then sneaking down to check on the kids. In her mind, that sewer of a mind, she listened out for us having sex and imagined our children perched on the bed and watching or rolling around in the sheets or whatever. It's so sick. I've paid her off. She's back in Hungary. And I can't bear to have anyone like her in the house again. I stripped her bed. Washed her sheets on ninety degrees but I'll give them away. Vacuumed the carpet and bleached her en suite. But that house must go. I've decided. It's clear. The whole place was wired to spy on us. Imagine that. And because it's too big to handle on my own we have a nanny there who turns out to have been her own sort of spy with sick fantasies swirling round her head. We're just a normal family, Steve. I want to just be normal.'

'Hayes told me about the photos. Of Colin and Amy. In the bath.'

'That's sick how that was shared. But they're just babies in bubbles, Steve.' She had spoken his name at last. Steve felt a pulse of relief at that. 'Those images on your computer. How can anyone do that to children? I threw up this morning. I thought about those little girls in Vietnam and I threw up.'

'You saw them?'

'One of them. The police wanted to know if I'd seen the images before and like a fool I said what images. I guess my reaction showed that I hadn't. You knew those photos were there. You'd seen them but you didn't tell me about it. We had dinner and a drink and sex and you never said a thing.'

'I was planning to courier the laptop and phone across to the office. Get them out of the house. Have the security team in to examine them, see the extent of the hack and work out what to do. I should have done, I was stupid, but you became my priority. When we spoke on the phone you were so upset. About the Nest Cams.'

'And I thought that was as sick as things could be, Amy faced with porno grunts. Hanga says she checked the Nest Cam's recordings every morning. You went in to see the kids in the night. Sometimes you were naked. And smiling, she says. But you never did anything. Not that she saw. That's what she said. She was using the Nest Cams to spy on us.'

'What would I ever do to them? They're my kids. I love them. I'd kill to keep them safe. You know that, Karen. Surely you know that.'

Karen looked at him, full in the eyes, for more than a second. She nodded her head, well the head trembled but it was a nod, it had to be a nod.

'My solicitor …' Karen checked to see Steve was watching her, then looked away again. 'She says if you've got those images on your computer and knew about them, you can't be innocent. It doesn't matter who put them there. Worst-case scenario, she says, we're looking at two years. You could be in prison for two years. She says I can use that time with visits to rebuild my own life. It's best not to make rash decisions. But of course we have to sell the house. I've booked three agents to give us valuations. I can't live in the area any more. I need to take the children away. I thought I might take up teaching. It takes training I know but a woman to teach Maths, that's what schools need. My life will need structure. And it will give me a private income. Overall, teachers aren't bad people. And that would leave me free to be with the children in the school holidays.'

Steve reached an arm around her shoulders. Karen stiffened. Steve waited. Would she tear herself away? Would she go?

Her body trembled. Slowly, Karen leaned left so that her head pressed against Steve's chest. Steve raised his left hand and stroked it through her hair. Karen's sobs felt like quiet shudders against his body. His eyes smarted. He kept them open, unblinking, so the summer air had a chance to keep them dry.

Chapter 29

A long concrete ramp led from street level and up into the Barbican complex. Tom drew up alongside hir.

'This is your den, isn't it?' he said. 'You've been all tense, but your shoulders have relaxed. This is where you live.'

The boy's head turned to take it in.

'Brutal,' he said.

Tom was slight, but his voice was deep. He picked his words. He noticed stuff.

Mel chose not to talk. To 'chat'. The mic was switched on in the handle of the bag. Let them listen to Tom if they had to. Ze would keep hir thoughts to hirself. Off the ramp, ze took the brick steps to the next level and kept on course.

'Follow the Yellow Brick Road,' Tom said, in a fast, made-up high-octane voice. Mel wondered what had got into him and then ze saw what was now normal to hir was funny to Tom, the yellow line on the walkway that guided visitors through the complex, and so Tom had adopted a *Wizard of Oz* voice. They were following the yellow line because that was the way, not because ze needed the line to find it. Mel had lobbied to have the line scrubbed away so that strangers grew lost. Londoners were on automatic pilot. They needed shaking up.

'And on the seventh day God gave up. And He made this place.'

Ze hadn't expected Tom to be such a talker. He was in a plaza that gave him space to walk beside hir, and he looked up and around and spoke on.

'It's your home. That's OK. It's not bad. It's just weird. Out there, London's made up of little pieces all stuck together. That's what I've noticed today. People need basics like houses and workspaces, but basic didn't do. People want to tart things up. When did architects become standard use? Centuries ago, did they use architects or have a go themselves? Most of London's a patchwork of effort and mistakes, it seems to me. Here's better. It's like someone discovered concrete and thought, that'll do, and slapped it everywhere. They didn't even polish it. All this flatness, the horizontal lines – a kid could have made this place out of Lego. It's like a quasi-futurist filmset. You could do a remake of *Clockwork Orange* here. How old is this place? I'm guessing the sixties.'

Mel felt responses stack up inside hir. One was on *A Clockwork Orange*. Kubrick filmed it in Uxbridge, on the campus at Brunel. Where ze happened to have gone to university. Mel had made the move from Brunel to here and never thought to link the choice of the two places. Tom had jumped in and made it for hir.

The rest of Mel's stack of responses was a version of hir in lecture mode. Ze wanted to tell how the Barbican was modelled on a Le Corbusier development in Marseilles, and reclaimed thirty-five acres of a Second World War bombsite. How walkways gave the place a community feel, people on foot while traffic was hidden far below. How that traffic below them now drove on the first carbon-free stretch of road in Europe. How the tracks of the underground railway were set on rubber so the complex was not shaken from its peace. How the place was called a brutalist masterpiece, but it was really people doing the best they could with what they had and leaving space for nature at its heart.

At Brunel, hir lecturers said ze should stay on for a PhD. Mel thought that meant they thought ze was like them, and therefore fit for a campus that acted as an asylum for bright, high-spectrum adults. Fuck that, Mel thought, I want to shake the world.

Whenever that temptation to lecture arose in hir, ze worked to quell it.

'Are dogs allowed?' Tom asked. 'I don't see any. This place could do with a few pets. Something random. Maybe they could import a beefeater and ravens from the Tower of London. And feed the birds raw and bloodied offal. The birds could caw and shit and dance around a patch of blood-soaked concrete that grows ever darker with every meal. Reconnect this place to the cycle of life and death.'

And voilà, Mel might have said, for if the walking route ze had picked out for Tom had a story to it, this was its climax.

They were at the top of a wide staircase and beyond was sight of what Mel felt was the best haven in London. There was the plaza, with its marble-top tables and white metal seats all filled with people on their breaks from work, and that was fine, but better was the rectangle of lake that stretched the entire length of the complex.

Its water was the muddy green of moss on the wet base of tree trunks, studded with reeds and grasses. The Barbican's concert and theatre halls made up the wall on the left, but you could say this view was like looking down from an arena at what was the real performance space, the people with their lunches were the performers, the lake was part of the set, but for Mel it was more like the safe insides of a garrison city. The tiers of concrete apartments kept the city at bay, and here you were safe.

Mel did not say voilà, though, or anything else. Tom's comment about hir shoulders made hir realize hir muscles were tense again. Tom could think what he liked about this place, Mel decided, he didn't have to love it just because ze did, but ze wanted him to like it.

If you care what others think it's best not to show it. That way you get less hurt. So Mel said nothing.

A quick wide scan gave her no sign of Samuel and his pink sweater and ginger head. Straight-backed, Mel tripped hir way down the flight of concrete stairs and moved toward the benches on the patch of false lawn. They were all full but as they drew close a young couple, she in her hijab and he with a thin beard, took hold of their cups of coffee and made to stand up.

'That's lucky,' Mel said. A middle-aged couple, he in a

puffer jacket and half bald and she with a Barbican bag like she'd been shopping for goodies, were seated on the neighbouring bench. Planted there by Samuel, ze suspected. 'We'll have our picnic there.'

But Tom had stalled.

Then he was off again, a walk angled to the right. He must have scanned the area from the top of the stairs and created a sort of map for himself and was now guiding Mel.

Concrete planters reached out into the lake and Tom worked around the edge of one of these runs. Thick-leaved foliage spread out from their squares of soil to what would otherwise be steps, but Tom trod down them in any case. By the water's edge you could sit down, still at a height where you could let your legs dangle and not get them wet.

Mel came down the other side of the planters.

'You don't like crowds?' ze asked.

Tom was staring out across the water. 'No ducks,' he said. 'You expect a pond to have ducks.'

'You're in London,' Mel snapped. 'Don't even expect a pond. Take what you get. Here, pass me the bag.'

Tom pulled the bag from his back and sat down. He swivelled his head from left to right, degree by degree to complete a full curve.

'Like you said, no ducks.'

'I'm looking for cameras,' Tom said. 'They're in the plaza behind us. I spotted five. I don't see any from here, though.'

'Relax. Pull down your hood.' Mel reached across and gave

the hood a slight tug. Tom grabbed its edges to yank the cover back over his head.

'Touchy,' Mel said.

Tom pressed his hands into his jeans pocket and pulled out the phone. A quick check to set it up, and he raised it and turned and it clicked. He had taken a close-up of Mel's face.

'Fuck off,' Mel said, and reached to grab the phone from him. Tom wheeled it round and far from hir and slid it into his left pocket.

'You don't want your photo taken?'

Mel held out hir hand. 'I'll wipe it.'

'Yes, you could do that. You could get rid of your photo that way. I couldn't. Not if a camera out there tracks my face. But you feel it's OK to pull back my hood.'

'Why should a camera track your face?'

'For facial recognition.'

'Don't kid yourself. We're not Beijing. We're not that advanced in London. Not yet.'

'How do you know? Daventry is.'

'Daventry uses facial recognition?'

'I did. In Daventry. All it took was a photo of someone. I got alerts sent from four cameras around the town. Whenever that person passed the camera, it recognized his face.'

'What person? Who?'

'Someone. Someone I cared for. He's gone now. He hanged himself. By mistake. His place is boarded up.'

'This was before I knew you?'

Tom turned to give Mel a full-on stare for a while, then looked away.

OK, it did sound lame saying ze knew him since they had only met that once on the train. 'I feel I know you,' Mel said.

Tom took the phone out of his pocket, opened up the screen and handed it across. Mel took it and stared at the picture of hirself.

It was a snatched picture. Mel had flowed into the moment when it was taken and ze flowed out the other side, but that moment itself was stuck on the screen, a separate thing. Mel was strong, but the creature in this picture, with its pale, wide-open eyes and shorn head and stick-out ears and albino eyelashes and thin, pinched mouth and jut of a chin and sucked-in cheeks and pedestal of a neck looked weak as fuck.

You can only kill or care for someone like hir.

Mel swiped hir thumb across the screen and pressed it down and the picture was gone. And the loss hurt a bit. One more act of erasure.

Now Tom had handed the phone to hir it seemed innocuous rather than dangerous. Ze gave it back and took out the two tubs of food.

Tom peeled the lid off his tub, peered inside then looked across to Mel. Ze was studying the food in hir own tub, like ze was checking how well it travelled but really to recognize it.

'It's vegan,' Mel said. 'Basically a buckwheat salad with beetroot, cashews, roasted peppers. And pickles on top.'

'Dill pickles.'

'Mini cucumbers and cauliflower florets.' Mel lifted it to hir nose. 'A few cloves of garlic were in the brine, stacked between layers of fresh dill.'

'My favourite,' Tom said.

His smile flashed broad into a grin. He picked out one of the cucumbers with his fingers and bit its top half into his mouth. Mel dipped into the bag and handed him a fork and a napkin. Tom wiped clean his hand then pulled the hood back from his head so that the curls of his hair sprang clear.

'Thanks,' he said. 'On the train that time, when you guessed my favourite food, I wondered how. It couldn't be from my shopping receipts. I pay cash, don't use loyalty cards. I've never typed the word "pickle". I've taped over my webcam lenses but haven't always. I eat my pickles from a jar. Eat one, and I can't stop. I started making my own. Some time, a year or two ago, you must have watched me eat dill pickle. You've been spying on me all that time.'

'Spying. That's an old-fashioned word.'

'Here's what I think I've worked out after that time on the train. You never had a brother called Max. Your last name's not Snelling. At school, kids didn't call you Smelly Snelly. That game you played on the train was a crock of shit. But you didn't plan it. That seat opposite me wasn't yours, but you sat in it. You'd been in Edinburgh. Was it you who interviewed me?'

'I wouldn't say interview. I asked no questions. I was part of a team working remotely from one of the conference suites. The perception analyst.'

Tom turned to hir and raised an eyebrow.

'In firmspeak, my job was to look for that which transpires behind that which appears,' Mel explained, and because that made nothing clear even to hir, ze carried on. 'Basically, who's showing off and who's ripe for action. You're good, Tom. You've got all the tech skills, of course you have, but it's how you've built those skills that stands out. In your life, has anyone ever said "Well done"? Told you you've done great?'

'Once. I took a plastic bag and picked up a dog turd. It was on the pavement outside my house. It meant I didn't want to go out and wouldn't want to come home, so I had to move it. This old woman saw me and she said, "Well done, boy." She said if only other young people were like me.'

'That's it? That's the praise in your life?'

Tom thought a moment and nodded.

'There you go. You work a keyboard like your brain's fused into the matrix. You learn languages but don't look for anybody to speak them to. You've gone ahead and learned all this stuff on your own without anyone giving you feedback.'

'I get feedback. I'm a community-minded guy.'

'Online tech chatrooms. Where you use aliases. You're invisible, Tom. That's why you're so good. No one sees you coming. Then you deploy the sneak slam and you've taken over their identity and still they don't know you're even close.'

'You say I'm invisible.' Tom speared a cauliflower floret on his fork, popped it in his mouth, ate it then spoke on. 'Yet you knew I was there. You've been watching. You've spied on me for ages.'

'You taped off the camera on your webcam.' Mel was thinking it through as ze spoke. 'Was that before or after you used facial recognition to track your now-dead someone around the streets of Daventry?'

Tom moved his fork to get even proportions of beetroot, cashew and buckwheat on its tines, put it in his mouth and made a show of chewing.

'You knew we were shadowing you.' It was a guess, but Mel watched Tom's face and saw no reaction so knew it for a fact. 'The facial recognition stuff, you put that through different routers. From a different system. But if that's so, why didn't you do your private work, that tracking of Steve McInnes, through the separate routers?'

'Some things are personal. Is your name really Mel?'

'What's that matter?'

'It's a new game. You started it. We're picking away at each other. Stripping back layers to find out what's underneath. I get to have a turn. I've started easy. Is Mel your actual name?'

Mel thought a moment. It didn't give much away. Ze nodded.

'This shaved head and the business look. Is that a disguise?'

'I contract out. This is my professional look.'

'If you work for Glyph, you don't contract out. There's no point. Your needs are cared for.'

'I do what Glyph says. How do you find out what the security forces know about you? You work for them.'

'So you work for MI5?'

Mel's brain had been in overdrive since hir encounter with

Samuel. Had ze believed in Glyph? Ze had. Now ze knew that it was just a front. What story should ze give Tom? 'Not exactly,' ze said, and could guess at the sudden bite of interest among the team listening in to their conversation. 'They keep me at arm's length. GCHQ are in the mix, too. But if you like.'

'You have to give MI5 something to make the deal work. So you told them about me. Is that right? That's why you sent me the EXIT message?'

'Here's what they think. You hack your way into the identities of bit-part players in fossil-fuel industries. All you do is collect info. They don't know about you taking over their identities and turning them into sleepers. They have you down as a researcher. I'm meant to shadow you. Copy any info you find that's useful to us. And wait to find out what you plan to do with the info. While you stay passive and act like a researcher, they let you be. When you turn active, they'll reel you in.'

'Which is what they're doing now. Why?'

'You must have gone active.'

'Must have? You don't know?'

'You've been pretty active with Steve McInnes.'

'The coal merchant? The merchant of doom?'

'That's pretty sick, what you've done to him.'

'You know what he's like. He had it coming.'

'You had him fund the child sex industry.'

'He offset it. Paid support for a kid with leukaemia. Contributed to environmental causes.'

'Those girls in Vietnam, did they have it coming?'

'All kids have it coming, Climate change spares no one. Steve's trades in coal are killing the whole planet.'

'Girls as sex slaves is not the same thing.'

'I did what I could for two girls. Brought them out into daylight. One grabbed Steve's watch and ran. Good luck to her. The other landed in the safe hands of the authorities. Did they let her go? Probably. The sex trade's like other trades. Men gobble things up and spit them out. I'd love to stop it but I can't do everything. We pick our issues.'

'They've raided your place. Found the extra routers.'

'They?'

'You knew I was tracking you. You could have hidden the Steve McInnes stuff on another router, but you let me watch you. Why?'

'Didn't you enjoy it? Seeing him brought down? You've met him. You know what a jerk he is.'

'Boys' stuff. You're a teenage hacker. You cruised for porn and dumped it on Steven McInnes. That's a teenage boy sort of thing to do. Did I enjoy it? No, Tom. It made me sick.'

'I'm a purpose-driven hacker. And I'm glad it makes you sick. That's the plan. Nobody's going to shun Steve because he profits from coal. Coal is child abuse. It stunts kids' lives and kills the planet. You know what's a really indecent image, one that makes me sick, literally sick? The sight of emissions belched from coal-fired power stations. Of gas flare-offs. Steve's work is harming children. He's committing planet-wide abuse. Does society care? No. Wait till it cares and we'll all be dead. So I use what I can.

Nobody's going to lock him up for the abuse he's doing, so we'll lock him up for the abuse they'll lock him up for. Job done.'

'Hardly. Steven McInnes is replaceable. He'll be replaced. His work carries on.'

'Fair enough. The way Steve pushed past me to take my seat on the train? It left me bruised. I hate coal and I don't like bullies. I took him down. Call that petty revenge. Does his work carry on? We'll see. That's a second router question.'

'You've targeted Hardbridge?'

Tom stared at her. 'Who's asking?'

'Steven McInnes is English, Tom. Or more importantly, his boss is. When you work against foreign companies, it's fair for MI5 to take an interest. Set your sights on British companies, you're up against the old school network. That's why I sent you the EXIT message. You've trodden on toes, Tom. They've decided to take you down.'

'And Glyph?'

'Glyph admires your work. You're a rogue. They like rogues. They gave me the OK to send you the EXIT note. If you get away, they want you to lead a seminar on how you played Steve McInnes. How you got away. If you don't get away, they want me to give that seminar. What you did right and where you fucked up.'

'So Glyph's getting into the seminar business?'

'It's an internal training session.'

'Have they told you that I tried to trigger one of my sleepers? I did it last night. As expected, it didn't work. Glyph's got a great message. Help us kill coal. It's pulled a lot of us in. And kept us busy. Together, we've infiltrated the global power industry. Got sleepers with their fingers on all the keys. But when we try to free them, we find those keys are locked.'

'It's a question of timing.'

'Indeed. The time is now. Your EXIT message was my trigger. It's all set in place. Step one, unless I stop it, takes place ...' Tom checked his phone. 13.58. '... two minutes from now. How do I stop it? Use this phone. Go online and input a code.'

Tom reached the phone over the lake and dropped it. It sliced into the water. The dorsal fins of black carp had been cutting the water between the reeds. They dived down in chase.

'Now I don't have a phone. Perhaps I'll find one by eight pm tonight. And if I do, maybe I'll input a separate code to stop what's coming next. We'll see how I feel. We'll see how the rest of the day plays out.'

'Is that a message you want me to pass on to MI5?'

'Glyph, MI5, same difference.'

'You're not at your keyboard any more, Tom. You're out in the world. Their world. You don't stand a chance.'

'Carve it on my stone,' Tom said. 'He never stood a chance.'

He stood and turned and walked up the brick stairway past the foliage and was gone.

Chapter 30

Tom's mind posted questions while he walked up the steps. Why had Mel coaxed him down to London? To warn him? To share a picnic by the lake? To confess that she was working for the secret services all along?

She lived in this weird concrete complex where she had a flat and a cactus. Was Tom ever going to see it? Did she plan to take him home?

She didn't know what the fuck she wanted, that was the truth of it.

Was she even a she? The dark suit, the shorn head, it wasn't a bad look, trans was OK with Tom, but he bet she wasn't even clear about that.

Tom climbed the last high step out of the red-brick pontoon and reached the level of the plaza. Where now? He scanned this concrete world and saw no way out. Well, there was that staircase to the left, but that took him back where he didn't want to go. He'd have to speak to someone and ask for directions. It was all he could do.

This man on the bench? His eyes were shut and he was

jigging his head to a beat from his phone.

That woman? Again, she had her headphones in. Not that she was listening. Her fingers were bunched around her phone and she was shaking it, yelling at it.

Tom scanned the courtyard. Everyone who was single had a soundtrack playing in their ears. They wouldn't hear him. He'd have to shout. He couldn't do that.

There, the couple on a bench. The man was pulling a light pink T-shirt down over his head. The woman was staring at the man's torso, stretched taut with the lift of his arms, hairless or maybe just blond; yes, there was chest hair, sunlight catching the sweat on his six-pack.

'Excuse me,' Tom said. He knew how to interrupt, to apologize for daring to speak, home life had taught him that. 'How do I get out of here? I'm looking to get to Liverpool Street Station.'

The woman turned to face him, the wet of drying tears below her wide eyes. She rubbed them with the backs of her hands. The man's sprout of hair, which was indeed blond, pushed out through the neck of the T-shirt and he pulled the pink cotton down to cover his body. It was a tight fit. The man faced Tom and his head tilted to one side like one of those Labradors in the park that wait for a ball to be thrown, he was trying to work something out, and Tom's mouth hung open a little as he saw who the man was and knew that Steve's memory was about to pinpoint him too.

For it was Steve.

This was crazy. Tom knew, like, had met in the flesh and got to know their names, only two people who lived in London, and one was Mel and the other was Steve, and here they both were in this concrete wasteland. What were the chances of that?

No chance at all. Chance had nothing to do with it. This was a trap. Mel had pulled him into London and set him up.

Steve wasn't ultra-bright, but he wasn't dim either. He looked up at Tom, that tilt of the head and a casual what-the-fuck-are-you-standing-there-for? kind of look, then he frowned to narrow his eyes and his face hardened.

'It's you,' he said.

Connection made. And then, to the woman on the bench beside him – Tom got it now, this was his wife, this was Karen, she looked different when she was not on screen – 'It's him. The boy on the train.'

Steve picked up his phone from the bench and poked at its screen.

'What boy? What train?' Karen asked.

Tom pulled the hood over his head and turned away. No way would he let Steve take a picture of him.

Where was Mel? Tom couldn't see her. Were there others? How wide was this trap?

Tom scanned the plaza. Nobody was coming his way. Nobody looked interested. Tom had to get out of here.

'Look at me!' Steve said.

Tom swung his head fast round and away again. He had guessed right. Steve had stood and angled his phone at Tom's head.

Tom wasn't a runner, and his bad leg didn't help, but he was quick in his head and on that fast scan of the plaza he picked what way to go and that was out along the lake. Steve had to swivel as Tom sped past him, and though Steve jammed his thumb on the screen again and again, no way had he got the picture of Tom that he wanted.

'Steve!' It was the wife's shout, long and loud and drawn out, calling Steve back, but you might as well call back a falcon and Tom was running.

To Steve it would have looked like Tom was darting from side to side, but this was Tom going as fast and as straight as he could and Steve came closer, like a fierce pink cloud, and while Tom ran, Steve flew.

It was a leap Steve must have learned in his boarding-school rugby days, a flying tackle, and Steve's hands clutched at Tom's thighs and Tom felt their fingers dig deep, and while Tom's feet kept pushing against the ground the ground was gone and Tom was scampering on air and he crooked his arms and his hands hit the brick paving and his arms crumpled. Tom turned his head so his hood took some impact when his left cheek hit the bricks and he felt Steve's head burrow into the small of his back.

Tom went limp.

That's what you do when men assault you, when they bring you down. His Dad had taught him that much. Fight back, and his Dad got extra excited. Squirm and his Dad loved it. His Dad's fingers would twist a hold in Tom's mop of hair and Tom's neck bent back and his spine arched and he was powerless. He didn't think of this now, his head didn't go there, but his body did. It knew what had happened when his hands clawed at his father to pull himself free and how his throat went so tight he couldn't breathe and pain and panic punched at his chest and he was small, he'd always been small and his Dad's weight just pressed down till he submitted. Fight, and he never won. He still lost, he always lost, but lost harder. Harder like you bled or your leg got twisted under you somehow and simply snapped.

And so Tom's body took the lessons his Dad had taught him and just went limp below Steve.

Steve pulled his hands from under Tom's thighs and the hands pressed their way up Tom's back, like Tom's back was a beach and Steve was a creature hauling its way out of the sea, and the heels of his hands pushed down on Tom's shoulders and Steve vaulted the rest of his body into position and breathed 'Got you, you fucker' into Tom's ear, and held his left hand on Tom's head to keep it fixed to the ground.

His right hand let go and Tom opened his eyes. Steve's phone lay on the ground in front of Tom's head. It buzzed and lit up and Steve's hand shadowed past to pick it up.

Steve knew who it was. The screen must have shown caller ID. 'I've got him,' he said. And sat up.

The weight of the man lifted off Tom's back as Steve shifted to his knees and knelt with Tom under him. This was the chance. You get one chance, and this was it. A quick slide forward and Tom could get his backside in front of Steve, and then there were only the legs and Tom could be free and up and away.

Tom had the thought and then he'd moved his hands, that's all he'd done, and Steve was on top of him again, one hand squeezed around Tom's neck and the other a fist punched above his left ear and held there. Tom heard the phone fall back to the ground, a tinny voice shouting through it.

'The hacker!' Steve shouted at the tinny voice.

Tom's muscles eased back. Steve was heavy. His body was hard. This happens; you have to wait it out. Tom let himself go limp again.

'I've got the hacker. Call the police. Get them here. I'm in the Barbican. The Barbican Centre. Just outside. By the lake.'

The voice in the phone jabbered on. Steve lifted his fist from Tom's head and levered himself up from Tom's neck so he could reach forward and stab at the phone's screen.

The tinny voice grew loud. It was a man. Steve had put it on speaker. And then shouted above it. Tom could see the legs of people standing nearby, pulled close to the scene, but not too close.

'Don't film *me*!' Steve called out to them. They must have had their phones out. 'Film him. Get a picture of his face.'

Steve moved so that his legs pinned Tom's upper arms to the ground.

'Karen!' he yelled. 'Grab a phone. Take a picture of this kid's face.'

'This is crazy, Steve.' Karen's voice came closer. 'What are you doing?'

Steve took no notice. He was shouting out at the onlookers.

'Anybody. You. A hundred quid. Two hundred quid. I'll give you two hundred quid for a close-up of this fucker's face. He's a hacker. He never shows himself. We need a picture of his face.'

Steve yanked back Tom's hood, wrapped his fingers inside the curls of Tom's hair and pulled it high like the head was severed, like it was his to display, and it was.

Tom could feel his body beginning to shake. Next would be crying. That's what happened next. Well, he wouldn't. Fuck Steve. Not any more. Tom had left home. He was an independent adult. He didn't cry any more.

Tom's neck strained. A boy not as old as Tom stood in front of him, one foot resting on a skateboard, baggy singlet, white skin, brown beanie pulled down to touch his ears and both thumbs working the screen of his phone. He was focusing in.

There. That faint click.

'I've got it!' the kid called out, and looked around to check out others, make sure he was the first, the reward his. 'It's me. I got it. I've got a picture of his face.'

Others kept back, too, making a circle, and Tom couldn't turn his head to see around but even so saw two more phones out, folk making movies.

His arms pinned to the ground, his head hung in the air, the side of his face raw, fibres streaking pain down his neck and out from his shoulders, a crowd standing and gawking and filming, Tom worked not to care. This is the crap of being in a body. Don't get stuck there. Think your way out. That's the way, and that's what Tom tried.

The man on Steve's speakerphone was shouting now, so Tom focused on that. He reeled his mind back to make sense of it. The man was from Hardbridge. They'd given Steve access to a phone and to all his work accounts, he said. Steve had passed their cybersecurity test. Not half an hour after that the accounts went haywire.

'Speak to us, Steve!' the man was shouting. 'Bev says to say we're not out to get you. You're upset. We can understand. But first we've got to stop it. Tell us how to stop it.'

Some of the anger got through to Steve, or maybe the pleading, the speaker's voice cracking a moment and bursting back. Tom could hear a woman, it must be Bev, though Tom didn't know of a Bev, yelling in the background. Steve still clung to Tom's hair, but with his left hand he brought the phone up to his mouth.

'Stop what?'

'Your accounts are emptied out. All commodities sold. At any price. You went into a junk spiral, Steve. That's over, you've bottomed out, you've nothing left to sell. It's not about you now, Steve, you're over. When you wiped out your accounts it started a run. Commodities are down across the board, but that's no use, we're frozen out, we can't buy in. And that moment your accounts zeroed out triggered sales across all our accounts. Panic selling's gone remote. All our holdings are getting wiped one by one and we can't stop it. Tell us what you've done, Steve. Tell us how to stop it.'

Steve acted first. That's who he was: act then speak then think. His grip on Tom's curls went so tight that his nails cut into Tom's scalp.

'It's the hacker,' Steve said. 'The hacker did it. I've got him. Got him right here. Talk to the hacker.'

Steve shifted, his knees now on the ground and not on Tom's arms, but what good did that do? Steve pulled Tom's head still higher so Tom's back arched. The phone glared blue in front of his eyes.

'Tell them,' Steve said. 'Tell them what you did. Tell them how to stop it.'

Tom tried. Tried to speak. You have to. In the end, you have to. You have to do what they say. But he had no voice. No sound. It was a gargle in his throat, then even that got shut down and saliva pooled there and Tom couldn't breathe and he started to choke.

Steve let go of Tom's head and took hold of his shoulders and wheeled Tom around, and the back of Tom's head hit the ground but didn't bounce because Steve held it there with his hands on Tom's neck and his face in Tom's face and Steve's hands wrapped around Tom's neck.

'Tell me, you fucker. Tell me what you did. Tell me how to stop it.'

Tom tried, he really did.

He panicked first, not able to breathe, then thought to try with his nose and took a grab at the air with that and found Steve's breath, a sick mix of mint and bacteria, and his legs started to shake and Tom was ready to speak, really he was, but he couldn't.

Steve must have felt the press of words in Tom's throat and pulled his hands off Tom's neck. He had dropped the phone but picked it up again and shoved it in Tom's face and wrapped his free hand into Tom's black curls again and picked up Tom's head and smashed it on to the ground.

'Tell them,' Steve said. 'Tell them how to stop it.'

Stop the sea stop the assault you don't stop things not some things when they've started. 'Can't,' Tom said, he managed that. 'Can't.'

Tom's head smashed on the ground once more, twice, three times. Steve's mouth was drawn wide to show a run of perfect teeth and the darkness behind them. Then the phone came back to glare at Tom.

It was five algorithms all tethered together, Tom could have said if he could have spoken, and those algorithms are looped through four proxy servers. When Tom set it all in place he didn't even know if it could work, not for sure, but clearly it had. He couldn't pull it back. Not now. He could have done. Before two o'clock. On the phone he had just chucked into the lake. But once the phone was gone the chance was gone.

Tom took the idea of how to do it from a suicide chat board. When you post you're about to chop yourself bells ring and calls go out so they can locate you and find you and stop you and you don't want to be stopped you just want to pull it off and show it can be done and bring hope to others, so on this chat board they take coding from your words and proxies take hold before they're even posted so even you can't retract what you wrote and no one can trace it and you get to watch what anyone writes back, and of course you could change your mind but why would you when people are watching, why let them down?

It's complicated, Tom could have said if he could have spoken. Why don't you let me go and we'll grab a coffee and we can sit down at one of these nice tables out here and take in the sun and I'll talk you through it? Have your tech folk join us, invite Bev along, and we can explain how they're fucked. They shouldn't be trading fossil fuels in the first place, coal was killing the planet, he'd done them a favour.

Steve banged Tom's head on the ground again and Tom heard a woman in what was now a crowd around him let out a shriek and he tried to work his mouth, but how could you it tasted of blood now and his throat was so tight and it was blocked but Tom gulped and that did something it cleared it so he could speak. He thought he could.

'You're fucked,' Tom said.

And Steve's eyes were still blue. You don't expect that, not blue eyes when someone's over you and has you down and beats you up, brown eyes maybe that happened once with a kid from school or steel-grey eyes like his Dad's not blue, blue is lovely.

Did Tom smile? Maybe he did. You don't talk back and you don't smile. Tom knew that, but sometimes you give yourself away and it's hard to stay safe.

Steve let go of Tom's hair and pulled back his right hand then swiped it into Tom's right cheek. Tom's head turned and he could see the crowd now, a lot of people, but tears started so he couldn't really see them for they all wobbled and Steve's fingers curled inside Tom's hair and Tom could speak now and did so. 'Sorry sorry sorry sorry,' he said.

'Steve!' It was a long call. Steve was pulling at Tom's hair to lift his head and slam it and lift it and slam it, but another hand had hold of Steve's and was pulling at it. It was Karen. Tom could see it was Karen. 'Sorry sorry sorry,' he said.

And then men came, men in brown vests, and they shouted at Steve and pulled him away so that Tom lay there on his own, and it was odd, it was like being naked without the weight of Steve pressed on top of him and the sun was bright and everyone was staring.

And Tom stayed put, not limp now but frigid and that tremble started. Steve was off him and men were shouting and Steve was shouting back and Karen was gasping and a woman was bending down to look at him close and Tom couldn't pull in his knees and hug them and tuck in his head and shake and cry they were all watching.

The woman dared to touch Tom's shoulder and say 'Stay put stay put we'll get help you're all right now,' but Tom reached up and pushed her hand away and he crooked his legs and they still worked and he got up.

Somehow he got up. He couldn't run but who's kidding who he could never run, but he ran as he quick as he could. He thought they would follow but he couldn't look behind, his neck hurt too much, and he could hear shouts but they grew more distant.

Lake to the right and theatre to the left and Tom went straight between them. He could spot no way out but away was away and that would do.

Chapter 31

Mel had this speed-walking thing, you keep your back straight and your arms by your sides as you would with time to stand still and gaze around but you push your legs out from the knee and near double the length of your stride and toe and heel hit the ground at the same time and it's all brisk so the speed carries your body forward into the next step and the next. Your head doesn't bob up and down because it's more like your legs create a wave and you're surfing it.

If people do spot you and think you look funny, it doesn't matter because you're gone. It's a way of fleeing without doing that stuff that men take as 'Chase me!'

And so when Mel saw Tom head one way ze sped the other, the route that took you through the theatre. Just five steps across its carpet inside the doors and desert boots trod beside hir. Samuel, still in his pale pink sweater.

'When we picked Snelling up at Euston he headed for the ticket hall. We checked. He bought an off-peak single to Lowestoft. Trains leave from Liverpool Street. That's where he's heading now. And you're going where?'

'The Barbican funnels visitors through the complex. They don't get offered much choice. There's a high walkway. He'll be coming out there.'

'At 13.58 he told you there were two minutes to go. The attack on Hardbridge let rip at 14.00. He could have stopped it. But he threw his phone in the water. We guessed right. He sets stuff to happen but keeps the ability to stop it.'

'You just had him surrounded. Yet you held McInnes back and let Tom go.'

'He's tough. You just watched McInnes smash his head onto bricks to make him speak. It got him nowhere. What else has Tom Snelling let loose Mel? You've got to find out.'

'And you think he'll speak to me? I led him into a trap.'

'You have to win back his trust.'

'You don't win back trust. When it's gone it's gone.'

'Shared victimhood. That'll do it. You've been duped, Mel. Tom Snelling went solo with his attack on Steve McInnes. Glyph doesn't want its players going solo. It teaches them the consequences. You told Glyph about the picnic. They made sure McInnes was there. Bang. Now you can't trust Glyph ever again. That's your story. You want to work together. It's you and him against the world. Tell him that.'

'That's crap.'

'The kid's concussed. He's bleeding. He's stumbling through a strange city. Maybe it's the kind of crap he wants to hear.'

They had made it through the theatre's hallways. Their route led them up a ramped entrance and doors opened to let them out onto the street. Samuel kept on talking.

'Snelling's a major asset but you've lost control of him. Look what he's just done to Hardbridge. He used McInnes's account to short the global commodities market, sell off Hardbridge's holdings and block them from trading while prices tanked. And this all happened while he was chatting to you. While McInnes was beating him to pulp. It didn't need his fingers on any keyboard. He'd set the algorithms loose. What's next, Mel. Find out what's next.'

Ze had left the backpack behind. On purpose. It was slung over Samuel's shoulder. He passed it across.

'We'll be listening in,' he said.

Just ahead were the stairs that spiralled up from the street to the level where Tom should appear. Mel climbed them and Samuel didn't.

Mel was breathing hard but made the breaths small and quick so hir chest didn't heave. It was best to look calm. Ze stood on the high walkway where Tom should emerge and waited.

It was only for seconds but ze began to have hir doubts. Maybe Tom had beaten hir to it and was gone. And then ze saw him. Ze caught the full wave of thoughts that crossed Tom's face.

First there was alarm when Tom saw that someone was waiting for him, then a spot of relief when he saw it was Mel, then the muscles beneath his skin all froze in what Mel would class as anger and Tom looked away.

'Wait a minute,' ze said.

Tom did stop, but not for Mel. A map of the complex and the roads around was fixed to the wall on his right, YOU ARE HERE in big letters at the top of it and the name 'Speed Highwalk', and Tom stood and studied it.

Mel knew Tom had a funny walk, but when he came into view it had looked more like a stagger.

'Are you OK?' ze asked.

Blood was thick and dark on Tom's cheek where the skin had been scraped away, and dribbling below it. More blood had caked the curls on the back of his head to his scalp. A ring of crimson stretched across the white flesh of his neck.

'My flat's near here. There's a lift. Come back. Let's clean you up.'

Tom turned from the map and walked away like ze wasn't there.

'I told Glyph,' ze began, walking beside him. 'They must have brought Steve there. I don't know why. You went off tangent with Steve. This is Glyph's way of putting you back on track maybe. Getting Steve to trash you. I'm sorry Tom. We can't trust Glyph now. Neither of us.'

Ze was doing hir best but it wasn't hir lie so was hard to tell. Better to do it hir way. Ze took the backpack off hir shoulders and set it flying as far as ze could to the side and put a hand on Tom's shoulder but he shrugged at it and winced so ze stepped in front of him and spoke a half-voiced whisper in his face.

'I left the bag behind but someone, MI5 I think, just ran up and gave it me. It's bugged. They told me there's a microphone sewn into the handle. They're listening in. We're performing, Tom. Our lives depend on it.'

His eyes stayed dazed. Had he taken anything in?

'I really do mean our lives, Tom, not just yours. MI5 raided my flat this morning. You guessed right. I didn't. I learned the truth today. Glyph's an off-the-books operation of MI5. You're an ecoterrorist in their eyes. I was meant to watch you, keep you under control. I've clearly failed. We're both expendable. I'm going to get the bag. When I get it, it's like holding up a microphone. Anything we say, they'll hear. Watch out.'

Ze hurried off and picked up the bag. Tom came forward with his head tilted down. He was following the yellow line. It angled left across the brick path and ended at a white metal gate, and beyond the gate was a drop and the road below. Tom slowed, looking around.

'That's London for you,' Mel said. 'This used to be the walkway. They keep knocking down and rebuilding.'

Ahead of Tom was a glass lift and to its right was a staircase with steps that twisted down to street level. Tom headed that way.

Tom was lurching. It was easy to keep up.

'McInnes started yelling for his phone. Said the hacker took it. He's right, isn't he, Tom? You've got his phone.'

Mel looked down at his jeans pocket to check for a bulge. It wasn't obvious, but an iPhone is slim. At the staircase Tom reached his left foot down the first step. He closed his eyes, breathed in, opened them again and brought his right foot down to meet it. He gripped the handrail.

'Take the lift, Tom.' Mel ran back to press its button. The cables unreeled at once. The lift rose inside its glass casing. 'Come on, Tom. It's here.'

Step by step, Tom made his way down the stairs. So let him. Mel let the lift close hir in and carry hir down. It was sweet, the electric motor, the glass case. Mel felt protected.

And then the lift doors opened to the street and its traffic and its press of people. Ze could press the button, be carried back up, go home. Mel owed Tom nothing. Ze owed Samuel nothing.

Yet ze stepped out. Waited for Tom to appear from the shaft of stairs and stood beside him while he worked out how to cross the road. The way was clear. Tom waited. A white van came barrelling along. Tom stepped out.

'Tom!' Mel yelled and pulled at his shoulder to keep him still. The shoulder was really bony. The wind of the van blew Tom's hair as it passed.

'I could have shoved you,' Mel said. 'Nobody's watching. Instead I saved your life. Pretend I'm on your side. Time for some home truths. McInnes slammed your head onto bricks. The back of your head's all bloody. You've got concussion. I see it in your eyes. They don't focus. I know where you're headed. To Liverpool Street. Unlike you, I know how to get there. You're staggering. Give me your arm.'

With hir left hand ze held out the bag and dropped it to the ground. Tom noted the move and offered up his arm for hir to hold. They crossed the road.

'This linked arm stuff,' ze said, 'it isn't easy for me either. I don't do touch. I should call an ambulance, but that's in effect calling the police. All the emergency services are one when it comes to the likes of you. Walk into Liverpool Street Station the way you look, the transport police will nab you. As a couple we're odd, but London's OK with that sort of odd. Let's stay linked and keep moving.'

They found a passageway that led them into a plaza set out with cast iron café tables and chairs. Mel settled Tom into a seat and sat opposite him. 'Give me your phone,' ze said.

He blank-stared at hir, like hir words didn't compute.

'Your phone.'

The repeat got through. He slid it from his pocket and handed it across. Mel set to work. Ze pulled a Sim card out of hir breast pocket and undid hir Timex watch. The prong that fit through the hole in its strap was filed to a point. Soon the iPhone was open and its Sim card replaced. Ze spent another four minutes working its keyboard and passed it back.

'Do you always carry a Sim card?'

'Tom speaks a whole sentence. There's hope,' she said. 'And yes I do. The most secure way of using a phone when I'm out is to borrow other people's. That's Hardbridge's phone. I used the bag's microphone back there to let MI5 know you had it. Whatever you set in place at Hardbridge for two o'clock clearly worked. You've announced you have another debacle set in place for eight o'clock this evening. Unless you use your phone to stop it. And that battering McInnes gave you, it impressed them. They think it proved violence won't make you talk. I suspect they're wrong but never mind. We'll take it. Now stand up. Hold on. You've got some walking to do.'

They made it through the plaza, used the lights to cross a busy street, and entered the approach road to the station. The pavement was narrow and oncomers stepped into the street to avoid them.

'At Euston, you bought a ticket to Lowestoft. They know that. I'm sure they're tailing us now and you're in no condition to shake them so you might as well keep to your plan. This thing you have planned for tonight … will you stop it, do you think?'

He said nothing. Just walked beside hir.

'Part of me hopes you don't. A big part of me. I'm curious, for one thing. I'm intrigued to know what you've pulled off. And I envy you a bit. I've made my choices. I pick security over freedom. I want a state that both respects and protects me. I'm outwardly radical yet want to be safe. I'm twenty-two but might as well be sixty-five. Look at you, a beaten up, passionate teenager who's taken on the world because you know best. There's a lot to like in that. When eight o'clock comes, Tom, will there be anything for me to see or to avoid? Any blackouts or explosions? Are we talking financial mayhem or something more tangible? Where should I be looking so I see it best?'

Tom brought across his right hand and freed his arm from her grip.

'Is it just you, Tom, or have you shared techniques with others in Glyph? I'm not the only watcher who's been duped, surely. Glyph's mission, total collapse of the fossil fuel infrastructure, I bought into it, Tom. I thought it was for real. Am I right that it is for real? That you've made it so?'

It was just hir talking.

'That's amazing,' ze said, to round it off. They reached the ramp that led down to the station and into a broad tunnel with plate-glass shops on either side. 'You're getting stares. From security guards. You look like the sort of guy they're meant to keep out. Let me take your arm again please.'

His arm was stiff but he didn't resist.

'There's a Boots at the end. I'll get you some painkillers. Will you wait?

He still gave no response but when she settled him at the end of an aisle he stayed still. Ze was back with him inside two minutes.

'I got you some Nurofen. Max strength. And water.'

He took the pills but made no move for the bottle.

'Single use plastic, I know. I never buy bottled water myself. But you don't know what you look like. Believe me, you're an emergency. Take the water, take the pills,' and she pressed them into his hold.

Black departure boards stretched high above the concourse.

'Ipswich,' ze read out. 'Platform 16. You've got ten minutes. Come on.'

He was silent but compliant. Ze led him to the barriers and took his ticket from him to open the barrier. With the credit card she drew out of her breast pocket ze opened the barrier for hirself and followed him through.

The carriage was largely empty. Ze settled him at a table, by the window, facing forward. It was the way he was sitting when they first met. Whistles started blowing outside.

'The train stops at Ipswich. You change there. For one that ends at Lowestoft.' She opened the pack of pills, popped two out of their plastic pouches, unscrewed the cap off the bottle, and watched as he drank the pills down. 'See if that has any effect. Give it half an hour and if nothing's happening take two more. I'm going to get off now. They'll surround me and interrogate me in moments. I'll make up some good stories. Buy you time. Good luck, Tom.'

He looked up at the sound of his name. Ze nodded goodbye but his head stayed still.

Samuel was waiting on the concourse, just the other side of the barrier.

'07207365412,' ze told him. 'The new number on his phone. I've set it to record. You can play back our conversation but I got nothing out of him. He's not fixed on tonight's action though. That's my guess. When the time gets close he'll open the phone, put in the code, and dither a while. McInnes has left him concussed. He's not in command of his own senses and knows it. He probably wants to be fully alert when whatever happens, happens, and will put it off for another twenty-four hours. In any case his head's muddled. He'll bring himself to the point when he presses stop, or he doesn't. So long as we're in his phone by then, that's our moment.'

'We,' ze had said, 'our', and the choice of pronouns made hir feel hollow inside.

Chapter 32

At Ipswich the train stopped and Tom roused himself from near-sleep. Three times Tom tried to stand up, and on the third he managed it. The pain in his left hip was the sharpest. Out in the corridor he had to stand still while his head swam.

Two women got on, thickset women with brown pony-tails and each with a big see-through plastic bag, and they walked in tandem down the aisle and wiped the tables with disinfectant and picked up rubbish, and when they got close they said, 'You have to get off here, love,' and their lips were in synch but apart, and it clicked. There was only one woman and Tom was seeing double.

The woman pressed herself against the seats to let Tom past, so he held on to the tops of the seats till he made it to the open door and stepped out.

He followed signs toward the exit and found a shop. It sold newspapers and sweets and other stuff. Tom needed other stuff. He found a box of paperclips.

The girl at the counter had frizzy hair and round glasses and stared at him. She swayed a bit. Tom placed his fingertips on the counter to hold himself still. A piece of cardboard was hanging on a rack with a SIM card inside a plastic pouch.

He unhooked it and handed it across. The girl scanned it and the paperclips and said something. Tom reached into his back pocket and pulled out a twenty-pound note. It wasn't enough. He gave her another one, and this time she took it and gave him some change.

Tom sat himself down on one of the wooden seats in the waiting area. The lid of the box of paperclips was stuck tight. He scraped away at the tape and pressed in his nail. The lid flipped open and the paperclips flew up like a fountain and scattered over the floor. Fuck it, he only needed one. This red one.

He bent the clip straight and pulled the phone from his pocket. The wire from the clip fit into the hole on the phone. He popped out Mel's Sim card, dropped it to the floor, stuck in his new one and threw its packaging on the floor too. This wasn't the Tom of old. Tom was a tidy guy who despised waste. He was acting out his new identity as Luke.

The Lowestoft train was announced. Four others in the waiting room, three men and one woman, all stood up at the same time and walked off. They looked ordinary. Were they tailing him? Is that what spooks would do, set off first so it looked like you were following them?

He followed them in any case. The train was small but empty. Tom sat next to the window with an empty seat beside him. If he slumped he couldn't see out and couldn't be seen. He checked out the phone.

Instagram came pre-loaded. Tom pulled up its screen and keyed himself in as Jodie Hayes. Jodie had 104 followers. She once posted a portrait of a grey sea that was bleak and featureless and oddly captivating. The tag #seaview pulled Tom in. Jodie's profile included her job which pulled Tom even closer.

Jodie worked at a bank in Lowestoft. She was entry level but they gave her a fancy job title: Universal Banker. Tom had laughed – well, a gust of air like coughing up a hairball – when he read that job title. It sounded massive, somewhere above President and CEO, yet when he looked into it the role was more like the bank's meet-and-greeter, or principal customer interface officer, if you wanted to get fancy. Later, reviewing Jodie's bank statement online, Tom would work out that she earned £21,734 a year. Pretty bottom rung.

High enough for Tom, though. All he needed from a bank was an entry point into its system.

When Tom first cracked Jodie, she was like an antidote to Steve. Someone nice to go to. Spells of time lived as Jodie washed him clean. She was English, like Steve, but everything Steve was not.

The former Luke Snape had died in a bike crash in Barrow-in-Furness, and when Tom saw his picture he thought, wow. He was a shaggy-haired thin blond kid of eighteen, but his chin was strong and his cheekbones were high and he had a face of light and shadows.

His death was sad. A boy like that had mileage in him. When his death certificate was released, Tom got himself a copy. He changed it a bit. It was easy to photoshop an electricity bill and a council tax bill to show the name Luke Snape.

It was ten days ago that Jodie was standing in the bank's foyer, all set for her meeting and greeting. Tom got to work. While Jodie was busy face-to-face chatting, Tom signed up Luke as her customer. He transferred funds into Luke's new account. Enough to live on for a year or two.

Jodie's WhatsApp account was quiet. That's because it was her day off and she was out shopping in Norwich with her best pal Suzie, and her boyfriend Nathan the plumber was busy on a house restoration in East London.

Ten p.m. was when Jodie's WhatsApp account hotted up. The phone sex was audio only, but Jodie posted some naked selfies to help it along. Nathan enjoyed them but sent no photos back. Jodie made do with a snap of him fresh from the sea in baggy blue trunks so Nathan was wet with his pale skin glistening. He had a long neck and was born to be slim but was developing a paunch. Nathan never had much to say, but his voice had an easy deep bass ring to it that Tom liked. He said things like 'baby baby baby' as he jerked off and never took long enough for Jodie.

They both thought they kept it quiet, Nathan in a guest-house with thin walls and Jodie with her parents in the next room, but when Jodie came she laughed then sobbed and Tom thought her parents might rush in to see what was wrong. They didn't, though.

Tomorrow, if he was up to it, Tom might walk by Jodie's branch and see how she was doing. He could snatch a glimpse through the glass door from the precinct outside. It was good to know someone in a strange town.

A hand took hold of Tom's right shoulder. He didn't move. The hand shook. Tom opened his eyes. It was a guard. In uniform.

Tom blinked. He managed to sit up. That didn't hurt too much. He pulled the cardboard ticket out of his back pocket and held it out.

'Lowestoft,' the guard read. 'Which is where we are now. Better get off if you don't want to head to Norwich.'

It was a dinky station with two tracks like an in and an out and no canopy. The passengers ahead walked past the closed ticket office and round the side of the building to the street.

There was a taxi rank but no taxi. Nobody was waiting. Tom lowered himself to the pavement, his back to the wall, and used the phone to call a cab. He gave his location and destination. Twenty minutes, they said. Wake me when you get here, he said. And he closed his eyes and heard the squawk of a gull and smiled and pretty much passed out.

Chapter 33

The cab driver squeezed his shoulder till Tom opened his eyes. 'You don't need a taxi, mate,' the driver said. 'You need an ambulance.'

The driver was older, tufts of grey hair above his ears. He wore a nylon shirt with a frayed collar. Tom didn't recognize his accent but could tell he had one. His car had the lettering and phone number of the cab company. If this was all part of a secret service operation then they'd gone way undercover. Tom trusted him. He stood up.

'No mate I mean it,' the cab driver said as Tom stepped toward his car. 'There's blood on you. I can't have you in my cab. I'll call you an ambulance,' and he took out his phone.

Tom opened the cab's back door and climbed in. He held out a twenty-pound note. 'I've got more,' he said. 'You can inspect the seat when I get out. I'll pay you double for any damage.'

A moment's pause and the driver snatched at the note. Doors slammed, he drove off. It was a short drive. Quicker to get the job done and be rid of the kid that way.

Tom hoped for glimpses of the sea. Instead he got industrial outskirts. The road was too busy to tell if they were being followed. In any case Tom wasn't up to turning his head around.

They turned off onto a quieter lane. Tom wound down his window and listened. No sound of a tracking car, just a constant shush-shushing. It took a while then he worked it out. Waves were hitting the shore.

The cab pulled up on a patch of asphalt with grass growing through it. It wheeled round so it was pointing the right way to leave. The driver got out first and waited for Tom to leave. He thrust in his head for his inspection. No blood.

'Thanks,' Tom said. 'Keep the change.'

He waited for the taxi to roar off. No other cars came. Weren't they tracking him? No need, maybe. His cab had its number on it. They could just phone up and be told where he got dropped off.

Ahead, ranged in rows in the lee of the seawall, was the mobile-home park. Tom pushed back his hoodie and wiped his hands through his hair and across his face. And tugged at a couple of scabs, one on the edge of his mouth and one on his chin. He might as well look presentable.

Pink letters across the faded pale blue of a wooden archway stated 'Welcome to Sunnydene'. Tom walked beneath it. A sign told visitors to report to reception. Another said this was a neighbourhood watch zone. And on another, NO BALL GAMES.

A ball, red plastic, came bouncing toward Tom. A boy in baggy shorts and long socks and Velcro trainers came chasing after it. Tom caught the ball. The boy juddered to a halt. His face grew wide and open in a silent scream and he turned and fled.

Tom placed the ball down and touched his chin and felt around his mouth. His fingers came back red. So that was it. The scabs were bleeding again. He could taste the liquid iron in his mouth.

He pulled his hoodie back over his head and walked into the camp. A path through it led to a concrete seawall. The waves he could hear must be crashing on its far side. He was meant to report in at the chalet on his left, but its door was closed and no light shone inside it. Tomorrow would do.

Tom had booked his caravan online. Block C, House 12. No pets, the advert said. No smokers. No children. No stag or hen parties. Holidaymakers only. It boasted of outside decking and the photo of this showed a paint-blistered length of railing rotted away from its post. Another photo showed a wooden table covered in a transparent plastic sheet and on it stood a bottle with three orange plastic tulips. That was the listing's concession to beauty. The caravan was by the sea and available, that's all Tom needed to know. He paid up-front for six weeks.

He passed a caravan. On its scrap of decking a man and a woman in matching baggy yellow T-shirts and white floppy hats sat in the fading light. A bottle of white wine leaned in its cooler. The couple raised glasses at Tom and smiled, but he turned his head to look away.

Its web photo had showed that his caravan was grey with white trim. It should be somewhere close.

Tom stopped. That old couple had been chatting away. They had gone silent. Tom pushed back his hood. Worked his blooded mouth into a smile. He turned to face them.

They were staring at him. The main glare came from the husband. The woman had her phone out, scrolling with her thumb.

'Hi. I'm Luke,' Tom said. 'I'm new here. Staying in C-12. My mum'll be here later. Nice to see you.'

He raised his right hand, bent and unbent his fingers like in a toddler's wave, and walked on.

Did that woman carry on with her call? Not yet. She was talking, but her voice was soft. People talk louder on the phone. Tom's bit about his mum was meant for her. You don't fear a youth who's on holiday with his mum. A boy who's polite and uses the word 'nice'.

Was that friendly enough? Did the woman still see him as a threat? Would she send out alerts to her crime watch network?

Tom listened. They were quiet. Still watching, though. He could feel them. He turned a corner round a dark blue caravan to get out of view.

He picked his nose to free it of clogged blood. That's when he got the first smell of sea air. It was constant, that sound of waves chucked at the seawall. A north wind skimmed sea chill into Tom's cheekbones.

He looked left. Someone else was staring at him. He felt it.

There, fork raised, a shave-headed guy with a skinny naked chest lifting straggles of spaghetti into his mouth and looking out.

Then another shape, bouncing up and down, stabs of high barking. A bull terrier, one of those thick-headed white stupid fuckers, leaping off the window bench and smashing its feet against the glass. The man chewed and stared and lifted a can of Fosters to his mouth.

Tom pulled his hood back over his head. Was that grey caravan his? Tom drew close. The lock box was where it was supposed to be, fixed to the side above the wheel. The wheel was flat. This mobile home would rot before it was mobile again. C-12 was painted on the black casing of the box in red nail varnish.

Tom tapped in the code, heard a click, and forced the casing open. A single bronze Yale key, no keyring, was inside.

The wooden steps bent as Tom walked up to the decking. The key worked. The air inside held a mix of damp and bleach. Drawn curtains were thin. Pale light from outside shone as bars between the folds. Patches of brown lino showed between the threads of carpet. The carpet and bench seats were a worn-out purplish red.

Tom tried the light switch.

Nothing.

A sheet of instructions lay on the narrow counter. Tom skipped down the list of what he mustn't do and got to the how-to section. The fuse box was on the wall to the right of the door. Flip the control switch.

Done.

Tom tried the light again. Two fluorescent bulbs flickered on.

Next job the gas. Turn the tap on the blue gas bottle under the sink.

Found. Done.

Take a match from the kitchen drawer, turn the knob below the boiler, light the pilot.

It worked.

Tom tried out a tap. Water gurgled then spurted out. The boiler shook and roared then settled. It went from lukewarm to warm to more or less hot.

This place would do.

Tom sat on the bench seat and took out his phone. Glyph wasn't wrong. Bigger is better. A whole crowd of Tom all acting at the same time would be great, never looking back, pandemonium guaranteed, but he was on his own. For days now he had been ready and then given himself an extra day, but just to tinker really. He had used everything he had.

It would work. Hardbridge today had proved that. But just how big it would be he couldn't know. Each act was set to trigger another. It would be chaos. Havoc. At eight p.m. all was set to go out of control. You can't predict that. So he had no need to wait.

But now he wanted more time. For himself. When he found Jodie and set himself up as Luke and got his new bank account and booked this place, he thought he might be able to disappear. No hope of that after today. They knew where he was and by now who his new identity was. They knew what he'd done to Hardbridge and so what he could do again. They'd be ransacking his hardware to know what he had done but it was a bit like a hostage situation. Come in heavy and snatch Tom and all he had to do was keep quiet and his algorithms would get to work. Leave him be and he could go in and stop it.

And that's what he'd do. Tonight at least. Today had been tough. Loads to process. Too much. He needed time. And his Luke identity was already shot. He needed a new one.

He picked up his phone. It showed him its clock. 19.05. His global meltdown wouldn't trigger till 20.00. He still had time.

He checked the little triangle of the signal bar.

It was blank. There was no signal.

The bathroom barely matched the size of the toilet on the train, with a fibreglass tray and pink flowered nylon curtain stuck inside to form the shower. To turn around inside the room, Tom had to squeeze his shoulders between the walls.

He stepped out into the corridor to strip off his clothes. To manage his jeans and pull off his trainers and socks, Tom went and sat on the bed. It was covered in a rubber sheet. He wanted to be clean. He wanted more pills. He needed to lie down. He didn't have time.

There was no soap, no shampoo, no towel. For seconds there was no water, then the boiler above the kitchen sink roared and the thin showerhead let through some drops and then enough water to call a stream. Tom pulled a switch to trigger a fluorescent bulb above the bathroom basin and climbed inside the shower and pulled the curtain.

He closed his eyes and let the water land on his head and rivulet down his body. His scalp stung, so did his hands and knees and face, but they were nothing more than layers of pain on top of his body. Pain means you're alive.

Tom bent his head to look down at his legs. The water ran pink through the whiteness and the hairs. Blood and water pooled around Tom's feet and gathered above the plughole.

A bang outside shook the shower tray.

Was it the boiler? No, the water kept flowing.

Bangs again. A male voice shouting. Tom turned off the shower so he could hear.

'I'm coming in!'

A crash. It was the caravan door flying back. Cool air flew into the bathroom and chilled Tom's wet skin. The whole place shook to the tread of feet. The shower curtain was ripped back.

'What the fuck are you doing?' The words were shouted down into Tom's face. Tom felt the warmth of the breath behind them. 'Get out!'

The man edged backward. It was a tight fit. His body was square, the buttons pulled tight on a cheap white shirt. Creases were etched into his shaved scalp.

'There's no towel,' Tom said.

'Fuck you with no towel.' The man reached in a hand that

gripped Tom's arm and tugged him out. Tom stumbled, hit the man's belly. The man pulled back, stared down at the patch of his shirt where his white skin now clung, then at the black hoodie and T-shirt under his feet. 'These are your clothes? Put them on. Get out here.'

The man stepped back. Tom grabbed his clothes and scuttled to the bedroom. It had a concertina door. It slid part way but wouldn't close. The man's fingers curled inside and slammed the door back into its frame.

'I said, get out.' He pulled at Tom's arm again. Tom's left hip scraped the doorway and he was out in the corridor. The man went into the bedroom, bundled Tom's jeans and underpants and shoes and socks into his hands and came out and thrust them at Tom. Tom clutched them against his chest.

'Get out there. Get dressed. Then you're coming with me.'

'I'm ...' Tom said.

'Shut it.' The man backed his way down the corridor and walked out the door. His voice yelled from outside. 'You've got sixty seconds.'

Chapter 34

The man was waiting on the shorn grass below.

'What's your name?' he asked.

Tom stood on the decking and blinked down. He didn't have an answer. He didn't even have a question.

'Are you Snape? Luke Snape?'

Tom nodded.

'And you were told to register at reception as soon as you entered the site?'

Tom stared.

'Well, were you?'

Tom nodded.

'So you're a fucking scumbag who thinks he can do what the hell he wants. Think again, Luke Snape. Say there's a fire. You could roast alive and we wouldn't know because you never checked in. Follow me.'

Tom came down the steps. He even hurried through a few hobbled lurches to catch up. Wind cut through his wet clothes and his body started to shake with cold.

The bull terrier barked and jumped at the window as Tom

passed and its owner had brought a can out on to the deck and stared as Tom went by. The couple in yellow had packed up their wine and little table but stood in their window and stared at Tom too.

Tom had been on display all day. Give him six months to process and he might have worked through all the incidents in detail. For now, it was like going white-water rafting without a raft. A force hurtles your body at speed. You bounce off rocks and on you surge. Tip back your head, open your mouth and gasp. Stay alive that way and maybe the river will subside and let you crawl back to earth. Maybe it will.

The man entered the chalet that was the reception and left the door open. Tom followed. 'Shut that door,' the man said, and Tom did.

The man moved around a desk of metal legs and cheap veneer. It held an old HP screen and a keyboard and a Wi-Fi hub. The man opened a drawer and pulled out a typed sheet that he slid forward for Tom to read.

Tom sat in the blue plastic chair on his side of the desk and placed his fingertips on the paper. It held a mass of single-spaced text in nine-point Comic Sans print. Tom let his eyes swim across the page. He couldn't bear to focus.

'Those are the rules. Agree to them, and sign here.'

The man pushed an open ledger toward Tom. In blue biro the man had filled in the first part of a column. 'I, Luke Snape, agree to abide by all the rules of Sunnydene Holiday Park.'

'Don't agree to the rules, then fuck off. You've already made a nuisance of yourself by walking through the park once. And when your mum gets here, she has to sign too.'

'My mum?'

'I'm told she's coming later. What's her name?'

'I've got no mum.'

'But you said…'

'To that woman? She didn't like the look of me. I thought she'd feel better if she knew I had a mother.'

'So you walked on to the park and lied to one of our residents. That's not against the rules, but I'm going to add it. Don't just stare at that paper. Read it. The rules are important. Do you want to rent a towel?'

Tom looked up and nodded. The man went through a door at the back. Tom heard a cupboard open. He tipped the Wi-Fi hub forward and checked for the password pasted on the bottom. Iv6Kklv1W.

As an image, it had some structure to it. Tom blinked twice, like he was taking a photo, and set the hub back in place.

The man returned with a thin grey towel. 'That's four quid,' he said. 'Up front.'

Tom pulled a twenty-pound note out of his back pocket.

'Nothing smaller?' the man asked.

Tom shook his head.

'You want sheets?'

Tom nodded. The man went away.

Tom spun the screen to face him. It showed a forum for Tractor-Boys.com. A fan site for Ipswich Town. Send this guy any link to Ipswich Town and he'd be bound to open it. But send it where?

The Gmail icon showed in the header bar. Tom clicked on it. The account was open. Tom clicked the + sign and wrote himself an email. Subject line Iv6Kklv1W. The Wi-Fi password. In case his concussion made him forget it.

He opened the Sent box and deleted the message. Then logged out of the account. He brought up the sign-on screen. PaulMTilley1979@gmail.com. Six dots to show a six-digit password. Shouldn't take long.

Tom heard a cupboard door close. He pushed the screen and keyboard back into place and picked up the biro.

'You've read everything?' the man asked.

Tom signed his name in the ledger. Well, he signed Luke Snape's name. 'You live back there?' he asked. 'On your own?'

'What's it to you?' Paul M. Tilley checked the ledger, closed the sheet of rules inside it and put it away in its drawer. 'That's a sheet, a duvet cover, and two pillowcases. Twelve quid. Sixteen in all. You get half the money back when you return them. Clean.'

Tom offered his twenty-pound note again. The man huffed and stood and went back out through the door, but not far. He came back with a pack of digestive biscuits, a box of long-life milk, and a forty-bag pack of Tetley teabags. 'You want sugar?' the man asked.

Tom shook his head.

'Don't think of this as a shop,' the man said. 'This is just a service. The essentials. That stuff takes what you owe me to £21.56. I'll waive the extra. We'll call it quits.'

He took a lined exercise book and a cash box out of a different drawer, entered the items and amounts into the book and locked Tom's twenty-pound note away in the box.

'That's it,' he said to Tom, looking up. 'Welcome to Sunnydene.'

Paul M. Tilley folded his lips and cheeks into a smile which he held in place till Tom stood up.

Tom collected the sheets and towel and foodstuffs into his hands, stepped outdoors and clicked the door shut.

The area in front of the reception had a patch of grass shaped into a lawn. It was surrounded by lavender. Busy in a last wedge of thin sun, bees were still at work on the blossoms. An iron pole stuck out through the lavender in the corner, a bird feeder hanging from its shepherd's crook. It was quarter filled with seed.

Tom looked through the window into the reception. The man was back on his keyboard, plugged in to the Tractor Boys fan forum no doubt, typing away. Tom pushed the door open and spoke from just outside.

'Is that your birdfeeder?' he asked.

'What's it to you?'

'What birds do you get?'

'Sparrows. All the tits. There's a robin and a blackbird work the grass where seeds fall down. And greenfinches. There's a whole flock of greenfinches. They must be breeding. I think they nest in the gorse. They suck the seed down.'

'Cool,' Tom said, and shut the door.

It was cool. Tom meant it. A man who takes care of birds has some good in him.

Holding the towel and sheets close to his chest made Tom warmer. He stood a moment and listened to the bees and, beyond that, the thunder of sea against rock. Across the park Tom could see steps that led up to the top of the seawall. Tomorrow he'd take a walk and stand there. Face the sea. Take it all in.

He'd send Paul M. Tilley an email before bed. Wait for him to click on it. Sign into Mr Tilley's account as Mr Tilley. Take back control. You don't raid a man's house and drag him naked out of the shower. You don't humiliate a man like that. Not without payback. Tom would activate his phone. He would assume Paul M. Tilley's virtual identity then go to sleep.

He didn't have to destroy Mr Tilley's life. It was just good to know that he could. He always could.

Maybe tomorrow Mr Tilley would let Tom stand by the feeder and watch the greenfinches. Tom had never seen a greenfinch.

He checked his phone. 19.38. Still time.

Tom opened up the Settings. Found Tilley's Wi-Fi. Put in the password from memory. It worked. The signal wasn't strong, but Tom was hidden behind a bush so didn't want to move nearer the chalet where he could be seen. He set the Linux program to instal. Rolled up his sleeve to reveal the URL. The ink had smudged a bit in the shower, but he could still read it.

There. The program was installed. He opened it.

19.47. Thirteen minutes to go.

'Oy!'

It was Paul M. Tilley. In a rage.

'What are you fucking playing at? I knew you were up to something. I've got a CCTV camera set up in the office. Just played it back. You turned over my router. Got the password I bet. Went online. I saw you. What are you, one of those identity thieves?'

'There's no signal in the camp. I need to send an email to my mum. I promised her. She'll be worried.'

'You lying cunt. You've got no mum. Here. Give me that.'

He snatched the phone from Tom's hand.

'Don't,' Tom said. 'Please. Let me use it. For a few minutes. You can stand there and watch. I've just got to type in this.' Tom pointed to the URL scrawled on his arm. 'Type it in and then a short code and press a button. You can even press the button. Save the world as you know it.'

'The world as I know it? Who the fuck would want to save that?'

Paul M. Tilley wrapped his fist around the phone and strode back to his chalet. The door closed and bolts slammed home.

Is that how it worked? Some old guy on a Lowestoft campsite turns out to be the agent of change?

It was hard to compute. Tom didn't even smile as he thought it through. He was hyper alert to CCTV cameras, but some amateur's ancient hobby camera had just caught him out. He should have noticed. But then Steve had bashed his head in. It wasn't Tom's fault. He wasn't at his best.

Tom left the teabags on the ground. He wasn't going back

to his caravan and its stove. When the world went into its post-eight p.m. meltdown MI5 or whoever they were would have nothing to wait for. The worst would have happened. They'd come for him. They'd surround the caravan. It was summer, dawn was early, and he wanted to see it.

Tom pocketed the biscuits. He wasn't hungry yet but he hadn't eaten. He kept hold of the bedlinen too. He could find a hollow somewhere and sleep out under the stars. Maybe on a clifftop. It would be good to get up high and maybe spot the lights of Europe over the sea. It would be fun to watch the lights go out.

Or maybe he could manage to walk to town. Find a bus. Head further along the coast. Get to Great Yarmouth. That was a holiday place full of strangers. Find a B&B. Borrow their computer. Hack Paul M. Tilley. Wipe his CCTV footage. Tom didn't need those pictures of himself in the news.

In the morning he could find a barber and get his head shaved. Barbers are good at telling stories. The barber would likely be Turkish. He could tell Tom how Turkey's coal-fired powerplants had shut down. How the country was on standstill. How the military had been sent in. How Brazil and India and Iowa and Australia were fucked too. How China thought it had got away with it then Mongolia crashed.

Maybe the barber would finish off the cut with scissors because his clippers had run out of power. Tom would stare at his new look in the barber's mirror by using the daylight that came in through the front window. Tom didn't know if the UK's power supply would hold up. Set these things going and it was all a bit random.

That was tomorrow. Maybe he could get as far as tomorrow and start again.

First though he'd climb that seawall and look out at the sea. He'd sit close. Listen to its roar. Let the spray from the waves wet him and chill him and their noise deafen him. That would be something.

My Thanks

The Boy on the Train has received a host of vital editorial support.

Sarah Walton and Roy Chapman brought their digital expertise to help steer the book more firmly toward credibility in the cybersphere.

Through Patrick Walsh and the Pew Literary Agency, Charlotte Van Wijk gave a terrifically helpful early reader's report. Her enthusiasm for the book's opening convinced me the novel was well on track, and she gave great pointers as to how to strengthen it for the home straight.

Sarah Day gave the manuscript a thorough professional edit, streamlining an earlier draft of the text.

George Biggs steered the book through a later edit, dropping a chapter or two to the cutting room floor and setting my sights on discovering the true nature of Glyph.

Sometimes negative feedback helps. Kate Johnston provided that, wishing for characters more like in my earlier fiction. The creation of Karen took strength from that.

I thought I was simply giving Maggie Hamand a good read, and she sweetly claimed I had done that. And then assumed her fierce and wondrous editorial aspect with clear directions as to how to fix both small points and larger ones.

Sometimes it's enough to be told a draft is really exciting and good by those who know such things, and Mike Johnstone and Brian Eno both came up trumps in that regard.

Year after year at the universities of Hull and Plymouth I set Patricia Highsmith's *The Talented Mr Ripley* as the novel for my creative writing students to study. I wanted to learn what made the novel so effective. I learned from teaching it, but also from the students' responses. How does Highsmith sustain the tension of a scene, page after page? How does she create effects through language? One student stayed behind after a seminar to say how she could sympathize with Tom Ripley because of his troubled backstory. That added aspects to this novel's Tom.

James Thornton shares my life and so the several complete drafts of this book, into which he has delved with his expert editorial precision, imagination and care.

Everybody has given me huge encouragement.

Mike Hart brought the book home with his final edit. And then typeset the book and designed the cover to boot.

Thank you all. This is your book too.